I0543680

BOOK ONE
OF THE
ST. EDMUNDSBURY
MYSTERIES

CRUSADER'S WAY

BOOK ONE
OF THE
ST. EDMUNDSBURY
MYSTERIES

CRUSADER'S WAY

ANNE-MARIE AMIEL

HEADLIGHT FLUID PRESS

Editing: Elizabeth Patrick, Headlight Fluid Press
Cover: Cathy Helms, Avalon Graphics
Formatting: Blue Valley Author Services

FIRST EDITION

Headlight Fluid Press, Spokane, WA 99202
Printed in the United States of America
ISBN: 978-1-956992-00-7

Headlightfluidpress.com

For Anthony Michael Amiel, beloved son and brother

No book is ever a solo project. This book would not have been possible without the unending encouragement of my sister of the heart, Pat Biegler, or the hard work of my editor, Libby Patrick. Thanks are also due to the many friends who listened to my ideas, eagerly awaited the next draft, and told me they loved it!

**MAP OF ST. EDMUNDSBURY IN
THE YEAR OF OUR LORD 1204**

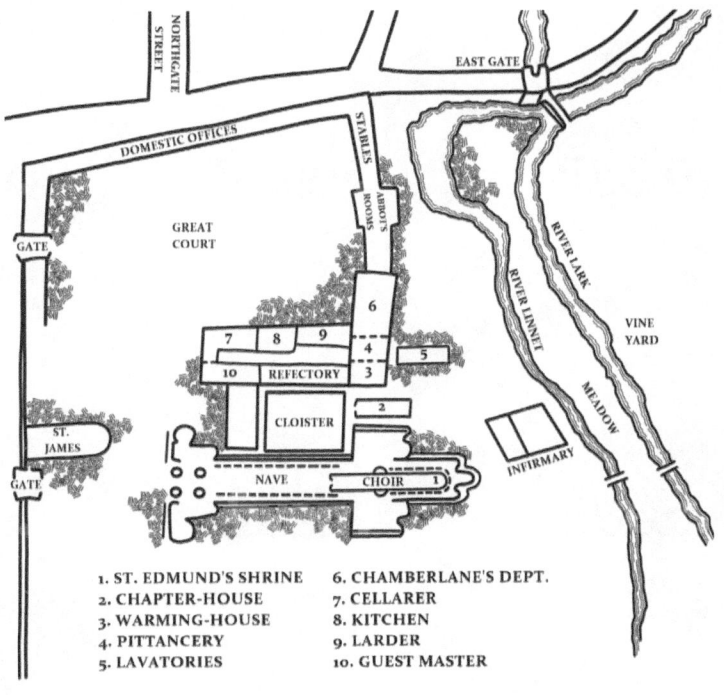

1. ST. EDMUND'S SHRINE
2. CHAPTER-HOUSE
3. WARMING-HOUSE
4. PITTANCERY
5. LAVATORIES
6. CHAMBERLANE'S DEPT.
7. CELLARER
8. KITCHEN
9. LARDER
10. GUEST MASTER

THE ABBEY OF ST. EDMUNDSBURY 1204

HISTORICAL NOTE

The Abbey and town of Bury St. Edmunds are real, and Abbot Samson and Prior Herbert really lived, as did the similarly named Sampson, the subsacrist, the town Reeve, Durand and Ralph, the gatekeeper. Bury St. Edmunds was founded about 600 years before the time of this was originally called Beodericsworth. The name was changed to St. Edmund's Bury in the 10th or 11th Century, the word "bury" coming from the Germanic/Norse word for a fortress, not because it referred to the burial of the saint whose bones pilgrims visited the town to venerate. Eventually the town became known as Bury St. Edmunds, and so it remains today.

Bury is still a market town, although the Abbey was destroyed in the time of Henry VIII and little remains today except for ruins. The streets mentioned in the book are still there, as is the market square (which still functions as an open-air market on certain days of the week). Moyses Hall, which has nothing to do with the prophet Moses or the Jewish population of St. Edmund's Bury, was built in 1180 and was in fact the home of a merchant. Although the original building is long gone, there has been a Moyses Hall standing on the site ever since, the latest one built in 1819.

Much of what we know about Bury St. Edmunds at the beginning of the thirteenth century comes from the journal of a monk of the Abbey named Jocelin of Brakelond, who recorded the daily events in the area from 1173-1202. Brother Jocelin was the Guest Master of the Abbey for periods of time during his life, and I have made him so in this story although we do not know anything of his history after the end of his chronicle in 1202. The quotes at the beginning of each chapter are taken from this chronicle (*see Chronicle of the Abbey of Bury St. Edmunds*, Oxford University Press).

Many of the events mentioned in this story actually happened, including the expelling of the Jews from the town in 1190. The stories of the death of the father of King Canute (the king who could not hold back the waves) and the paralysis of the former abbot were also widely known at the time of this story. The story of Samson's trouble with his fellow monks when he was subsacrist at the Abbey is also true.

Little is known of the saint whose shrine was the center of veneration in St. Edmund's Bury. By tradition, he was an Anglo-Saxon king killed by the Danes around the year 855 A.D. He was beaten and beheaded when he would not deny Christ. During medieval times he was regarded as the patron saint of England.

King Richard the Lionheart of England and Philip Capet, King of France led the Third Crusade from 1189-1192, seeking to recapture the Holy Land from the Sultan Saladin. This followed the fall of Jerusalem to Saladin's forces in 1187, an event that struck at the heart of Christendom. Although the campaign of the Third Crusade was largely successful, the European soldiers failed to recapture Jerusalem, their main goal.

The Fourth Crusade (1202-1204), the Crusade from which the knight of this story returned, was the next attempt to recapture Jerusalem. Again, the Crusaders failed to retake the Holy City. They did, however, capture and loot the Byzantine city of Constantinople and install their own king, Baldwin, on the throne.

Maimonides was a highly regarded Jewish Rabbi, philosopher and physician of the 12th Century. He was born in Cordoba, Spain, but lived a large part of his life in Egypt and worked in the court of the Sultan Saladin for some years. His skill as a physician was so widely known that he was consulted by Jew, Moslem and Christian alike. Some of his words as quoted in this story are taken from his works.

The story of the du Lac and de Vere family feud is not drawn from history, but the account of the betrothal of King Richard to the sister of King Philip, and his subsequent marriage to Berengaria of Navarre, is true.

GLOSSARY OF MEDIEVAL TERMS

Some words and descriptions that were in common use in 1204 may not be known to you. They include:

Alb: An alb is part of the clothing worn by a priest during church services. It is a full-length white tunic with sleeves.

Cellarer: The cellarer was always one of the most powerful officials in any monastery, and the Abbey in the town of St. Edmund's Bury was no exception. It was the cellarer who was responsible for supervising the tenants of all the Abbey's lands and for making sure all the food and drink that the Abbey needed was provided.

Chamberlain: The chamberlain was responsible for the monks' clothes and other linens, such as the altar cloths and vestments.

Charcoal: In medieval times charcoal was used for heating, cooking, and even for medicine. Most settlements had charcoal burners. They would chop down wood and stack it in a certain way, covering the entire pile with earth or brick to make it into a kiln. Then they would light a slow-burning fire which needed to be watched in order to prevent a destructive fire breaking out. It would take several days for the wood to turn to charcoal.

Chasuble: The sleeveless, ornate vestment worn by a priest. In the Middle Ages a bishop's chasuble might be decorated with gold thread, pearls and gems. It could take years to complete.

Combat: In the Middle Ages a trial by combat was sometimes used to settle accusations in the absence of witnesses or a confession. There were very strict rules governing the conduct of these battles. They would continue until one combatant was dead or disabled, or until one cried "craven," which was the old French word for "broken." These trials, while prohibited by law by the 16th Century, are an early version of the private duel, which continued into the 19th Century.

Cope: A cope was a long mantle worn by the clergy. Those worn by bishops and cardinals wereoften extremely richly decorated and were very costly.

Couching: This is an embroidery technique that was used extensively in medieval times, and usually included the use of thread made of gold or silv er.

Crusader's Cross: Otherwise known as the Jerusalem Cross, this symbol represented Christ's command to spread the Gospel around the world, a mission that started in Jerusalem. It was part of the coat of arms of the short-lived Jerusalem Kingdom (1099-1203 AD).

Great Hall: The Great Hall of any castle or manor was a large room on the lower floor. The family and their servants would all gather there to eat and keep warm. It was a large room so that there could be some degree of privacy, with the servants staying far away from the family and the hearth.

Hazard: This dice game was popular in medieval Europe after being brought back from the Arab world by the Crusaders. King Richard the Lionheart put restrictions on the amount that his knights could wager and forbade foot soldiers from playing it at all. He also passed a law that forbade masked men from entering people's houses for a dice game during Christmas!

Hippocras: Hippocras was a spiced wine which was very common in medieval times.

Hue and cry: This is an expression we still use today to describe a big fuss. In medieval England it was the official term for the search for a criminal.

Humors: One of the basic principles of medieval medicine was that a human body was composed of four humors (blood, phlegm, yellow bile and black bile). A good balance of these humors was essential for good health.

Liberty: The Liberty of St. Edmund was the term for all the land under the control of the Abbot. He effectively stood in the king's shoes, levying taxes and acting as the judge in civil and criminal cases.

Reeve: In most towns, the Reeve was the man who did the police work for the nobleman appointed Sheriff of the whole district. In Bury St. Edmunds, though, there was no civilian sheriff, and the Reeve had less power. He reported directly to the officials at the Abbey.

Sacrist: The sacrist of a monastery was one of the most powerful officials. He was responsible for the maintenance of the buildings. The power of the Abbey at Bury St. Edmunds meant that the sacrist there had even greater power, for it was the sacrist who ran the court for the town and surrounding area. Samson used his power and influence as sacrist to eventually become Abbot.

Salerno: The medical school at Salerno is often called the world's first medical school. It flourished from the 10th to the 13th Centuries, reaching its height of influence in the 12th Century. It remained open until 1811.

Scutage: In medieval times land was held in return for service to the lord. Scutage was a tax levied upon knights who wanted to avoid military service ordered by the king.

Serfs: In the feudal system of the Middle Ages serfs were those who worked parts of their lords' lands in exchange for protection and the right to farm fields to provide for their own living.

Small Ale: This drink, which contained very little alcohol, was also known as small beer. Often more like porridge than pure liquid, it was commonly drunk in the Middle Ages because the water supply was often polluted, and true beers and wines were too expensive for most people to drink on a daily basis.

South Sea: This was the name given to the English Channel in Anglo-Saxon times, and it remained so until later in the Middle Ages.

Surcoat: A surcoat was a sleeveless gown, usually of cotton or linen, worn over chain mail. It had deep slits in the front and back so that horses could be ridden with ease. By the time of this story, it was common for these gowns to include simple designs, such as the Crusader's cross.

CHAPTER ONE

Behold, "the acceptable time"; the long-desired day has come, which ... I am particularly happy to describe.

"WAKE UP, SLEEPY HEAD!" Aileen dimly heard the words, but it was too warm to stir, snuggled down as she was in the big feather bed she shared with her sister.

"Wake up, or you'll be late. You can't be late on your first day at the Abbey."

Oh, no, I've overslept! Aileen sat up with a start, staring at the window to see if it was yet dawn.

"It's all right," said her mother, coming into the room from the stairs. "You have more than an hour before you need to be there."

Now Aileen could hear the sounds of the town stirring. Close at hand, doors and windows were banging open in Looms Lane as housewives got ready to throw slops into the street. Merchants shouted to each other as they began setting up their wares. Loud orders to apprentices to hurry up and get to work interrupted the

1

racket of hens clucking and dogs barking. Already the smells of dyes and wet cloth from the workshop in the back of her father's shop downstairs were beginning to tickle Aileen's nostrils.

Farther away, there were other sounds: the creaking of cart wheels rolling down Northgate Street toward the Abbey, cocks crowing as their slumber was disturbed, other animal calls as they were carried to market, and beggars crying for alms in the first rush of the day.

Today was a day Aileen knew she would never forget, and she wanted to remember everything about it.

Today, she thought, is the day it seems I have longed for all my life. When I greet my father this morning he will see a woman who brings honor to our house and coins for our purse He will see someone who no longer thinks only of small, unimportant matters, or sits at her mother's knee learning of plants and dyes and the embroidery of fine cloth. On this first day of September in the Year of Our Lord 1204 I am to begin work at the great Abbey of St. Edmund's Bury. From this day forward I will use my needle for God.

As she went downstairs, having dressed and braided her light brown hair carefully in an attempt to control its distressing tendency to curl, Aileen felt herself standing tall, somehow changed from the day before. She was somewhat disappointed to find out that her parents didn't seem to appreciate the change quite as much as she had expected.

"Ah, good," said her mother, tying a scarf around her greying hair as she headed toward the dying shed.

2

"Before you go, Aileen, would you milk the goat please, and then make sure that Richard and Henry drink all their milk and eat their bread. I have to get on with mixing the madder root and alum so your father can dye that cloth Mistress Palmer ordered. If I don't get that done this morning, I won't have time to begin couching the medallion for the bishop's cope, and that would never do!"

"Yes, Mother," said Aileen.

"Important day," said her father as he rose from the breakfast table. "Make sure you do me proud, Aileen. You have all the skills needed to do a good job, and I expect you to bring honor to our house." The words were softened by a smile. Aileen's father was a big, bluff man with iron grey hair and eyes to match. He was well-respected by the townsfolk of St. Edmund's Bury and well-loved by his family.

"Yes, Father," said Aileen.

Well, it was probably too much to expect everyone to notice immediately just how different she was on this great day.

Aileen milked the goat and coaxed her young brothers through their breakfast as she hastily swallowed hers. Then, with a kiss and a word of encouragement from each of her parents and her sister Mabel, she walked out into Looms Lane. As dawn broke over St. Edmund's Bury, Aileen began her new life.

3

For Aileen and her friends, it seemed as though the Abbey had always been there, like the trees and the sun. It was a great house, built to venerate a saint whose tomb was known to be a place of sanctuary and healing. Walking along Mustow Street towards the Abbey gate, Aileen thought of the pride in her father's face when he received word that Aileen was to be permitted to work within the walls of the Abbey. Smiling, she remembered the times her strict, law-abiding father had talked about the great privilege bestowed upon the Liberty of St. Edmund by King John in granting Abbot Samson the power to impose taxes and sit in judgment over lawbreakers. Such a high honor was not only rare, but valuable. As her father said, the townsfolk of St. Edmund's Bury might grumble at what they sometimes considered the heavy hand of the Abbot, but they were keenly aware of the wealth the honor brought to their town.

"It's best to test the Abbot's coin before testing the Abbot's mood," was something she had oft heard her father repeat when discussing a dispute that was to be brought before the Abbey court. Aileen wasn't sure she wanted to test either, so it was with some degree of nervousness that she came to the Great Court

4

Gate, hesitating before she passed through into the courtyard itself.

This was not the first time Aileen had peered through the shadow of the gate into the sunshine of the Great Court, but always before she had been merely an inquisitive child on her way to attend services in the Abbey's church. Now the scene she viewed seemed somehow different.

As she looked around, she realized the scene before her was indeed different. There were many more people than she was used to seeing in the Great Court this morning. Today, as well as the monks she had expected to see, there were men and women in working clothes scurrying from one place to another, carrying provisions, tools, timber and cloth. There were young boys who were surely scholars of the Abbey school, some of them chosen by their parents to enter the cloister when they were of age. The boys all seemed to be hurrying to complete some appointed task in time for some unknown but exciting event.

There were even knights and their ladies present, their squires and servants adding to the general air of confusion and expectation that was heavy in the air.

"And what can I do for you this morning?" said a voice close by. Aileen turned to face the speaker. Sergeant Ralph, the Abbey's portly gatekeeper, was standing before her, hands on his hips and a slight frown on his face.

"Excuse me, sir," she said, smiling nervously. "I am to start work at the Abbey this morning and was told to report to the chief robemaker."

Much to Aileen's relief, the gatekeeper's frown was replaced by a smile. Turning, he pointed her to an open door in a building across the courtyard. "The linen room is where you need to go. Ask for Mistress Taylor. She will give you instruction."

"Thank you, sir," Aileen said, dropping a small curtsy before crossing the courtyard.

In the doorway of the linen room she paused, looking around. The room was quiet, tables and stools neatly set in rows, and racks for cloth lining the back wall. Ceremonial cloths for the church covered some of the tables, and under the windows in the same wall as the door sheer white linens held fast in their frames lay ready for fine stitchery.

"Hello?" called Aileen, unsure of what to do next.

"Oh dear," said a woman behind her. "It's Aileen, isn't it? Master Arundel's daughter?" Without pausing for an answer, she gently pushed Aileen through the door and went on talking.

"I meant to be here when you arrived, but with all that's going on today I'm in a terrible muddle!"

The woman plopped down on a stool, breathing a sigh of relief. "I'm Mistress Taylor. I am in charge of the Abbey linens. Well, I'm not exactly in charge of the linens, but I suppose many would say that I am."

Seeing the look of confusion on Aileen's face, Mistress Taylor shook her head as though to clear her thoughts. "What I mean to say is that I'm in charge of the linens under Brother Michael's guidance. He's chamberlain here and keeps a close eye on all within these walls."

The seamstress gestured to the table by which she sat, on which lay several altar cloths. "These brothers may be all very well, and it's God's call that they answer, but it takes a delicate touch to keep the Lord's cloth in order. And cloistered monks need an awful lot of help! Thanks be to God, for it's the Abbey that keeps us all in bread!"

Seemingly without pausing for breath, Mistress Taylor rattled on happily, moving from the fine linens woven especially for the Abbot's table to the work Aileen would be doing in her first days at the Abbey, the disgraceful price of gold thread, the amount of time they had to spend on drawing candlewax stains out of an altar cloth, and even the care of fine cloth.

"Of course," she said. "We only wash and bleach the most delicate cloth as robemakers. We leave the general washing duties to the washerwomen, whose duties do not include the detailed work that we must do."

Mistress Taylor picked up a beautiful piece of embroidery. "This is one of the vestments worn by the Abbot during high mass. As you learn more, I am sure that we will be able to use you for work such as this. Your parents will have taught you well how to handle and stitch fine cloth."

At last, as she took a short break in order to quench her thirst, Aileen managed to ask the question she had

7

wanted to ask ever since arriving this morning. Nerves had prevented her asking the gatekeeper, but she didn't feel at all nervous with the talkative robemaker.

"Everyone seemed very excited this morning," she said. "And I had not expected to see so many people in the Great Court. What is so special about today?"

"You mean you haven't heard!" exclaimed Mistress Taylor, clearly delighted that she was to be the one to impart great and exciting news. "I thought that all within the Abbey's rule must know by now. Today our holy place will be blessed by the addition of a piece of the True Cross on which Our Lord suffered and died." The robemaker crossed herself as she mentioned the holy relic.

"Today!" said Aileen. "I knew it was rumored that such a treasure was to be given to the Abbey by a knight returning from the Crusade, and I'm sure that all within the town know that the goldsmith and the master mason have been building a wonderful shrine to receive the gift. I had not heard, though, that it was today that the knight was expected."

"He sent word to the Abbot last week," said Mistress Taylor. "He landed from France just three weeks ago and stopped only to pay his reverence to King John. He pleaded with the king to be allowed to complete his vow to God that he offer the holy relic to the Abbey of St. Edmund. The king not only granted his request but said that he would send abroad a great proclamation to honor the gift and the giver. The king delayed the knight only a few days so that the proclamation could go forth, and then the Crusader was sent forth with a royal escort of knights to ensure both speed and safety in his journey to St. Edmund's Bury."

"A royal escort," breathed Aileen.

"Yes, and that is why all the gentlefolk of the Liberty are here, and why there is much preparation for the ceremony. There will be many people to house and feed tonight, and many horses that must be found room in the stables. It seems that every spare hand in the Abbey precincts is seeing to the hanging of cloths in the Abbey church and the needs of the guests, and food for a feast is being prepared as we speak. Oh, it is going to be so exciting, and just think how the pilgrims will flock to our beautiful Abbey when they know we not only have holy St. Edmund within our precincts, but a piece of the True Cross!"

Aileen's thoughts drifted as Mistress Taylor continued to talk. It would be a splendid scene, with knights and ladies, armor polished to a jeweled shine, proud horses and festive banners. The ceremony to place the holy relic in the Abbey would be glorious, and the feasting and celebration would be greater than anything St. Edmund's Bury had ever seen. And she, Aileen, daughter of Jude of Arundel, was to be at the center of it all.

CHAPTER TWO

*The abbot was commended for his
splendid and generous hospitality.*

"YOU SHOULD HAVE SEEN IT!"
Aileen and her best friend, Ruth, sat on the banks of the River Lark in their secret place, chewing on blades of grass and talking over the day.

"I could hear the crowd cheering the procession as they rode down the hill toward the Great Gate," said Aileen. "The sound of the horses' hooves striking the stones was like that of the smith's hammer."

"Were there very many of them?" asked Ruth quietly. Ruth was always quiet. It was almost as though the girl thought that if she drew no attention to herself those around her would forget that she was one of the outcasts, a Jew. But she had been Aileen's closest friend since they were two years old, and nothing could tear them apart.

"Oh, yes," said Aileen. "Three knights carrying banners of the Crusader's Cross led the way. They wore linen gowns over their mail, and their helms had been polished until they shone. Even the horses were dressed in the colors of their lords."

Aileen paused, as she remembered the scene, with the sunshine picking out the glint of the helmets, shields and swords carried by the parade of knights.

"Go on," urged Ruth. "Tell me about the rest of the procession."

"Well, following the three knights rode the Crusader knight himself. His name is Sir Henri du Lac. And behind him rode a squire and the royal escort of knights. The knights all carried lances and shields, all polished until they shone in the sun like ... like ..."

"Like polished metal in sunlight," said Ruth. Both girls laughed.

"You have no imagination!" said Aileen. "Well, anyway, they rode two abreast, and I could just imagine the army riding to the Crusade thus. They were so straight and true. And there were so many of them, I thought the procession would never end. It was wonderful!"

"What about the knight?" asked Ruth. "What about Sir Henri? Did you hear anything about him?"

"I heard the monks talking about him as I stood beside the gate," Aileen said. "They said that he fought bravely in the East. When the great city of Constantinople fell to our soldiers, Sir Henri was rewarded with one of the most holy of the relics hidden within the city's walls.

"Sergeant Ralph, the gatekeeper, said Sir Henri swore a vow to God before the great altar at the Church of Saint Sophia in Constantinople, the very church where the new king of that city was crowned by the Crusaders. He swore that he would dedicate his life to peace from henceforth. As a sign of his intent, he swore to bring the holy relic to St. Edmund's Bury."

"Why should he bring this relic here?" asked Ruth.

"I'm not sure, but one of the monks said something about his mother's family being from this part of England."

"Oh. Well, go on with your story," said Ruth.

"Sir Henri was dressed in a white surcoat with a red cross down the front and back, and his shield and horse were decorated with the same design. He sat tall in the saddle, proud and like a king, with dark hair and a thin face. I confess I thought he looked somehow sad."

The girls sat silent for a moment in the gathering twilight, watching the water as it flowed slowly by. Then Aileen roused herself and turned excitedly to Ruth.

"Behind Sir Henri rode a squire, as I said. He carried a cushion on which rested a beautiful gold box. It must be in that box that the holy relic lies."

"I don't really understand all this fuss about some piece of treasure from a city far away," said Ruth.

"It's not just a `piece of treasure,.'" said Aileen, a little hurt by her friend's unenthusiastic reception of her news. "It's a part of the cross upon which our Savior died. I know you don't believe Jesus was the Son of God, but for us Christians, the cross is the most

12

important sign of the truth of what we believe." Aileen was quoting from her father, who had listened to her account of the day's events with the close attention of a man who had fought in the Holy Land on the Crusade led by King Richard the Lionheart.

"Ah," said Ruth. "Then this golden box is for Christians what the Ark of the Covenant was for us Jews, except that your box contains a piece of the cross and our Ark contained the Commandments given to Moses upon Mt. Sinai. This box, and what it contains, is the most sacred symbol of your faith, and any unconsecrated one who touches the box will surely die."

To Aileen this seemed a little drastic. Her father had said nothing about people dying if they touched the relic. Of course, she knew about those who had been struck dead for threatening the Abbey's shrine. It was said that King Canute's father had been struck dead at St. Edmund's tomb for daring to threaten its destruction if he were not paid a large ransom, and one of the abbots before Samson had been paralyzed when he handled the body of the saint in an irreverent manner.

However, her father had always told Aileen that touching a holy relic without evil intent was considered one of the greatest blessings that could be given to anyone. Many people believed that touching the tomb of St. Edmund would cure them of disease, and certainly many who feared the power of the law had sought sanctuary in the shadow of the tomb, for none would dare take a man by violence within the church's walls. The power of even the smallest part of the cross

13

upon which Jesus had died was greater even than that of any saint's relic, and Aileen knew that it was not just Mistress Taylor who looked to see more pilgrims within the precincts of the Abbey of St. Edmund's Bury now that such a powerful talisman was to be seen and touched.

"I don't think it's quite the same," Aileen said slowly. "Holy relics are God's gift to us, gifts of great power by which He blesses us and lets us know that He rules over us and cares for us." Her mother had tried to explain all this to the children that very evening, so Aileen was sure that Ruth would understand.

"But why do you need pieces of wood and the bones of your saints to know all that?" asked Ruth. "Do you doubt His power?"

"No, of course not," said Aileen.

"Well, then, why are relics so important?"

Aileen thought for a moment. She had never really thought about relics in this way before. She had always just accepted what she had been told. Relics were a sign of the power of God and of His grace. Accepting this was a part of faith. One accepted what one could not understand — on faith. But if one accepted things on faith, why were relics necessary? Shouldn't faith be enough?

It was enough to give one a headache!

"People are healed of all sorts of diseases by touching and visiting the tombs of saints and other holy relics," said Aileen. "That must mean that God wants us to honor them."

14

Ruth didn't look very sure of this explanation, but Aileen changed the subject before she could ask any more questions.

"Anyway, when the procession reached the gate of the Abbey Church, the Abbot and Prior came down to meet the knight," said Aileen. "The Lord Abbot, the Prior and several other brothers whom I had never seen before all stood on the steps of the church awaiting the arrival of this great gift."

"I have, of course, heard much of the Abbot," said Ruth. "But I know little of any others of the House."

"The Prior is nice. His name is Brother Herbert, and he looks as though he is always happy. He spoke very kindly to a servant who tripped and spilled a flagon of ale over his habit. I think that no one is afraid of him, even though he is second only to the Lord Abbot in power."

"What about Abbot Samson?" asked Ruth. "It is said that he is an ambitious man."

"I don't know," said Aileen. "He is stern, I think. He doesn't look as though he should be, because he really isn't very tall, and with his bushy eyebrows and large nose it would seem that he is made for laughter, not power. But his gaze is very hard, and I would not like to try lying to him."

"Well, you probably won't see much of him, Aileen," said Ruth. "So I wouldn't worry about it unless you do something likely to bring yourself to his attention!"

Aileen laughed, and said she would do her best not to do so.

"So what happened next?" asked Ruth.

"The knight dismounted, and he and the Abbot greeted each other very formally. Then Sir Henri's squire gave him the cushion with the box. Sir Henri knelt in front of Abbot Samson and held up the box. I heard him say, `My Lord Abbot, I have come to fulfil my vow to God. I present this holy relic to you, as abbot of this holy place, and I offer it in humility as a small penance for my sins.' He speaks with a strong Norman accent, so I had to pay close attention to understand all his words."

"Go on," Ruth urged when Aileen paused.

"It was so still," said Aileen. "All those within the gate and, it seemed, all those who had pressed forward as far as they could outside the gate, were still as statues, straining to hear what passed between the Abbot and the knight.

"The Lord Abbot laid his hand in blessing on Sir Henri, and reverently took the box from the knight. Then he said, `Sir Knight, you have faithfully fulfilled your vow to God. In honor of the completion of your journey and your faithfulness to our Blessed Savior, we will hold a mass in two days' time to thank God for the coming of this great gift to our House and to place this holy relic in its place of honor within our walls. Tomorrow, the whole town will feast and celebrate this momentous day in the history of our Liberty, and you will be our guest of honor.'

"The knight said, `I thank you, Lord Abbot. But ere this sacred mass is held I must keep vigil and pray. I

16

ask that the time for celebration be after the ceremony of offering. I pray you to let me keep vigil beside the tomb of St. Edmund for these two nights..'"

"What did the Abbot say?" asked Ruth.

"He couldn't very well say no to the knight's request," said Aileen. "Even though all at the Abbey had been preparing for a feast, Sir Henri could not be denied. So, tomorrow, there will be no celebration. It will be in two days' time, after the mass, that there will be great feasting in the Abbey. There will even be meat and ale for the people of the town, by order of the Lord Abbot."

"I'm sure that made everyone happy," said Ruth. "So what happened next?"

"Nothing much as far as the relic is concerned," said Aileen. I had a very busy day, learning my duties and getting to know all the people I'm going to be working with. And I must have heard a hundred times about how careful I need to be in everything I do, since I am working with the Lord's linen now!"

"One thing's for sure," said Ruth. "Your first day at the Abbey was certainly not dull!"

"No, and I wish I had time to tell you more," Aileen said. "But it is full dark now, and even though I am now bringing home the Abbot's coin, I do not believe father will fast change his mind about my being out beyond time!"

"You're right. I didn't realize how dark it had grown while we talked of knights and relics," said Ruth. "Father will be very worried, and I have three miles to

17

go before I get home." The girls rose, brushed the grass off their skirts, and turned for home.

Darkness snatched at Aileen's feet as she sped on her way. I'm in trouble for sure she thought as she ran. Father will be very angry! But even the thought of her father's wrath seemed less scary than the rustling night filled with nocturnal creatures and strange sounds.

If I can make it in five minutes, thought Aileen, everything will be all right. Thus urged on by her promise to herself, and by the sudden hooting of an owl close by, Aileen sped down Mustow Street, longing for the safety of a glowing fire and a warm bed.

CHAPTER THREE

He concentrated all his efforts on making a most precious canopy above the shrine of the glorious martyr Edmund.

AILEEN'S RETURN HOME LAST NIGHT was not something she cared to remember. She had broken curfew, and her father had been very angry. Useless to exclaim that now she was of age she should have more freedom. That had just made her father more determined than ever not to amend the rule. It had taken the calming influence of her mother to cool the temperature.

It is strange, Aileen thought, how love often expresses itself in curious ways. I know my father loves me, but I really wish he wouldn't keep on treating me like a child! On the other hand, maybe mother had a point. Perhaps I wasn't being very responsible when I stayed out so late without telling them. I know they were worried.

As she arrived at the Abbey, Aileen determinedly put aside her personal problems, and set her mind on the coming day.

"Good, you're early," greeted Mistress Taylor. "So much excitement yesterday, it quite threw me out of sorts. It's all very well, having these lords and ladies and a blessed relic in our Abbey, praise be to God, but some of us have to get on with the daily work that keeps everyone content."

I can see life working under Mistress Taylor will never be dull, thought Aileen as she followed the robemaker to a bench at the other end of the room. Mistress Taylor sat down and waved Aileen to a stool beside her.

"Now," said the good woman, "I want to see how delicate are your couched threads. I have no doubt you have skill in laying down woolen threads, but we use much silk and gold thread here. It is too expensive to waste, and I allow few of my women to work with it."

"I understand," said Aileen. "My mother has taught me the balance between beauty and cost, and I will gladly show you an example of my skill."

"Your mother is known throughout the Liberty for her skill in design and embroidery," said Mistress Taylor, handing Aileen a piece of linen and a needle threaded with fine silk. "I will return in a few minutes to see how you progress."

So saying, the robemaker bustled off to see to the assignment of the day's other tasks.

Aileen bent to her task happily but had been working for only a few minutes when she became aware of people hurrying by the window under which she was sitting. Looking up, she saw the other women huddled in the doorway, looking out at the courtyard and whispering among themselves. I wonder what is going on, she thought, setting aside her work and getting up to join the rest of the women at the door.

She beheld a strange sight. The Abbot and Prior Herbert were hurrying across the court, robes flapping around their legs. Several other brothers followed in their wake, worried expressions creasing their brows. The sight of the hurrying monks was sufficiently unusual to cause many in the courtyard to cease their activities and stand still, staring after them.

"What do you suppose is happening?" asked one of the women.

"I'm sure I don't know," said Mistress Taylor tartly. "But whatever it is, it is not cause for anyone to cease their work and stand around gossiping."

Thus admonished, the women went back to work. Silence fell over the workroom, more from the stretching of ears to pick up any hint of what exciting event had occurred than from any virtue of restraint.

So it was that, within a matter of minutes, the sound of soft footsteps and calming voices could be heard coming from the direction of the guest hall. Aileen stole a look out of the window and saw the Abbot and Prior Herbert walking across the court with Sir Henri du Lac. The two monks were gesticulating and speaking in quiet tones. The knight was white in the face, and returned only short, angry responses.

I wonder why the Crusader is so angry, thought Aileen. Should this not be a time of joy and peace for him?

"Aileen," called Mistress Taylor. "Come over here. I wish you to see the fine work that is being done on this chasuble."

Obediently, Aileen crossed the room. "Oh, how beautiful!" she exclaimed, seeing for the first time the golden vestment upon which the most senior of the women were working.

Mistress Taylor beamed with pride. "Yes, it is," she said. "We have been working on this for nearly two years, but it should be finished in time for the mass celebrating the Feast of St. Edmund."

Aileen bent to take a closer look, aware of the eyes of all her colleagues upon her. This is some kind of a test, she thought. Silently praying that she had learned enough from her mother to pass, she took her time examining the fine work.

The chasuble celebrated Christ victorious, surrounded by the apostles. Aileen knew this was not uncommon in such vestments, but in the work before her she saw that the shrine of St. Edmund was stitched in beautiful detail, and the blessed saint himself was kneeling before Christ on His throne. The whole chasuble shone with the reflection of light on the gold thread. No one could fail to feel the power of the faith woven into the cloth.

22

"Such delicate couching," she said finally. "The gold thread on the background of blue silk twill is breathtaking!"

Almost it seemed as though a collective breath was released. I must have said the right thing, Aileen thought as they all smiled and nodded.

"To be sure, the Abbot will testify to the importance of our saint's resting place when he wears this for the Feast Day mass," said Mistress Taylor happily.

"Now, everyone back to work. We have too much to do to be spending our time chattering like magpies." Clapping her hands, she walked over to inspect the work held by another frame on the other side of the room, and her obedient workers scattered to their various tasks.

While Aileen and her colleagues were admiring the embroidered shrine, Sir Henri du Lac was standing in front of the shrine itself, deep in thought. He frowned at the memory of that morning.

It is insupportable, he thought. That I should be so accosted in the midst of this great celebration! I, who brought a gift of such holiness. Why should this happen now!

The knight dwelt for a moment on the Abbot's words as they sat in his chambers after the confrontation.

"My son," the Abbot had said in soothing tones. "Please do not distress yourself. Where there is greatness, there is also jealousy."

"My Lord Abbot," responded Sir Henri. "I thank you, but my heart is heavy with the taint of anger at a time when all should be at peace."

The Abbot looked at him thoughtfully. "Sir Henri," he said. "I was summoned to the guest hall by Brother Jocelin only after he became concerned that members of two such noble families should be in dispute in his hall. I sense that there is something more to this than meets the eye. Is there anything you wish to tell me?"

"Father," said the knight, "I will confess to you that there is some ill-feeling between my family and that of the young man who spoke with such passion. I had not thought to encounter him, or his mother, within these walls, and I crave your pardon for the disturbance."

"I am grieved that any conflict should attend this joyous time, but such is the nature of man that complete accord is rarely to be found," said Abbot Samson.

Seeing that his words were having little impact on the Crusader, Samson sighed. "Mayhap it will be of help to you if I recount a particular event from my own past. It is rare that I would do so but, in this situation, I judge it to be beneficial."

Pausing for a moment to collect his thoughts, the Abbot continued:

"Before I was anointed Abbot of this great Abbey, I was the subsacrist in charge of the workmen. It was a source of pride to me that, under my leadership, the abbey was maintained in such good repair that all who visited could not fail to comment that the Abbey of St. Edmunds was one of the greatest in the land. Why, I even arranged for the beautiful choir screen you see now in our church to be built."

"It is indeed beautiful, my Lord Abbot," said the knight. "You can be justly proud of your work."

The Abbot smiled. "Yes, I was proud. Perhaps too proud."

"I am not certain that I understand," said Sir Henri.

"You see before you now," responded Samson, "a man of maturity, who has labored in the fields of God's creation for many years. At the time of which I speak, however, I was both younger in years and in the understanding of men's hearts. In pursuit of my work for the glory of God and the blessed saint whose bones rest within our walls, I failed to notice that some of my brothers had become jealous of the attention which I received as a result of my endeavors."

"These brothers conspired against you?" Samson had captured the knight's attention.

"You may say so," said the Abbot. "Some would find it shocking that such low emotions might be found within the walls of this sacred place, but I doubt not that your life has taught you that all men are capable of ill will, however lofty their beliefs or their declared intent."

The Crusader sighed. "Truly, I fear it is so."

Sipping from his goblet, the Abbot returned to his tale.

"It was my intent to build a great tower in the Abbey church. It would reach to the sky and all men, near and far, would be awed by the power of God shown through the labor of His children.

"At the time of which I speak there was no Abbot to guide the brothers, for Abbot Hugh had died and no choice had been confirmed to succeed him. It is well said that where there is no order, there is chaos, for I found that some of my brothers and some others of the town had joined together to oppose my plans. The sacrist and these conspirators petitioned the custodians of Abbot Hugh's estates to forbid the construction of any building while there was no abbot to provide direction. The petition was granted."

"Yet is there not a tower in the church?" asked Sir Henri.

The Abbot smiled. "Yes, there is," he said. "This is why I tell you my tale, so that you may know that jealousy and malice cannot stand against the light for long.

"It came to pass that those who opposed me were removed from their positions," continued the Abbot. "With their departure, I was given the power to fulfil my vow to God. The tower was built, and it was though I heard my Father saying to me: 'Well done, good and faithful servant. Thou hast been faithful over a few things. I will make you ruler over many things..'"

Silence fell between the two men. Eventually, the knight stirred. "Father Abbot," he said. "I am honored that you would tell me of this. I understand what it is that you are saying, and I hope you will not think me churlish if I ask to take my leave of you now. I must think a while on what you have said."

"Go in peace," responded the Abbot. "May God bless and keep you."

Standing now before St. Edmund's shrine, Sir Henri thought of how the Abbot had urged him to calm his troubled thoughts and focus only on the holy ceremony to come. Yet he found it impossible to put behind him the memory of that young man declaiming the infamy of the Crusader's noble family.

He had no right, thought the knight. Angrily, he turned on his heel and went out to the stables.

"Seward!"

His groom came running out of the stable. "My Lord?"

"Saddle my horse," said his master. "I am riding out to see the country around this great Abbey."

"Do you wish that I accompany you?" asked Seward.

"No, I shall ride alone. I seek to put my mind at peace, and for that I must be alone."

"Of course, my Lord," responded the groom. "I will bring Raven out to you at once."

As he rode out of the Abbey gates, Sir Henri saw little around him. He rode through the town and out into the countryside, thinking only of the importance of the relic and how it might be installed in its rightful place beside the blessed St. Edmund without any more conflict to disturb the peace of his hopes or those of the people of the Liberty.

CHAPTER FOUR

Five knights came and tried out the abbot by asking himwhat they should say on oath ... "When it comes to your oath,speak the truth as you know it."

THE PRE-DAWN SKY PROMISED A fine, clear day after a cold night that spoke of the winter to come. As Aileen walked to the Abbey, she thought of the day ahead, and wondered if she would be allowed to attend the ceremony to install the holy relic in its place in the church. She had been lucky on her first day, when the knight had arrived with his offering of the relic. But she was not sure that Mistress Taylor would tolerate any more time spent away from the work at hand, and there were many linens that needed tending. A cloth that remained stained for too long would not be fit for use in God's house, and no amount of fine embroidery would make it so.

No sooner had she crossed the threshold of the Abbey, though, than she realized all was not as it should be.

In many ways the scene was like the one that had greeted her that first morning. Servants hurried from place to place, boys ran across the courtyard, and monks moved between the courtyard and cloister with serious expressions on their faces. But the excitement was not the same. There were no smiles, no laughter. The gatekeeper was not even at his post.

Aileen stopped a young boy who was running past her. "What is going on?" she asked.

"It's gone," he cried. "It was taken in the night!"

"What is gone?"

"The Cross," he replied. "Someone has stolen the holy relic!"

I can't believe it, Aileen thought, as the boy shook himself free of her hand and ran off. How can that be!

She ran over to the linen room, seeking Mistress Taylor or one of the other workers. As she ran, she bumped into Brother Herbert, who was walking swiftly across the courtyard toward the Abbot's lodging.

"I'm sorry, Brother Prior," stammered Aileen. "I was so shocked to hear about the relic that I wasn't paying attention to where I am going."

"I have taken no injury, child," said Brother Herbert. "I am afraid we are all a little distracted this morning. Do not worry yourself, though. There is little you can do except pray for the safe return of the Cross."

"That I will do willingly, brother" said Aileen, and watched the prior continue on his way.

Mistress Taylor was in the linen room, talking with two servants who were gathering linens for the wash.

"God have mercy on us," she was saying as Aileen entered. "He will surely not be pleased that we take so little care of this holy gift."

Oh no, thought Aileen, she is beginning to sound the way Ruth did when I told her about the relic. Is God such a wrathful God that he punishes even those who have no hand in desecrating His house?

"What has happened?" Aileen said, sitting down next to one of the women and picking up some altar cloths to check for stains. "A boy just told me that the relic is gone, but how can that be?"

"It's terrible!" cried one of the servants, hearing Aileen's question. "Last night, as the knight was praying by the tomb of St. Edmund, he heard a noise behind him. Before he could see who was disturbing his prayers, he was knocked unconscious!"

"Who knows how long he lay there without his senses," continued Mistress Taylor. "But when he recovered them, he found that the relic had been stolen, and there was neither sight nor sound of the thief!"

"Was the knight alone then?" asked Aileen. "Was no one with him in the church?"

"No, no one," said Mistress Taylor. "He kept his vigil alone and would allow no one to share it with him. Oh, if only he had, perhaps the relic would even now be in its place and there would be rejoicing instead of wailing!"

"Is he all right?" Aileen asked.

"Yes. He has a nasty headache, but it is his honor that is most offended by this theft." Mistress Taylor gave a sniff, as though she thought that personal honor was not something to be considered when such a tragedy had occurred. "He is with the Abbot and the Prior even as we speak, and the Abbot has told Durand, the Reeve, to begin a hue and cry after the thief. Though how they are to find someone about whom they know nothing, and who is surely long gone now, I do not know!"

"Is that why Sergeant Ralph is not at his post?" asked Aileen. "He is out with the Reeve pursuing the thief?"

"No," said the robemaker. "The Reeve is waiting for the men to gather. They have not even left the Abbey grounds yet." Another sniff. "Isn't that just typical! A thief runs off in the night with a priceless relic of our Lord, and they wait around all day before they begin to chase him!"

Aileen could think of no good answer to this, especially as only a minute before Mistress Taylor had so dismissed the idea of chasing the villain as to make it appear to be a worthless endeavor.

"As for that gatekeeper, it would appear that sore heads are abundant today. Apparently they had to rouse him from a deep sleep this morning after they discovered the theft, and he has been of so little use that the Abbot ordered him to lie down and keep out of their way until the Reeve is ready to ride."

"He wasn't attacked as well, was he?" asked Aileen sympathetically.

"No, I think it more like too much enjoyment of the vine through the night," responded Mistress Taylor in a tone that was clearly designed to squash any sympathetic tendencies in her worker.

"Well, enough of all your gossiping!" she declared, returning to her role as taskmaster and clapping her hands. "It's about time you all got to work. Time's a'wasting, and there is much to be done!"

The women did as they were bidden, their mood low but their hands busy. Aileen mended a small tear in an altar cloth and hemmed it before passing the cloth to her neighbor, who had worked at the Abbey long enough to be permitted to embroider some of the linens which adorned St. Edmund's shrine.

It was more than an hour later when they heard the sounds of men gathering in the Great Court and voices crying out orders. Unable to contain their curiosity, most of the women got up and went to see what was going on. They weren't alone. It seemed as though all work around the Abbey had ceased while everyone within listened to the instructions to those who were going to search for the thief.

Aileen slipped out of the linen room and found a place in the doorway of the stables next to the Abbot's quarters. From there she was able to hear and see all that occurred as the search was ordered.

The Crusader knight, the Abbot, the Prior and the town Reeve all stood on the steps of the Abbot's lodgings. Before them stood a mixed group of men and boys, carrying sticks or knives, slingshots or short swords, according to their position in the town. To the side were ranked the knights of the royal escort, standing beside their horses.

"Men," said the abbot. "You know that there has been committed a most foul crime within these walls. We do not know who would do such a thing, although surely no true Christian would dare to so tempt God's wrath!"

A murmur arose amongst those gathered, and the Abbot was forced to raise his hand to command silence.

"You have been brought together to search for the thief and recover the holy treasure. I think you will never have a task of more importance, for there are few of you called to take the Cross in a Crusade, as was the noble Sir Henri here. As a young man it was my desire to fight with King Richard the Lionheart, but it was God's will that I enter the cloister. Now, I tell you that it is God's will that you search for the holy relic and bring the thief to justice!"

The men seemed to stand taller as they listened to the Abbot's words. Seeing themselves as Crusaders, they turned to attend to the injured knight as he stepped forward.

Sir Henri waited until all eyes were turned upon him. Then hesitantly, as though he searched for the right words in a foreign tongue, he began to speak.

"You see before you a man who has travelled many strange paths, and who has seen much that is painful to recall. I have fought in the heat of the desert and struggled through mud that rose to men's knees."

No one stirred. The knight had started softly, but as he continued his voice grew stronger and the words seemed to flow more smoothly.

"I took an oath in Constantinople, on the very day that King Baldwin was crowned by the soldiers of the Cross, that I would bring this most holy of relics to the great Abbey of St. Edmund. Yesterday I had thought my vow fulfilled, but last night I failed in my duty to God."

The men murmured denials of this, but the knight had not finished, and he would suffer no interruption.

"This morning I say to you, on my life, that I shall not rest until the piece of the True Cross that I brought across the seas is restored to the shrine of St. Edmund. This I promise you all!" As he swore this new vow, the knight knelt and held his sword upright in front of him, as though offering it to the men of St. Edmund's Bury.

A great cheer broke out in the courtyard of the Abbey, and Aileen felt tears pricking her eyes. It was a great moment, and she understood for the first time what her father meant when he talked about the tide of emotion that had carried him across Europe behind the banner of King Richard.

The Abbot again raised his hand for silence.

"Let us pray," he said, and all those present knelt.

"Oh, mighty God!" he cried. "You who have said 'Woe unto them that call evil good, and good evil; that put darkness for light, and light for darkness.' Hear us as we cry to thee, asking for your strength and wisdom to seek out that which is evil and which has taken the

34

light from our midst! Guide us to the sinner who has defiled Your holy house and stolen the sacred Cross. May our deeds today be a symbol of repentance for our failure to protect Your holy treasure and may Your anger be turned from us and Your forgiveness granted us."

"Amen," echoed around the courtyard.

As the men rose, the town Reeve stepped forward.

"We do not know who it is we are seeking," Durand said. "But we know that he must have been on the roads in the dead of night, and he was in a hurry. It is also possible that there was more than one man involved, and they may even be lying low in a nearby village or in the forest.

"Sir Henri and his escort will be riding in the direction of the villages of Glemsford and Long Melford. The rest of you will divide into teams of ten and will fan out towards the villages around Bury. Seek out all who live along the road and in the forests and ask about disturbances in the night. Search for signs of any who might have paused to rest along the way overnight and question any strangers to the area."

The Reeve paused for questions, and then asked the Abbot if he wished to say anything further.

"May God bless you in your holy quest," said Abbot Samson. "Your first task must be to bring the holy relic home. If you also bring the blasphemer to my court for trial, you may be sure that justice will be wrought!"

With that, the men were dismissed to begin their hunt.

In the confusion of organizing the men and preparing for departure, Aileen heard many people discussing the possible identity of the thief. There was deep anger in all that was said, and a desire for revenge that frightened Aileen without her quite knowing why.

"No Christian would do a thing like this," said one man as he passed close by Aileen. "Only a heathen would dare defile the shrine of the saint."

"Everyone I know would be terrified of doing something that would be sure to bring down God's anger on them," said another.

"Whatever can they hope to gain?" asked one of the monks as he held the bridle for one of the knights to mount his horse.

"It must be a stranger," said one of the stable servants.

"Or a Jew," replied his friend. "Abbot Samson threw most of the Jews out of the town over 10 years ago, but there are still a few around. They wouldn't care about stealing a part of the True Cross!"

"You're right," exclaimed another of the servants who had been listening in. "I bet it's one of those Jews who still live at Fornham!"

"Who's going in that direction?" asked the first man. "We had better tell them to go for the Jews first."

Aileen turned cold. Ruth and her family lived in Fornham!

Before either Aileen or Ruth had been born, there had been a large Jewish community in St. Edmund's Bury. But then there had been some trouble when a Jew was accused of murdering a young boy. The townspeople had rioted on Palm Sunday in 1190, and many people had died. Abbot Samson had expelled the Jews from Bury, and none had been allowed to settle in the town since.

Ruth's father was a well-known physician and had done great service to the Abbot over the years, curing him of fevers and pains, and helping the monks in the infirmary at the Abbey and at the hospital founded by Abbot Samson just outside the north gate of the town. For his service, the Abbot had rewarded him with the tenancy of a small holding at Fornham, and there Isaac of Cordoba had settled and raised his family. Two other Jewish families had also been allowed by the Abbot to settle in Fornham, and together they formed a small community which kept itself largely to itself and tried not to inflame the passions of the townspeople of St. Edmund's Bury.

Aileen knew that feeling still ran deep against the Jews in the town, but she had never really understood why. Ruth had told her that it was because most Christians never even saw the Jews as people. They hated the whole race. "The only thing that most people see when they look at us is the people who killed your Messiah," she had said.

To Aileen this seemed stupid. How could you blame a whole race for the actions of a few? It would be like hating all people with yellow hair because a little girl with yellow hair had stolen your favorite toy as a child.

Now, however, for the first time, Aileen felt something of the fear that she knew Ruth and her family often felt. For these men seemed interested only in avenging themselves upon an unpopular group for the theft of the relic. They were not at all interested in looking closely at any evidence of wrongdoing on the part of the Fornham community.

I have to warn Ruth and her family, thought Aileen. But how? I can't leave the Abbey without being noticed, and if I do, I will lose my position here.

Robert! Aileen suddenly knew how she could warn her friend. She ran across the courtyard to the cellarer's gate. She knew that one of her best childhood friends was delivering some gold plate to the Abbey today in preparation for the feast, and she was sure that he would have stayed to listen to the speeches of the Abbot and the knight if he could.

Skidding to a halt at the gateway, she looked around, hoping against hope that she would be able to catch him before he left. Where is he? Oh no, I've missed him!

No! There he is, going towards the cemetery gate.

"Robert," she called. "Robert!"

Her second call, carrying its desperation on the breeze, had the desired effect. Robert halted, and turned towards the voice. Seeing Aileen coming towards him, Robert smiled and started back towards her. He was a tall, gangling teen, a year older than Aileen and just becoming conscious of his manhood. He and Aileen had always been great friends, as had their parents. It brightened his day when he could talk to her.

"Aileen," he said. "I wasn't sure that I would see you today. I didn't want to come in search of you in case the robemaker did not like my disturbing you in your new work."

"Robert," Aileen said. "There isn't time for all that now. You have to hurry and warn Ruth and her family!"

"Warn them about what?" asked Robert.

"The men searching for the relic. They're blaming the theft on the Jews, and I just heard some of them talking about going after the people in Fornham." Aileen's voice was rising as she desperately tried to get Robert to understand.

"Calm down, Aileen," he said. "Are you telling me that they are going to attack Ruth's family and the other Jews in Fornham?"

"Yes! Please hurry, Robert. You have to go and warn them and tell them to get out of there before the men arrive. They haven't left yet, and you can get there ahead of them if you go now!" In her distress, she was pulling at his sleeve.

Robert took Aileen's hand and gave it a squeeze.

"It's all right. I'll leave right away. I have the cart outside, and I can take the shortcut through the woods. Don't worry. It will be all right."

Giving her a quick smile, Robert turned on his heel and ran towards the gate. Watching him go, Aileen at last felt some of the tension drain out of her body. Keep him safe, Lord, she prayed. And please, please let him get there on time!

CHAPTER FIVE

The abbot asked the king [in 1190] for written permission to expel the Jews from St. Edmund's town, on the ground that everything in the town ... belonged by right to St. Edmund.

"YOU WERE RIGHT TO DO it, Aileen," said her father. It was evening and Aileen was tense, straining to hear any sound of men returning from the hunt. "Men will do in anger things that they would never do if they thought about it first. But, and I want you to listen to me very carefully, I do not want you getting involved in this any more." Jude looked directly at his daughter, and Aileen recognized his "there is to be no argument on this point" look.

The candle on the table, marked to show the passing of time, showed it was but an hour past dark. All the evening chores were complete. The shutters were closed, the floors swept, the evening meal had been eaten and cleaned away, and the cloth to be dyed on the morrow had been prepared. Sage, marigold flowers and dandelion leaves, needed for the dyes, had been

40

collected from the garden in the back, and the goat and chickens had been fed.

It was the family's "together time," and they treasured this hour of the day. Aileen and her mother were both working on part of a big order from the wife of one of the town's most important citizens, her mother putting the finishing touches to an embroidered sleeve and Aileen hemming a kerchief. Her sister Mabel was watching her mother's careful work with rapt attention, while Richard and Henry played in front of the hearth and their father counted the day's takings at the table.

"The theft is a terrible thing," said Aileen's mother, Anne. "I can't imagine who would do something like that. And I am glad that you were able to do something to make sure that innocent people were not hurt. But it makes my blood run cold to think what could happen if you were to interfere any more. Your father is right. Do not get involved!"

"But how can I ignore it when I know that my friends are in danger?" Aileen protested. "And, after all, mother, they have been your friends too!"

"That's enough," said her father, sharply. "We are not talking about friendship here. We are talking about your keeping out of danger. You will obey me in this, Aileen."

"Yes, father," she said.

Aileen was saved from further comment by a knock at the door. Jude rose, opened the door, and invited the visitors in.

"Robert," said Aileen, getting to her feet. "I'm so glad you have come!"

Remembering her manners, she greeted Robert's father, John Palgrave, and invited him to take her place in front of the fire.

"I thought Robert and I should come this evening to discuss the day's events," said John. "The mood of the town is dangerous, and I am concerned that our children not become involved."

"We were just discussing the very same thing," said Jude. "Aileen, get Master Palgrave a cup of hippocras, please, and then you and Robert may talk together if you wish."

Aileen and Robert looked at each other. They recognized dismissal when they heard it.

Aileen fetched the cup of spiced wine for Robert's father, and then the two of them moved farther away from the group at the fire, to a corner where they could talk undisturbed. When her sister made a move to follow them, Aileen shook her head and told her to watch their brothers for a little. Mabel stuck out her tongue at her sister, but good-naturedly went back to her stool near the fire.

"What happened?" asked Aileen softly. "I know that you must have got to Fornham on time, for I heard that the searchers found no one there. But I have been dying to hear what occurred when you told Ruth's father about the theft of the holy relic."

"I only just made it in time," confessed Robert. "When I got to Fornham I found Ruth and her mother

42

tending to the herb garden, but it took quite a while to find all the members of the other two families.

"I had thought I would have trouble persuading them all to leave," Robert went on. "But it was strange. When I told them what you had heard, they quietly put together a few things they might need for a period of hiding and moved into the forest."

"You mean they didn't question anything that you said?" said Aileen.

"No. Ruth's father said to tell you he was grateful, and that they would say prayers of thanks to Yahweh for your kindness. Ruth told me that they are always prepared to run, and they have a hiding place prepared in the forest for just such a day as this."

"That's sad," said Aileen.

"I thought so too," Robert replied. "I never thought about what it would be like to always live in fear of attack and to always be prepared to run at a moment's notice. But, in this case, I'm glad they did react so quickly."

"Why?" asked Aileen.

"Well, as soon as they had left, I turned the cart for home. I had gone only a few hundred yards when I heard men coming towards me. I turned into the woods, so as not to meet them, and in less than a minute they rushed past me. They looked to be in the heat of anger, and I do not think that they would have stopped to ask questions had they found Ruth and the others at home."

"Aileen, Robert, come over here," Aileen's father called.

The pair went over to join the group in front of the hearth.

"Robert, Aileen," said John Palgrave. "What you did today was brave. But, having talked to some of the returning searchers this afternoon, I am very concerned that you should have acted so. You are both old enough now to think before you act."

Robert was surprised at his father's tone. "What do you mean, father?" he asked. "I thought you would be pleased that we had helped our friends."

"Do you know what happened after you left Fornham today, Robert?" asked Jude, looking at his daughter's friend.

"No, sir," replied Robert. "I thought it wise to leave as quickly as possible after the men had gone past."

"I'm glad you had that much sense," said his father, gruffly.

"The men burned down one of the houses at Fornham," said Jude. "They were so angered by not finding anyone there that they trampled the plants, ransacked the homes, and then burned one of them down. Had you been there, you could have been hurt."

Aileen was horrified. She had been so concerned about Ruth she had never thought of the danger in which she could be putting Robert. But she had also never thought of the possible reaction of the men when they found nobody at home in Fornham.

"But I saw Peter Fuller at the Abbey," said Aileen. "And Henry of Thetford's sons, John and Edward. I used to play with them. I can't believe they would do something like this!"

Her father shrugged. "As I have said, men do strange things when they are in a rage. And when they found no one at Fornham, they became even more convinced of the guilt of the Jews. To them, flight means guilt."

John Palgrave turned to Aileen and took her hands in his.

"I know it is a hard thing," he said. "But are you so sure that your friends are *not* guilty of this crime?"

Aileen pulled her hands out of his clasp. She couldn't believe her ears!

"Of course! How can you think such a thing?"

"Aileen," said her father. "Do not speak with so little respect to Master Palgrave!"

"I'm truly sorry," she said. "I did not mean to be rude. It is just that I could never believe anyone in Ruth's family, or any member of the other families of Fornham, would steal the relic. Why should they?"

No one seemed very sure of how to answer this question.

"I know they are your friends," said her mother. "Indeed, we have never had cause to think anything but good of them before." Anne paused, obviously trying to think of the right way to express what she was thinking.

"Aileen," she said. "You know that this is a sacred object, and it is very hard for Christians to believe that any other Christian would risk his soul to steal something that would bring him only sorrow."

"I don't know about Christians or Jews," said Aileen. "I only know about these people. And I *know* that neither Ruth not anyone else in her family would ever do such a thing."

Her father and mother shook their heads, and an uncomfortable silence fell. Then Anne asked John Palgrave if he desired another cup of wine, and Aileen and Robert had the chance to slip away into their corner again.

"We're going to have to do something, you know," said Aileen.

"What?" asked Robert. "The town is in an uproar, and there isn't much we can do on our own. Even if we wanted to hide the Jewish families, with the way our parents are feeling at the moment that is out of the question."

"The only way to make sure that Ruth and the others are safe is to find out who really took the relic." Aileen made it sound like the only sensible course of action.

Robert looked at Aileen as though he couldn't believe what he had just heard.

"Aileen!" he said. "That's impossible!"

"Why?" One of the reasons Robert had always been so fond of Aileen was because her clear grey eyes and slim build hid such a determined will. Now he wondered why he had never seen the disadvantages of that quality.

"Why?" he repeated. "Because we are only two. Because we wouldn't know where to start looking.

Because if the king's men can't find him, we have absolutely no hope. Because…"

"All right," said Aileen. "I know it might be a bit difficult, but we do have some advantages that all those powerful people don't have, you know."

Aileen was laughing, but Robert was becoming increasingly suspicious. He wasn't sure if he really wanted to ask the next question.

"What advantages?" Robert asked finally, resigning himself to the inevitable.

"Well, for one, no one takes any notice of us," she said.

"How does that help?" he said.

"When people don't notice you're there, they say all sorts of things that they would never say in front of people who matter."

"I'll grant you that," he said. "But I don't see how that's going to help unless we happen to be talking to someone who knows who took the relic."

"That's only partly true," said Aileen. "People often don't realize they know something important. They may not know the whole story, but I'll warrant there are a lot of people who saw something strange last night."

Robert looked unsure about this.

"It's like a riddle," Aileen insisted. "If you only hear a part of it, you can't possibly find the solution. But if you hear it all, then you can work out the answer."

Aileen was warming to her argument.

"That's what we need to do," she said. "We need to find the information that completes the riddle, and

47

then we can find out who really took the relic, and where it is now!"

"Well, I don't suppose it would hurt to try," said Robert. "I'm not sure you're right, but I'll certainly do anything I can to help."

Aileen smiled. "Thank you," she said. "I knew I could count on you."

Robert blushed, then coughed to hide his embarrassment. Aileen's confidence meant a lot to him.

"So," he said, hurriedly. "How do we go about this?"

"Let's think," she said. "We need to find out if anything unusual happened at the Abbey last night. Apart from the theft, that is!"

"We also need to check outside the Abbey," said Robert. "The searchers were right about that. The thief must have gone somewhere after he struck the knight and stole the relic."

"Unless it's still in the Abbey," said Aileen. "Perhaps the thief is on the inside!"

"I hadn't thought of that," Robert said. "We do need to cover both possibilities."

"All right," she said. "I'll take the Abbey and see what I can find out. At the very least I can find out what the fuss was about yesterday morning. It may have had nothing to do with the theft of the relic, but we cannot afford to ignore any possibility."

"Absolutely!" agreed Robert. "I'll take the surrounding areas. I have to make some deliveries for my father tomorrow anyway, so I'll talk to the people who live along the road and in the woods."

48

"Didn't the searchers do that today?" asked Aileen.

"Yes," said Robert. "But, as you said, it's the little things that people don't particularly notice that we will be asking about. And some of the people around here might not be very happy talking to the king's men. Poaching is one way for a poor man to put meat on his table, but it is not looked upon with favor by the owner of the land!"

Aileen nodded her head. "Yes, you're right. And even if they have no cause to fear the soldiers, many folk would be unlikely to tell strangers anything if what they saw or heard wasn't something they thought was important."

"Let's do it!" said Robert, catching Aileen's enthusiasm.

"We had better get together tomorrow evening and talk about what we have found out during the day," said Aileen. "We'll meet by the river, shall we? And if you can, will you bring Ruth with you? She may have some ideas that we can use."

Robert nodded. As he rose to rejoin the group around the fire, Robert squeezed Aileen's hand and smiled at her.

"Don't worry," he said. "We'll do it. Between us, I know that we can solve the riddle and save Ruth!"

CHAPTER SIX

The abbot had incurred many expenses in his journey overseas, but brought back a golden cross and a precious gospel-book worth 80 marks.

AILEEN HAD LITTLE SLEEP THAT night. Where to look, with whom to talk? These were the questions which occupied her mind as she tossed and turned in the room she shared with her ten-year-old sister Mabel and their little brothers.

If we are to succeed, we're going to have to act quickly, she thought. Otherwise the townspeople are sure to find Ruth and the others. Aileen didn't even want to think about what would happen in that event. She wasn't sure she knew her neighbors anymore, not after this day.

When the first birds began their morning wake-up call, Aileen rose and dressed quickly and silently. She stole downstairs and milked the goat, preparing the morning oatmeal before her mother stirred. By the time her mother came downstairs, Aileen was ready to leave.

"Why are you leaving so early, Aileen?" asked her mother. "Are you all right?"

"Yes, I'm fine, mother," said Aileen, giving her a hug. "I just had trouble sleeping, and you know that I think best when I'm doing something. So I thought I would get started early."

"What were you thinking about?"

"Oh, about the relic, and Ruth, and all that."

"Aileen," said her mother, looking worried. "I know how much your friendship with Ruth means to you. But you really must hold your peace for now. The town is in an ugly mood, and I don't want you getting hurt."

"I know," Aileen replied. "I promise. I'll be careful."

Her mother didn't look completely satisfied with this response, but Aileen gave her mother another quick hug before she could say anything more. Then she greeted her father as he came downstairs for his breakfast and left the house.

As she entered the Great Court that morning, Aileen came across Seward, whom she recognized as one of the Crusader knight's servants. He was walking the knight's horse around the yard, checking that all was well with his favorite charge.

"Good morning, Seward," said Aileen. "I hope that your master is improved this morning?"

"I have not seen him yet today," said the young groom. "But I believe that he is well, thank you."

"Were you with Sir Henri in the Holy Land?" asked Aileen, stroking the horse's black coat.

51

Seward was used to being asked questions about his master. To those who had never travelled far from home the very idea of "taking the Cross" and going to the Holy Land was filled with romance.

"Yes, I was. My father served Sir Henri's mother, the Lady Eleanor de Clare," said Seward. "When Sir Henri joined the Crusade, she sent me to be his groom. She knew that I would serve him well on a difficult journey." He spoke with pride, as one who felt himself as much a part of the family as any son of the house of Clare.

"You must have seen great things," Aileen said, encouraging him to continue.

"I saw many things, both wonderful and terrible. I had never thought to see such splendor as the city of Constantinople, with its golden towers and its bright colors and strange scents. But before we reached the city it was a terrible time, and many brave men died."

"What about the knight?" asked Aileen. "What about Sir Henri?"

"As you must have heard, he fought bravely in the campaign, and he was rewarded for his valor." Seward gave the knight's horse one final pat and began to put on the saddle. "Of course, without such a noble horse as Raven here, he would not have been able to achieve so much!"

The horse nudged his companion and whinnied, as though understanding what was being said.

"Were there many treasures in the great city?" asked Aileen.

"Oh yes, many, and even I was given a share. But the richest treasures went to the noble lords, of course. And the most prized relic of all went to Sir Henri. He made sure of that!"

"What do you mean?" Aileen asked.

"I'm sorry," said Seward. "I did not mean that to sound harsh, and perhaps I shouldn't have said anything. It's just that Sir Henri is very conscious of the position of his family, and sometimes his desire to show that he is among the very best can be hard on others. But he's a very fair master," the groom added hastily.

Aileen thought about this for a moment.

"He is ambitious, then?" she said, cutting to the heart of the matter as usual.

"Well, yes," said Seward. "But that is no very bad thing in a strong knight, is it?"

"Oh, no," said Aileen. "But perhaps ambition may make enemies where gentleness would not."

"That's true," said Seward. "Why, when the treasures were being gathered in Constantinople, it was a French knight of royal blood who first was given the piece of the True Cross. But Sir Henri came to the new king in Constantinople and claimed a favor he was owed from the battlefield. He swore his oath before the high altar in the cathedral and told the king he must have the relic in order to fulfil his vow. What was the king to do? He had to take the relic back from the royal knight and award it to Sir Henri!"

"What did the French knight say in response to that?" asked Aileen.

"He was furious!" replied Seward. "King Baldwin thought he would not react so, for Sir Henri had stood by the knight in the heat of battle when many had run away in fear. But the son of a royal house is not used to having his wishes opposed!"

"What did he do?" asked Aileen.

"He said that Sir Henri only swore the vow to advance himself in the eyes of kings and lords, and that he was no genuine pilgrim seeking God's forgiveness and grace."

"Why would he say a thing like that?" Aileen asked.

Seward was silent for a moment, obviously thinking about whether he had already said too much. Aileen waited, stroking Raven's nose and trying not to look too eager for more information.

"Well, it's like this," said Seward, making up his mind to hold nothing back from such an attractive and interested audience. "Sir Henri grew up in France, and his family was long in favor with the French king. I am told that his father had hopes of becoming an ambassador for the king, and certainly he rose quickly in power. But then something happened."

"What?" said Aileen, as Seward paused. "What happened?"

"I'm not really sure," said the groom. "I did hear that Sir Henri's father was accused before the king of some great crime. I do not know what but, whatever the insult, the king was greatly angered, and the whole family was banished to some estate far away from court."

"Sir Henri was banished as well?" asked Aileen.

"Yes. It is rumored that he begged the king to be allowed to remain at court, and to serve in whatever manner the king should choose. But the king was very angry indeed and told Sir Henri that he was not interested in helping the son of a traitor achieve power he might use one day against the Crown. I think if it was treachery the king truly meant, then it is God's mercy that the family was only sent away from the court. Many have died for less than that!"

"But it was the end of Sir Henri's hopes," Aileen said. "How sad."

"You don't need to be too sad," said Seward. "It was not long before the Pope called upon the kings of the West to take the Cross once more. At once the king commanded many of his favored lords to be a part of his Crusading army. And, at the request of one of the king's nephews, with whom Sir Henri had once been friends, Sir Henri too was permitted to join the retinue that accompanied the king's army. I do hear he was valiant in battle, even saving his friend's life, and so his reward could not be withheld once they reached Constantinople."

"That's how he came to ask for the relic?" said Aileen.

"Yes," said Seward, simply.

"Did the French knight try to fight Sir Henri for the relic?" Aileen asked.

"No, but he swore an oath of his own to avenge himself upon my master. He said that his honor had been called into question and he would neither forgive nor forget!"

Aileen was fascinated by all that Seward was telling her, and it was certainly giving her some ideas

"Did that knight travel back from Constantinople at the same time as Sir Henri?" she asked.

"I do not know. I think he was still there when we left," said Seward. "Sir Henri had decided to come to England, to visit the home of his mother, and he left the city before most of his fellow Crusaders."

"Does Sir Henri intend to stay here?" asked Aileen.

"My, you do ask a lot of questions!" said Seward. "But I suppose you do not hear much of the outside world here in St. Edmund's Bury!"

Aileen rather resented this attitude toward her hometown, but she knew that anything she might say at this point would only stop the flow of information. Finding out the answers to her questions was more important than taking offence.

"I'm sorry if I'm being over curious," said Aileen. "But you must admit that it is of great interest to us here if Sir Henri intends to settle in this country."

"I wish I could tell you the answer," said Seward. "But I don't really know. He did visit King John when he first landed in England, and I am told that he was received warmly. His vow to give the holy relic to the great Abbey of St. Edmund's Bury was well known, and I heard some of Sir Henri's knights say that King John would be only too pleased to be able to claim the relic as a sign of God's favor on England rather than have the French king claim any such favor for France."

56

"So Sir Henri may have hopes of favor from the English court, even if the French court is closed to him?" asked Aileen.

"That is what many of those closest to Sir Henri say," said Seward.

"More reason for the French knight to be angry with Sir Henri," said Aileen.

"If he knew of it, yes," agreed Seward.

"Do you think the disturbance in the guest hall the day before the theft might have had anything to do with the French knight?" Aileen pondered out loud.

Seward merely shrugged and said he didn't know anything about that.

At that point Mistress Taylor came through the courtyard and, seeing Aileen, called to her. Aileen hastily wished good day to the groom and ran to answer the robemaker's call.

"Ah, Aileen," said Mistress Taylor, looking rather flushed this morning. "I don't know what the world is coming to. Really I don't! First it's the holy relic stolen and the noble knight injured, and now it's the vestments for the high mass. Whatever are we going to do!"

As the distraught robemaker continued, Aileen tried to get a word in edgeways. It was no use.

"I just knew it," wailed Mistress Taylor. "As soon as I heard about the theft of the blessed relic, I said to my husband: 'Mark my words. We will all be punished for this. Just mark my words!' And see, I was right. I just knew it!"

"I don't understand," said Aileen, finally managing to ask a question as the robemaker paused to take in another breath. "What has happened to the vestments?"

"Look!" said Mistress Taylor, leading the way into the linen room. "Look at them!"

All of Aileen's fellow workers were gathered round one of the tables, apparently examining something laid out before them. As Aileen joined the group, she saw the source of the robemaker's distress.

On the table lay the white tunic, the alb, worn by the abbot at high mass. Its usual clean whiteness was marred by streaks of dirt, and a whole section of the front had been roughly torn out. The stole which was worn over the alb, beautifully embroidered with gold thread, had been cut in half, one end being left with the ruined tunic and the other taken away.

"We found them like this when we went to check everything was in order for the mass today," said Mistress Taylor. "They were all bundled up in a corner of the vestry. It must have happened during the night, but I can't understand why anyone would do such a thing!"

Aileen thought for a moment. "Did the Abbot wear these robes yesterday at mass?" she asked.

"Of course," said Mistress Taylor.

"No, he didn't!" said one of the other women. "He wore the robes he wears on ordinary days. Don't you remember, Mistress? After the men had left to search for the thief of the relic, a special mass was held to pray for the recovery of the relic? One of the young

58

brothers came rushing in to say they couldn't find the high mass vestments!"

"I'd forgotten," said Mistress Taylor. "I just thought they were in such a muddle that they weren't looking in the right place."

"If the vestments were missing yesterday, then that means they were damaged on the night of the theft," said Aileen.

"It must have been the thief," said Mistress Taylor. "That just proves it was a heathen who did this terrible thing. Why else would anyone ruin church vestments!"

Aileen didn't like the way this conversation was going.

"Did anyone hear about anything else strange happening that night?" she asked, trying to change the subject.

"What more do you want!" cried Mistress Taylor. "All this is more than enough already!"

"Yes, but you know, there was something else," said one of the women. "One of the stable lads told me that he woke up in the middle of the night when the horses started moving around in their stalls and whinnying. He sleeps in the stable loft, you know," she added.

"Was there someone in the stables?" asked Aileen.

"He didn't hear anyone, but he didn't go to check," said the woman. "When he heard about the theft, he just decided that the horses must have sensed the disturbance and were upset."

"That could be," said Aileen. "But did he hear anything other than the horses?"

"He didn't mention anything, and I think he would if ..."

"That's enough," interrupted Mistress Taylor. "We have lost enough time already with all the problems in the last couple of days. Just get on with your work, all of you. And Aileen, you ask too many questions. Don't be so nosy!"

"I beg your pardon, Mistress Taylor," said Aileen, getting down to work. What a wonderful crop of information she was going to have to tell Robert this evening, she thought. I just know we are going to be able to solve the riddle!

Ruth, hold on. Everything is going to be all right.

CHAPTER SEVEN

*I will not be deflected from carrying out my
intention for your sake any more than I would
for this young whipper-snapper there.*

ROBERT'S DAY WAS GOING WELL, too, even if not as well as Aileen's. For the past year he had been an apprentice to his father, and it was one of his first duties of the day to make sure that the goldsmith's furnace was ready, and to lay out his father's tools. Today he had risen well before dawn to get his morning chores done and was on the road by the time the sun rose above the Abbey.

His errands took Robert to the east of the town as far as Cottishall and then back to the north gate, near the hospital founded by Abbot Samson. That suited him very well, since he thought it most likely that any thief would take the quickest route out of town from the Abbey, and the road east was safe and easy to follow.

As he went about his father's business that morning, Robert asked questions of everyone he met. Had they heard anything out of the ordinary the night of the theft? Had they seen any strangers in the area? Had they found any signs of campfires?

It was not until he reached Cottishall and talked to the servants who worked at the local manor that Robert found his first clue to the events of the night of the theft.

The first person Robert came across as he neared the gates of the manor was the gamekeeper. He was sitting at the entrance to his cottage, right by the road, sharpening his knife, a pile of willow bark by his feet.

"Good morrow," said Robert.

"For some, mayhap," said the gamekeeper. "For others it is a day of work that should not be."

"Truly, it is a strange week, of that I am sure," said, Robert, not quite certain how he should respond to such a declaration. "The theft of the relic from the Abbey, and the search for the thief, has caused much distress in our part of the land."

"Thieves and wastrals," grumbled the gamekeeper. "I don't know anything about relics and knights, but I know a lot about theft. And I don't just mean the poachers I spend my life chasing!"

"What do you mean?" asked Robert.

"My lord is a hard man. He would tell you that himself," said the gamekeeper with a hard look in Robert's eyes, "so I am telling you nothing that is not truth.

"No doubt my master feels the burden of the king's taxes on his back, but he would have me manage the deer and game on his land, bring him meat for his table and capture poachers in greater numbers than in days past. I have no time for petty thieves and lazy beggars."

"Petty thieves?"

"Yes, and a lot of time it cost me when I have better things to do with my time!" said the gamekeeper angrily.

"What is it that has been stolen?" asked Robert.

"My best fish trap," responded the gamekeeper, his color rising. "It took me three years to grow the willow withies to the right size, and much time to strip away the bark and weave the basket chambers. I set it outside my door, ready to take to the river and catch the fish my lord commanded for his dinner the next day. When I came home for my supper after a long day chasing poachers, it was gone."

"When was this?" asked Robert.

"I don't know why you should care, but I remember the riders coming out the next day asking all sorts of questions about strangers in the night, so it must have been the day before that. I only know I had to use the old trap, and that doesn't catch near enough fish to please my master. Had my lord not been so taken up with all the fuss in St. Edmund's town I would have caught the rough edge of his tongue, you can be sure. As it was, he scarce noticed there were few fish and much fowl at his table that night."

Robert was excited. This was the first clue he had found, even though he didn't know how this could be related to the theft of a piece of the True Cross.

Bidding farewell to the unhappy gamekeeper, Robert continued on his way. He thought to talk to

63

the forester's wife, who lived nearby. Her husband was an important man in the community, an official of the Liberty who would not be interested in talking to a mere craftsman's son, however well-regarded the craftsman, about holy relics and thieves. Robert, however, did not come from a large family for nothing. The forester's wife was probably a much better source of information than her husband and, unless she was of a similar frame of mind as the gamekeeper, much more likely to be interested in passing the time of day with the son of the goldsmith.

Not more than a mile farther along the road from the gamekeeper's cottage he came across a short track leading to the forester's home. He turned down the track, hearing a humming and grunting growing ever louder. Turning a bend in the track he saw the forester's wife at work outside her home. Her arms were deep in a wooden bucket of water, the air heavy with the smell of wet wool.

"Good morrow, Mistress," said Robert.

"The Lord be praised for your coming," the woman said. "I'm sore tired of cleansing this fleece. My hands are cold and my back is sore. Will you sit with me a spell and take a mug of ale?"

"Gladly," responded Robert, thinking that this day was improving by the hour.

As the woman fetched him some ale and sat down with a heavy sigh Robert thought with pride of how well he had gauged the prospects of her friendly disposition. I'm better at investigating than I thought. Aileen will be impressed.

For a few minutes the pair sipped their ale and spoke of small things. Then Robert turned the conversation to the theft of the relic. Of course, all within the Abbey's rule had heard of it, and so the good woman was eager to talk to someone who might have news from the very place where all the excitement had happened.

"That was a strange night," she said. "Nothing was as usual. It seems as though heaven would let no one sleep while such a terrible thing was being done!"

"What do you mean?" asked Robert.

"Well, I had scarce laid my head down that night when my youngest started crying. She's less than a year old, you know, and her teeth are causing her pain just now.

"No sooner had I bathed her gums with a potion of chamomile and settled her back to sleep then I heard the sound of horse hooves on the road. We are not so far off the road from St. Edmund's Bury, you see, and sound carries far in the dead of night."

"You expected no visitors that night?" Robert asked.

"Indeed no, or else we would not have gone to bed," said the woman, indignantly. "Good Christian folk have too much work to do from dawn to dusk to tarry long after the sun sets. And, in any case, the rider did not come here. I think he turned off the road into the woods, though, for the sound did not fade away as it would if he had continued on the road."

"Where do you think he could have been going?" asked Robert.

"I don't know, and I really didn't give it much thought at the time," she said. "It just struck me as strange that anyone would be abroad at that time of night."

The woman could tell Robert nothing more, beyond the fact that she thought there might have been two horsemen, although she could not say for sure that it was not the sound of only one mount. Bidding her farewell, Robert led his horse and cart back to the road, looking for any signs of disturbance in the undergrowth.

Reaching the road without having seen anything other than fox tracks in the grass, he left his horse to graze and started searching along both sides of the way. It took him a while, for it was not unusual for foresters (and poachers) to use this road to reach their destinations. Eventually, though, he found signs of at least one horse having left the road within the last few days.

Following the trampled grass, Robert walked through a belt of trees and came to a pond. There he lost the trail and tried without success to find it again anywhere around the water or in the surrounding woods. All he found was a hovel some distance from the pond, and it was clear from the burnt ashes littering the clearing that this was the home of a charcoal burner. No one was home, but probably the man and his family were all abroad in the woods seeking wood for the pile. Returning to the pond, Robert tried to put himself in the place of whoever it was who had taken this way from the road.

"Whoever rode in here must have returned to the road the same way," thought Robert. "But what was he doing here?"

He looked around, and even climbed up into one of the trees to see if there was anything other than the pond in the area. Nothing! There seemed to be no other clearings in the woods that he could see, and there were no signs of digging or other disturbance of the earth, or even signs of anyone having stayed any time in this clearing. A few tree stumps surrounded the water, but that was all that marred the fresh smoothness of the grass.

"This might have nothing whatsoever to do with the theft, of course," said Robert to himself. "I had better go on and see if I can learn anything else from others in the area."

Having made his decision, Robert returned to the cart and continued on his way.

Halfway through the afternoon, Robert had finished his rounds, and was approaching the north gate of the town. He was tired, and somewhat discouraged. He had learned nothing more from anyone whom he had questioned.

Just before reaching the north gate, Robert turned off the road, going towards Fornham and the surrounding forest. Checking carefully to make sure no one was within sight, he ducked into the woods, moving northwest along a barely visible track.

After about half a mile he came upon a clearing with a big oak standing sentinel in the middle. Going to the tree, he placed his back against it and walked straight into the forest at right angles to the track along which he had come. After a couple of minutes, he reached a holly bush, and stopped.

Robert whistled softly, and within a couple of minutes Ruth came towards him through the trees, looking from side to side as she moved soundlessly, and accompanied by a tall young man.

"Robert," said Ruth. "I'm so glad to see you. We were wondering what had happened since you came to warn us yesterday. Thank you for offering to come and tell us how things progress."

Ruth introduced her companion as her friend, Avraham. "Avi watches over my safety as you do Aileen's," she said. Robert, surprised at her words, cleared his throat in embarrassment and quickly returned to the matter in hand.

"The townspeople are still very angry," Robert told them. "They blame you for what happened, so it would not be safe for you to return to your homes."

"We feared that it would be so," said Ruth. "We will stay where we are for the moment."

"That's not all," said Robert, not quite sure of how to go on. "When you do return to Fornham, I'm afraid that ... well ..."

Ruth laid her hand on his arm. "We saw the smoke rising through the trees, Robert," she said. "They burned our homes, didn't they?"

Robert was stunned that Ruth could be so calm, and so unsurprised, when faced with such a disaster.

"Only one," he blurted out. "They only burned one. Although that's bad enough!" he added hastily.

"So it's not as bad as we had thought," Avraham said, breaking into a smile. "We appreciate your coming to tell us. Do you by chance know which house was burned?"

"No, I'm sorry," replied Robert. "I did not wait to see what the men would do when they did not find you at home, and I only found out about the burning of the house last evening."

"Never mind," said the young man. "We'll find out soon enough. In the meantime, we must offer prayers of thanksgiving for the saving of our lives and for what remains."

"Ruth," said Robert, as the pair started to say their farewells. "Will you come this evening to the riverbank? Aileen and I have decided we are going to try and find the thief so that we may clear your name and the names of all your friends."

"But how are you going to be able to do that?" asked Ruth.

"As I travelled for my father today, I asked about strange happenings the night of the theft, and Aileen was going to do the same at the Abbey. We are meeting this evening to discuss what we have found out during the day, and we thought it would be best if you could come as well."

Tears came to Ruth's eyes. "I am fortunate indeed to have such good friends," she said. "But it would be impossible for me to leave the shelter of the forest. My father would never permit me to take such a risk."

"I understand," said Robert. "We probably should have thought of that for ourselves. I'll tell you what, though. I'll try and come back to this place late in the afternoon tomorrow, although I cannot tell if that will be possible. I can tell you what we have discovered and perhaps even get your ideas on what it means. Would that be all right?"

"I would be very happy if you would do this," Ruth said. "And do not worry if you are unable to come. Avi and I will return to this bush at this time each day and hope to see you when you have some news.

"But Robert, you and Aileen must be very careful" she continued. "Whoever did this evil thing is a ruthless man, and if he suspected that you and Aileen knew anything that could lead to him, he might harm you."

Robert started to protest, but Ruth would not let him interrupt her. "I know you both very well, Robert, so it would not surprise me if you were to succeed in finding out something important. But I would never forgive myself if any harm came to either of you because of what you do for me."

"We will be careful," said Robert, unconsciously echoing Aileen's words to her mother that very morning.

With that, Ruth and her companion returned to the forest, and Robert turned once again for home.

70

Reaching the north gate of the town late that afternoon, Robert talked to the gatekeeper about the events of the past few days.

"Aye, it has been hard for the town," said the man. "So much celebration at having such a gift, and then so much shame that we should lose it!"

"Do you think they will catch the thief?" asked Robert.

"I 'xpect so," the man replied. "It'll be one of them heathens, you mark my words."

"Did you hear anything that night?" Robert wanted to keep the man on track.

"I sleep sound," the old man said. "But I seem to remember hearing noises just afore dawn. That's not so strange, though. Farmers must get here early if they're to get prime space in the market."

"That's true enough," said Robert. "But what about horses? Did you hear any horses that night?"

"I disremember," the man said, unhelpfully. "Could have, but one night's much like another here."

Robert nodded, and turned away, disappointed in the information he had managed to obtain from the man.

"Mind you," said the man, as though suddenly remembering something. "It could have been that night I heard what sounded like the metal of harnesses in the middle of the night. I remember thinking that it was strange I should hear the sound of the harness but not the hooves or the cart wheels."

"Yes, that is strange," said Robert, turning back to the man. "Perhaps the hooves were covered to prevent anyone hearing the thief leave the city!"

"Could be." The man thought for a moment. "But I 'xpect it was more like the rain earlier that day making the mud soft, so's I wouldna hear nuttin' anyway!" The gatekeeper burst into gravelly laughter at having so succeeded in pulling the leg of the serious young man before him.

Much against his will Robert acknowledged the joke gracefully. Even more reluctantly, he was forced to agree with the gatekeeper's rather down-to-earth explanation for the lack of hoof sounds in the night. He went on past the beggars who always sat in the shadow of the strong gate that was only closed when the town was in danger and returned home to report back to his father in the workshop. As his hands busily worked the bellows which pumped in the right amount of air to keep the furnace at the correct temperature, his mind was working equally hard at trying to find some meaning to what he had learned that day. The thought of letting down Aileen — and Ruth of course — was not to be borne. Therefore, what he had learned, put together with whatever Aileen had found out, had to lead them to the next step. It just had to!

CHAPTER EIGHT

A struggle is dangerous when it is started and waged against a stronger and more powerful adversary.

"PERHAPS THE FRENCH KNIGHT FOLLOWED Sir Henri to England, and it was he who stole the relic!" Robert turned to Aileen eagerly. "He probably believes it to be his by right!"

Aileen and Robert sat on the riverbank, heads together to ensure that no one heard their conversation. The evening sun at their backs, they had each told their tale and were now at the stage of discussing what it all might mean.

"Well," said Aileen, slowly. "Perhaps. But do you think that such a high-born knight would come to England alone, without a big escort? And if he came with many knights, how would they travel the roads of England without being noticed?"

"That's a good point," said Robert. "I wouldn't think he would come alone, and any large force of knights would not only have been seen but would have been challenged by the lord of any land through which they rode. I suppose it is just possible that a knight bent on revenge would not wish to risk bringing a large force with him to a foreign land, but we have heard nothing about any knight but Sir Henri returning from the Holy Land to the Liberty. We'll have to think of something else."

"I agree," said Aileen. "I spent some time today just talking to those around me about the visitors in the guest hall, and no one mentioned any other knights at all. I think it would be hard for a knight of royal blood to so disguise himself as to not give himself away to those with whom he shares common space."

"So at least for the moment that is one less theory for us to consider," said Robert. "What do you think we should do now?"

"You know, the idea of the French knight has started me thinking," said Aileen, after a pause. "When we first heard about the theft, we all assumed that it was the relic itself that was important. But perhaps that's the wrong way to look at it."

"What do you mean?" asked Robert.

"Well, if the power of the relic was behind the theft, then it either had to be someone who hated what it stood for, as everyone in town believes, or it had to be someone who thought that actually having the relic himself would give him what he wanted."

Aileen looked at Robert questioningly. "Am I making myself clear at all?"

"Yes, I think so," he replied. "You mean that a thief would either have to hate Christians so much that he would take away anything that was important to them, or he would want the piece of the Cross in order to gain power for himself."

"Or perhaps even to use it to heal himself or someone he loved," said Aileen, always seeking the best in people rather than the worst.

"It's a thought," said Robert. "But why do you say that focusing on the relic itself is the wrong way to look at it."

"Oh, it isn't," said Aileen, further confusing her companion. "Not necessarily. It may be the right way. But there is another possibility." She paused, gathering her thoughts, looking out at the quiet water as twilight slowly crept along the banks of the River Lark.

"If it were the French knight who had stolen the relic," she went on. "Then it would have been done out of hatred for Sir Henri, not because of the relic itself. Perhaps the Crusader has other enemies, enemies who would be able to travel around England more freely than a member of the French king's house. Perhaps the theft was done to bring dishonor to Sir Henri, and so the relic itself was not the important thing. What was important was that it harm Sir Henri."

"If you're right, that would change everything," said Robert. "It would completely clear Ruth and the others. The Jews would have no reason to steal the relic. They didn't even know Sir Henri."

"Neither did anyone else in town," Aileen pointed out. "It would have to be a stranger, if harming Sir Henri were the reason for the theft."

"Yes," said Robert. "We really must find out about any strangers in town that day." He sat, deep in thought for a moment, and then went on.

"The problem, of course, is that there were plenty of people in town that day to see the procession and attend the offertory high mass. Word of Sir Henri's arrival spread very quickly. And it's not just people from the surrounding area coming for the festivities. There are plenty of people staying in the guest hall at the Abbey who have come from parts far distant from our town. It's not every day that one of the greatest abbeys in the land receives a gift such as a piece of the True Cross."

"I know," Aileen said. "And we know that at least one visitor held something against Sir Henri because there was a disagreement between them the day after the knight arrived. I have yet to find someone who can tell me all about it, but at least now that we have an idea of where we are heading, we may be able to ask better questions and get better answers!"

"That's true enough," Robert said. "But you know, Aileen, if that really were the reason for the theft, I'm not sure that it didn't all go wrong for the thief."

"What do you mean?" asked Aileen.

"If the relic was stolen in order to discredit the Crusader, it really hasn't worked. The whole town is buzzing with tales of the honorable knight, and his vow to recover the piece of the Cross."

"I know," said Aileen. "It's hard to find anyone who can talk about anything else!"

"You told me people say Sir Henri is very ambitious," Robert said, and Aileen nodded.

"Well, I could see how an enemy would want to stop him from achieving his ambitions. But after he vowed to bring the relic back to the Abbey, there is no one doing anything but praising Sir Henri. It's almost as though this knight whom no one had ever seen before this week has been adopted by the town, isn't it?"

"It certainly is," said Aileen. "It's usually impossible for an outsider to become accepted by the townspeople. But it's hard to believe that Sir Henri didn't grow up in St. Edmund's Bury, the way people are treating him."

"So, what's going to happen?" Robert said. "The knights of the royal escort are bound to tell the king all about it. That will only make the king look with more favor on Sir Henri. So, in the end, this theft will probably *help* the Crusader's plans for the future, not hurt them!"

"Wouldn't that be strange," said Aileen. "Someone who hates the knight tries to do him harm, and in fact helps him rise to power."

They watched as late summer leaves slowly drifted by in the gloom of the evening, each thinking about how strange it was that things never seemed to turn out as one expected.

"Well, at least we have some ideas we can look into," said Robert. "Where do you think we should go from here?"

"I think we should follow-up on both ideas," said Aileen. "If the relic was stolen by someone who wanted

77

to use its power, there might be talk by now of a man who is claiming sudden blessings. Or there may be word of a miraculous cure. Let's see if we can find out if there is talk of anything like that."

Robert nodded, and made a mental note to ask his father if he could deliver the pieces commissioned by the lord of Long Melford tomorrow after he had bought supplies and the rough work in the workshop was complete.

"On the other hand," Aileen went on. "I can't imagine why the healing power of the relic should work for a thief who violated the Holy Church, so if he used it for himself, it may have had the opposite effect! We should check into that, as well."

"I can ask around tomorrow," said Robert. "I must visit the market in the morning, but in the afternoon I should be able to ask questions of those on the road to Long Melford."

"As far as the idea about the thief being an enemy of Sir Henri is concerned, we can go on asking about strangers in the area," said Aileen.

"I can talk to some more people tomorrow," Robert said. "Perhaps the thief went south, instead of east."

"Good," said Aileen. "And I'll see what more I can find out at the Abbey. I need to see if I can find out more about that altercation in the guest hall involving Sir Henri, and perhaps I can find out whether anyone knows anything more about the other visitors in the Abbey precincts. Some of them are clearly from noble families, though, and may well know something about the French knight, or even Sir Henri. Why," Aileen said excitedly, warming to her theme, "it's even possible that one of the visitors knows the French knight and can help us rule out that theory completely!"

"I suppose it's possible," said Robert, "But I wouldn't set your hopes too high on that being the case. I agree that someone may know something of his family, though. Just be careful. Some people may take exception to your questions."

She gazed out over the darkening water, thinking that Robert wasn't the first person to comment on her curiosity. But there was something else ...

"What is it?" asked Robert. "You look as though you've thought of something."

"No," she replied. "But something is tickling at the back of my mind, and it's just out of reach. Does that ever happen to you?"

"All the time," said Robert. "It's maddening, because you know that if you can just put your finger on whatever it is, you'll have the answer to your question."

"Exactly!" said Aileen. "If I could just put my finger on this, I think it would help solve the riddle."

"Really?" Robert thought hard. "What were we talking about when you started getting that feeling? Can you remember?"

"No," she said. "It just started creeping into my mind, and I can't think why."

"Well, stop trying so hard," Robert said. "If you think about something else, it'll come back to you."

"You're probably right," Aileen said.

The pair sat quietly for a few more minutes. The breeze tickled the reeds into a slow, lazy waving motion, and wildfowl called to each other as twilight crept over the water. Somewhere a branch cracked ...

"What was that?" Aileen asked, startled out of her thoughts.

"What?"

"That sound." Aileen stood up and turned to look around. The quiet of the riverbank was unbroken and no one was in sight. "I thought I heard a branch break as though someone had trod upon it."

"I'm sure it was nothing, Aileen," said Robert, standing in his turn. "It was probably just a falling branch or a badger treading on a dead limb."

"Yes, I'm sure you're right," Aileen responded, doubtfully. "I suppose all this anxiety and distrust in the air is getting to me."

Robert put his arm around Aileen's shoulders. "You wouldn't be normal if it wasn't." He laughed. "Of course, I'm not sure I would exactly describe you as 'normal' anyway!"

Abandoning all pretense of adulthood, Aileen stuck out her tongue at Robert and then ran off toward the town. "Let's go home. Whatever was in the back of my mind has gone now, and I don't want to get into trouble with my father again."

"Whatever it was, it'll come, just when you least expect it," Robert said, running to catch up with Aileen and provide her with a proper escort home.

As they walked companionably back to town Aileen thought about the way in which the townsfolk had turned into an angry mob after the theft of the relic. I grew up with some of the young men who joined the search, she thought. Never would I have dreamed that my fun-loving friends would have turned into men who could hate others just because of who they are. I am so glad that Robert is not like that. He is a true friend and an honorable man.

Robert and Aileen walked all the way back to Looms Lane, each remaining silent within their own thoughts. Saying goodnight, Robert started for his own home along the dark, unlit streets of St. Edmund's Bury. As he turned into his own street, his mind elsewhere, he just caught sight of a shadow slipping into a doorway on the corner. Was someone following him to rob him of his purse? He had been thinking so hard about this evening's events that he had paid no attention to anything around him. Should he head for home as fast as he could go, or should he check to see if anyone was really in the doorway?

As he stood, undecided, the door of the tavern two doors down opened, and light spilled out on to the street. Three men, obviously full of ale and good cheer, erupted from the doorway into the street, turning in Robert's direction. Distracted by the sudden appearance of the men, Robert almost missed the shadow move quickly out of the doorway and down Paddockpool towards the Abbey. Casting aside as foolhardy a sudden urge to follow the stranger, Robert headed for home and safety.

Safety, that is, for this night. But what about tomorrow, he thought? Was Ruth right? Are we in danger? Seeing the shadow of a stranger seemingly dogging his steps tonight rang a warning bell in his mind, one that was hard to ignore. Robert's last thought as he opened the door to be greeted by his noisy, boisterous family was of Aileen: How do I make sure she's safe?

CHAPTER NINE

He swore that he had never lamented so much as this over anything ... because of the stain of an evil report that had already made our dissension publicly known.

AILEEN ARRIVED AT THE ABBEY early the next morning. The events of the past few days had thrown everything into chaos, and she knew she had to impress Mistress Taylor with her skill and efficiency. If she could show herself to be an asset, she was sure there would be time enough for her to find a way to ask more questions and, hopefully, solve the riddle of the theft before any harm could come to her friends.

Entering the work room Aileen came to a stop in the doorway. It seemed as though she had witnessed this scene before.

"I don't know what the world is coming to," declared Mistress Taylor indignantly, face flushed and hands trembling. "It's not as though we have nothing to do, what with the need to make new vestments for the High Mass, repair linens that have been soiled and torn by the visitors in the guest hall … and what do you suppose they were doing to damage them in the first place, I'd like to know … and making sure that the altar cloth is without stain before Sunday. And now this!" The robemaker, hands on hips, looked around the room as though daring someone to contradict her.

Aileen scarcely liked to speak, but apparently none of the other women present felt up to asking the question that was clearly hovering on all their lips.

"Mistress Taylor?" The robemaker turned to Aileen, seemingly surprised to find her standing there.

"May I ask what has happened to cause you so much distress?"

"Why, the Lady Alyse de Vere of course!" stated Mistress Taylor, as though that would explain everything.

Twelve pairs of eyes under twelve puzzled brows continued to look at her.

Exasperated, Mistress Taylor swept up a cloak from the table and shook it at them. "Dame Alyse sent her maidservant over here not even one hour ago with instructions to have us mend and clean this cloak," said the robemaker. "Does she think that the craftswomen of the Abbey are hers to command? Does she believe that she only has to demand it and we will abandon our work for God's house and set our needles to her earthly needs? Has she no servants of her own who have any talent with a needle?" Her voice rising with each question, Mistress Taylor finally ground to a halt.

Looking around her, the robemaker saw her women looking anywhere but at her. No one was inclined to offer any answers to her questions.

"Well, that's as may be, and I suppose it is not the place of such as us to question the commands of our noble lords," she sniffed, clearly working to regain command of her own emotions. "I doubt not that we can do a better job than any of her household."

Turning to Aileen, she handed her the cloak. "Aileen, you have the least experience of my women in tending to the Lord's linens, but I am sure you will be able to do the work necessary to satisfy the Lady Alyse de Vere. As for the rest of you," she said, turning to the gathered women and clapping her hands, "Be off with you and get on with your tasks. Do you think we have the time to tarry and talk, when there is so much to be done! How would it be if Brother Michael were to come in and see you all standing around gossiping like fishwives?"

The women, well used to Mistress Taylor's moods, bobbed their curtsies and returned to their needlework. Aileen was left holding the mysterious cloak, questions already forming in her mind.

Aileen laid the cloak on the table. It was a rich cloak, made of velvet with a lining of fur. A jeweled clasp at the neck was clearly made by a superior craftsman. "Robert would know how much skill it took to make something so grand," thought Aileen, fingering the intricate gold filigree and precious stones.

85

Turning the cloak over, Aileen saw several long rips in the back and dark stains marring the soft nap of the velvet. To her eyes it seemed that the cloak had been dragged through bushes.

"Mistress Taylor," Aileen spoke up as the robemaker passed by, "What happened to this cloak? Do you know?"

"There you go again, asking questions! I take my oath that I never met anyone so full of questions in my whole life!" But the good woman, hesitating for a moment, sat down and turned to Aileen.

"I don't suppose it matters if I tell you what the maidservant said," she said, not unkindly. "After all, mayhap it will help you as you clean and mend the fabric." Thus having justified her actions in her own mind, she continued with her tale.

"According to the maidservant, Lady Alyse de Vere's son William is a wild lad. Well, after all, that is not to be wondered at. He's his father's heir, and I do hear that his family is thought of most highly in the French court." Hearing this, Aileen drew closer to the robemaker, encouraging the woman to continue.

"The maidservant, Agnes, told me that her mistress was sore displeased when William came back late to the abbey, wet and cold, and without his cloak. She was already disturbed that he had become involved in an argument with the Crusader knight earlier in the week, but she had scarce seen him since to say her words to him."

So that is what happened that morning, thought Aileen. I little expected to find my answer in the linen room!

"The young lord's mother asked him where was the cloak she gave him only a month since, and he replied that it was lost some days before." Mistress Taylor laughed out loud, then lowered her voice conspiratorially when the other women looked up to see what had so amused their mercurial mistress.

"I think I would not have known where to look had I been present in that room," she said. "Agnes told me that Dame Alyse never raised her voice, but the very quiet of her tone did send chills up Agnes' spine."

Mistress Taylor paused but, seeing Aileen's rapt attention to her every word, she leaned in closer and continued.

"The Lady Alyse told her son she did know that he had left the precincts of the Abbey on the night of their arrival and had done so each night since. When he would say something, she raised her hand to silence his protest and told him that this was neither the time nor the place to discuss his conduct, but that he must be assured she was not blind to his failings. She said she had no doubt but that he must know where he may have put aside his cloak and that it was his duty to retrieve it. Dame Alyse told him that she would not tolerate such treatment of her rich gift. She said she was about to visit the Shrine of the blessed saint," here the robemaker crossed herself in reverence, "and that, when she returned, she expected to find her son

87

awaiting her, with the cloak in his hand. With that, she rose and walked out of the room."

"Ohhh," breathed Aileen. "What happened next?"

"Well, the noblewoman prayed before the shrine for an hour or more, but when she returned her son was indeed waiting for her. He had retrieved the cloak, he did not say from where, but it was as you see it now. The Lady de Vere merely looked at it and then instructed Agnes to bring it to me first thing this morning for repair. Then she turned on her heel and left the room!"

"If her son was able to return with the cloak in that amount of time, he surely must have known where it was to be found," said Aileen. "Where do you suppose he went after his mother left to pray at St. Edmund's shrine?"

"Well, I'm sure I don't know," exclaimed Mistress Taylor, apparently remembering her position and with whom she was speaking. "And you don't need to know either! Just get on with mending and cleaning the cloak. We will need you to help hem the new altar cloth as soon as you can finish this task."

With that, Mistress Taylor stood up and left the room. Aileen was left to her work and her thoughts.

The end of the workday was drawing near as Aileen crossed the cloister to return the cloak to Brother Jocelin in the guest hall. It had been a busy day, and the scent of the grass and the warmth of the sun slowed her steps.

"Aileen!" She turned at the sound of the call.

"Hugh," she greeted the young man loping toward her. "It's so long since I've seen you!"

"I know," he said. "I heard you were coming to work at the Abbey, so I've been looking out for you. You certainly picked an exciting time to begin working here,"

"Didn't I?" she replied, ruefully. "I've scarce had time to think since arriving, let alone show Mistress Taylor what I can do.

"But what about you?" she asked. "I did hear you had been accepted as a scholar at the Abbey school. Your father must be very proud." Hugh's father was a skilled blacksmith. Robert and Aileen had known Hugh since they were children but had not seen much of each other in the last couple of years.

"Yes, he is," confirmed Hugh. "Were it not that the Lord Abbot pays a stipend to the schoolmaster to take poor scholars such as I there would be no possibility of my being able to attend the school. My father has great plans for me. I just hope I can live up to his expectations." Hugh hung his head slightly.

"Why would you not?" said Aileen. "You were always one of the quickest among us at your letters. Are you not still shining at your studies?"

"Well, yes," Hugh said. "Master Edward, the schoolmaster, does tell me that I do well in my lessons."

"There! Did I not say you need have no fear of failure?" said Aileen, smiling.

"You always did make me feel as though I could do anything," said Hugh. "It is so good to see you!"

"And I you," replied Aileen. "But now I must be on my way. I must needs return this cloak to its owner and there is yet much to be done today."

"I will delay you no further," said Hugh. "Mayhap I will see you again soon?"

"I hope so," said Aileen, waving goodbye to her friend.

As she proceeded on her way to the guest hall, she heard anxious whispering behind the pillars on her left. Thinking it may be Robert trying to attract her attention, Aileen moved toward the sound.

"I will not allow our family name to be besmirched by your behavior." Aileen stopped in her tracks. Clearly this was not Robert, but how to retreat without being discovered?

"Mother, it is no concern of yours what I do on this journey." The young man spoke with bravado but could not contain the tremor that crept into his voice. "I am of age, and my father's name is in no danger of being harmed by anything I do in this little burgh."

"This 'little burgh,' as you put it," said the woman scornfully, "is under the control of a powerful man. The Abbot of St. Edmund's has the ear of the English king, and your father's influence does not extend this far. I require your oath that you have no part in any deed that might delay our departure from this place."

"By my oath I will not be accused so," declared the young man. "When we traveled to this place, we

90

both knew who it was we risked seeing and how hard it would be to avoid association or remembrance. Yet you still chose to make the journey. If I were so churlish as you obviously believe me to be, I could as easily accuse you of unbecoming conduct, but I would not so despise you!"

"How dare you!" For a moment the woman's voice rose in anger. But when she spoke again her icy control had returned.

"My motives in making this journey are none of your concern," she said. "Your conduct, however, has given neither your father nor I cause for confidence," she continued. "I had hoped to be able to report to your father that you have grown in wisdom in the course of the past year, but I fear I cannot do so. First you begin an argument with Henri du Lac, and now I find that you lost your cloak in some unknown wanderings. Do you now wonder that I fear you have returned to your old habits, or that I find your account of events leading to the damage to your cloak less than believable?"

"It is of no great matter to me whether or not you believe me," cried the young man. "I have striven hard to atone for the sins that led to the loss of favor in my father's eyes, but it would appear to me now that there is nothing I can ever do to regain that regard. If that be the case, then mayhap I should pledge fealty to another lord who may find my service more acceptable!"

Silence fell in the cloister.

"We will continue this conversation in our quarters," said the woman at last. "I would risk no other hearing how the son of such a proud house as ours should speak so to his mother." The woman's voice was low but brooked no argument. "Come!"

Aileen was desperately looking around, seeking some place to hide, when she heard the pair walking off in the opposite direction. Sighing with relief, she continued on her way, thinking furiously about what she had just heard and determined to get to the bottom of the mystery that was keeping her friends from returning to their homes.

Coming to the door of the guest hall, Aileen hesitated. She had never been within the lodgings before, and she was unsure of how to proceed. She could hear sounds from within, but there was no sign of anyone close by the entry.

"Brother Jocelin?" she called, softly. "Are you here?"

Silence.

"Brother Jocelin?" she tried again, a little louder.

"Oh, dear me," she heard from a room to the right of the entrance. Brother Jocelin came to the door, quill in hand and ink on his fingers. "I beg your pardon," he said. "I was deep in my writing and did not hear you call." Seeming to suddenly realize that he still held his quill pen he quickly turned around and put it down, then turned back to Aileen.

"May I help you?" he asked, smiling at the young woman before him.

"I have come to return the cloak belonging to one of your guests," Aileen said, holding out the garment to the monk. "I believe that it belongs to the young lord

William de Vere. His mother sent it to Mistress Taylor to be cleaned and repaired."

"Ah, yes," said the Guest Master. "I remember that the Lady de Vere did ask who we might have within the Abbey walls who could make repairs to this fine mantle. I was loathe to direct her to the robemaker, but she was most insistent that no gossip should attend upon the damage done to the cloak and thus did not wish it to be taken to anyone in the town itself. She is a most determined lady," he added.

The monk seemed almost apologetic about directing the noblewoman to the Abbey's robemaker.

"I was glad of the opportunity to work with such a fine garment," Aileen told Brother Jocelin, earning herself a broad smile from the monk.

"Come," he said. "Let us go in here and see what you have been able to do to restore the cloak." He led the way into the room from which he had exited upon hearing her voice.

The room was clearly an office, for there was a table upon which rested papers and what Aileen supposed to be some kind of ledger to keep the accounts for the guest hall. There was little else in the room beside a stool and a few shelves upon which rested bound parchments. The window above the table was small, and Aileen was not surprised to see a pile of candles, both whole and mere stubs, lying on the table.

Sweeping aside papers and candles, not seeming to mind that half a dozen of the latter rolled onto the

93

floor, Brother Jocelin placed the cloak on the table. Bending over it, he exclaimed with pleasure.

"You have a deft hand with the needle," he said. "I saw the rents and the dirt on the cloak before the maidservant took it over to Mistress Taylor. Had I not done so I doubt I would have been able to tell that there was ever any damage."

"Thank you, brother," Aileen said. "My mother is Anne, wife of Jude of Arundel, and she is well known for her skill as an embroiderer."

"Ah, that would be why you are employed in the linen room, and why Mistress Taylor trusted you to restore this cloak," said the brother. "Mayhap the skill of the work will calm the ire of the Lady de Vere."

Feeling a little embarrassed, Aileen changed the subject. "It must be a great responsibility, to be the Guest Master of this great Abbey," she said, thinking that perhaps this monk might be a source of some helpful information.

Jocelin smiled. "It is indeed, and it is also an honor. For many I am the only Benedictine that they come to know well, for it is certain that they are more used to seeing monks in the choir or at the market."

"Do you spend much time with your guests?" Aileen asked.

"I do not seek them out, but of course I attend upon their needs, and some travelers do ask about the town and its surroundings."

"Yes, I had never thought about it before, but visitors to our great shrine must often need to find out where they may be able to obtain goods to fulfil their needs," said Aileen. "Have many of the guests who came to see the relic asked you such questions?"

"Several have asked how they may obtain supplies for their return journey," responded the monk. "And a few have asked about the country around St. Edmund's Bury."

"Why would they do that?" asked Aileen. "Did they desire to travel about, or were they just curious?"

"I do not know," Jocelin said. "I confess that my mind is oft on my duties or, perhaps too frequently, on my writing. I scarce bother to ask the reason for a question, but merely respond to the extent of my knowledge."

Oh dear, thought Aileen. How to overcome such a lack of curiosity?

"I wondered only if perhaps the Lady de Vere's son may have been one of those who asked you about the villages around our town," said Aileen. "His cloak cannot have become so torn and dirtied within these walls, and I must admit I am curious as to how the damage was done."

"It is not our task to pursue such enquiries," said Brother Jocelin with mock severity. His eyes twinkled, however, and Aileen knew he was not angry. "Yet, your curiosity is only human, and I see no great sin in attempting to satisfy it."

The monk paused to think. "Yes, I do believe that I remember the young lord asking me about the town on the first day that he was here. I do not think he asked much about the surrounding villages, however, but merely about the town. I seem to remember that he asked also about the other visitors in residence, which is not perhaps as common a question."

"Perhaps he was interested in whether he knew any of the other visitors," said Aileen.

"Well, of course he did know one of them," said Jocelin, ruefully. "For, in spite of my attempts to provide a safe and calm place for all who have come to our Abbey, he got into an altercation with the Crusader knight the day after the great gift was delivered to the Abbot.

"Bad enough that there was bad blood between them, of which I could have had no prior knowledge," the monk continued. "But that they should become so violent in their language in the presence of so many gentlefolk was deeply disturbing to me."

"What was it that so upset them, do you think? asked Aileen, holding her breath in anticipation.

"I do not know for certain," said the monk. "I was writing in my chronicle when I heard loud voices. When I went out to see what it was that was causing the commotion the two men were red-faced and shouting about honor and infamy. Others of our guests were attempting to hold them back, else I do believe the two men would have come to blows."

"What did you do?"

"I endeavored to quieten the dispute myself, just as I would were it an argument between any two visitors within our walls," replied Jocelin. "Regrettably, neither man would desist in his struggles against those whose

96

arms prevented them from reaching the other, and it was becoming clear that it would take more than my meagre efforts to separate them. Since one of the visitors involved was the Crusader knight, I felt it necessary that Abbot Samson be involved, and so I hurried to fetch him."

"That must have been the morning I saw Abbot Samson and the Prior walk swiftly through the courtyard," said Aileen. "Were they able to calm the dispute?"

"A little," responded Brother Jocelin. "Father Abbot asked Sir Henri to return with him to his quarters and, once one of the disputants had left the guest hall, it quieted down rather quickly."

"Did you find out what had caused the fight?"

"No, I did not ask, for it is not my place to enquire into personal matters," Jocelin said. "As I said, their cries were of a lack of honor and a betrayal of trust. These are matters into which no one has the right to enquire, particularly not a lowly monk of the great Abbey of St. Edmund's. Nor, for that matter, a young woman of the town."

This time the meaning of the monk's admonition was clear, and Aileen decided to heed the warning.

"I believe you are right," she said, earning herself another smile from the Guest Master. "And now I must allow you to return to your duties, as must I to mine. Thank you for taking the time to talk to me, brother."

"It has been my pleasure," said the monk. "You may trust me to return this cloak to its owner, and I hope that I may see more examples of your work in the future."

Dropping the Guest Master a small curtsy, Aileen passed out of the door into the courtyard, mulling over what she had heard and eager to tell Robert all about her day and the information she had gleaned.

CHAPTER TEN

*As his wisdom increased, so also did his carefulness
in the management and improvement of property
and in making proper arrangements for expenses.*

As AILEEN AND HER FAMILY walked to church the following morning, frustration creased her brow. She had hoped to see Robert the evening before when she came to confession, but they had barely had time to greet each other before Aileen's father told her to hurry up. When she suggested they get together later Robert would only respond with a quick "I'm sorry, but father has need of me tonight. We will have to talk tomorrow."

She had lain awake much of last night turning over and over in her mind what she had heard yesterday and trying to make out of it some sense. If only she and Robert could talk about it, she was sure they could figure out between them where this information fit in the events of the past week. One good fact put in its rightful place should surely lead to another and another. But now it was Sunday, and how are we going to find time to talk about it today, she wondered. I know mother will expect me to stay at home and help prepare the sauce for the goose. Perhaps later on, in the evening?

"Aileen," said her mother, interrupting her train of thought. "Did you not hear me?"

"Oh, she's just wondering if she'll see Robert today," said Mabel. "She's sweet on him!"

"I am not!" said Aileen, scowling at her sister.

"Yes, you are!" declared Mabel, dancing out of reach of Aileen's hand.

"Stop it!" said Aileen, giving chase.

"Aileen's sweet on Robert. Aileen's sweet on Robert!"

"Stop that right now!" said their father. "Can you not see how people are staring? Think you not that the Lord expects better behavior of you, especially on the Sabbath?"

"I am sorry, father," said Aileen, giving her sister one last scowl. "I should have known better than to allow Mabel to make me behave so. After all, she is still but a child and I am full grown."

Mabel stuck out her tongue at her older sister.

"Enough!" commanded their father. "Mabel, you will be quiet. And Aileen, I expect you to remember that part of being of age is knowing that sometimes you must resist the temptation to react in a childish manner to childish behavior."

Perhaps, she thought rebelliously, but that doesn't mean I have to like it!

Keeping her thoughts to herself, Aileen meekly followed her parents through the doors of their parish church of St. James for the morning mass.

Try as she might, Aileen found it hard to focus on the Latin mass that morning. Her body went through all the proper motions, but her thoughts were elsewhere. She kept looking around to see if Robert and his family were there, although she knew well that his family was a part of the congregation of St. Mary's, which stood at the far end of the Abbey grounds close by the great cemetery. Twice her mother had to gently nudge Aileen to return her attention to the priest, and once Mabel even dug her in the ribs so that she would move forward in the line to take communion.

Aileen could say nothing of the purpose of the priest's sermon even though, as decreed by Abbot Samson, the sermon in this church that stood on Abbey grounds was given in English, the declared intent being that the homily should be edifying rather than just a matter of a priest showing how well he knew Latin.

The mass over, Jude and his family began their walk back home.

As they drew close to the Great Court Gate, she heard footsteps coming up fast behind them. Turning, she saw Robert running to catch up with the family.

"Good morrow, sir," he said to Jude. "I trust that you and Mistress Anne are well?"

"Very well, thank you," said Jude, smiling. "And how fares your father and the rest of your family?"

101

"Well, thank you," said Robert. "I saw you come out of the church, and I thought to greet you on this sunny Sunday morning."

Jude smiled, not for a minute fooled by the young man's enquiries.

"Thank you, Robert," he said. "Please send my greetings to your father and mother, and bid them God's blessings from my family and me.

"Aileen, you may spend a few minutes talking to Robert if you wish," he went on, turning to his older daughter. "But see that you return home promptly so that we may break our fast together."

"Thank you, father," Aileen said.

Jude and the rest of the family continued on their way home, leaving Robert and Aileen to walk over and stand in the shadow of the gatehouse to talk.

"Robert! I'm so glad to see you."

"And I you," he said. "I'm sorry about last night, but father wished to show me how to tell gold from latten or copper. That is something every goldsmith must be able to do, and I couldn't get away."

"I understand, Robert," said Aileen, "but we need to talk properly soon. Yesterday I found out something really interesting about one of the families staying in the guest hall. I don't know what it means, but I need to tell you all about it."

"Can you tell me now?" Robert asked eagerly.

Aileen drew him aside from the entry to the Abbey, away from all the people hurrying hither and thither.

"Well," Aileen began, "there's this family staying in the guest hall named de Vere, and they are very important people in the French court."

"Do you think they know Sir Henri?" Aileen frowned at the interruption. "I'm sorry," said Robert. "Please go on."

"The Lady de Vere and William, her son, are among those who are come to see the relic installed in the abbey. Yesterday morning Mistress Taylor had me repair a cloak that belongs to the son. It was torn and stained, and apparently his mother is very angry because he has not been conducting himself as she believes he should. I heard them arguing in the cloister, and Lady de Vere accused William of besmirching the family name. She said …"

Aileen stopped suddenly and pulled Robert around, ducking her head.

"What's going on?" asked Robert.

"Shhhh! That's him – that's the son!" Aileen jerked her head in the direction of a young man exiting the Great Court Gate.

"Really?" Robert stole a quick look. "He doesn't look anything like I expected a high-born French nobleman to look," he said.

"I'm not sure how high-born French noblemen are supposed to look," said Aileen, "but he's looking around as though he has something to hide."

"I think you may be right," said Robert. "It is yet early for one such as he to venture forth. Were it not Sunday, and thus a day when Christian men and women are to be found in church, I would expect him to be lying abed or ordering his servants to prepare for him some tempting delicacy."

Aileen looked at Robert in surprise. "Why, Robert, you don't even know him. Yet you sound as though you dislike him very much!"

"I'm sorry, Aileen," he said, looking somewhat shamefaced. "I do not know why the sight of him puts me out of sorts."

"You have already apologized to me enough for one day," laughed Aileen. "You have no need to do so again."

As they spoke, the young nobleman left the shelter of the gate and set off up the hill from the Abbey.

"He's walking off toward Abbeygate," said Robert. "I wonder where he is going in such a hurry on a Sunday. I'm going to follow him."

"Are you sure? Will your father not be expecting you?"

"I have some time before I must be home," responded Robert. "If he tarries too long, I may have to stop pursuing him, but at least I should be able to see where this young lord is going. Do you think we'll be able to meet this evening at the usual place?"

"I will try, but I think that my father will not look with favor upon my wanting to leave the house this evening."

"I think you're right," said Robert. "I doubt not that my father will expect me to stay at home on a Sunday evening. If not this evening, then, tomorrow for sure!" With that, he was gone, leaving Aileen staring after him and hoping that he would be careful.

William de Vere walked quickly up Abbeygate, a man with a purpose. Every now and then he would stop to look around him. Robert had to wonder where this stranger to St. Edmund's town was going, but for once he was glad that so many people in town knew him and his family.

"How is your father this fine day?" called out the wine merchant, walking back to his house with his family in tow. "I have some fine French wine that I know he'd like!"

"The Lord forgive you for talking business on a Sunday," admonished his wife. The merchant winked at Robert, who smiled at him and hurried on.

"Robert, I'm glad to see you," said a burgess a few buildings further on. "Please tell your father that I would like to see him about a brooch for my daughter's wedding."

While all the greetings made it impossible for him to remain in the shadows as he followed William de Vere, he was not concerned about it. He was sure anyone who cared to take note of his progress would consider him just one more craftsman meeting other townsman as he returned home from mass. Certainly the young man ahead of him appeared to look with no more interest directed at Robert than anyone else even though he seemed to look back over his shoulder more

105

than one might expect from someone merely walking through the town on a sunny day.

Turning into the market, William began to walk down the line of empty stalls. Tomorrow the market would be filled with produce and loud with the voices of stall owners crying out their wares to the crush of women thrusting through the throng, baskets on arms and toddlers hanging on their skirts. Robert, fearful that he might be spotted by the young lord, turned aside and proceeded along the line of stalls parallel to William de Vere, catching sight of him between the stalls and slowing his steps to match the Frenchman's progress.

Eventually William stopped outside a merchant's house close by the hog market. The house had only been built about twenty years ago and was known as Moyses Hall. Robert did not know much about the people living there. It was rumored that the merchant was rich, but few knew for certain what it was in which he traded.

Looking around him one last time, William knocked on the door of the house. Robert moved closer, hoping to hear the conversation when the door was opened.

A big, rough looking man answered the knock. He looked William up and down and then stood aside for him to enter. Neither man said a word. Puzzled, Robert decided to wait and see if anything further happened.

Shortly after William de Vere had entered the house another man, clad in a long cloak and with a hood hiding his face, knocked at the door of the Hall. Again, not a word was spoken when the door was opened by the same large man, but the stranger was admitted. This is getting interesting, thought Robert. I wonder what it is about Moyses Hall that is so attractive to strangers to our town, and what could possibly be taking place on the Sabbath.

It was not long before Robert decided that following people and waiting for things to happen was not so very exciting. He had seen no one else enter the house, and neither had anyone left. No sounds emitted from the house, and no one seemed to cross in front of any of the windows that were within Robert's view. There was simply no sign of activity at all.

Of a sudden, Robert thought about a back door, and wondered if perhaps the young Frenchman had seen him following close behind after all. Should he check to see if William might have left by a back way, or should he remain where he was and wait a little longer?

Tiring of the curious glances he was getting from those passing by him, Robert finally made up his mind to walk around and see if he could find any sign of William de Vere. He walked slowly past the house, trying to look as casually as possible into the small windows that faced the street.

"Just keep walking," said a voice behind him. Startled, Robert began to turn around, but an insistent hand pushed him on for several more yards before directing him around a corner and allowing him to stop.

"Master Durand!" exclaimed Robert, disconcerted to see the Reeve standing right behind him as he turned.

"So, Robert Palgrave," returned the official, eying the young man with interest, "What is it that has prompted you to keep watch over Moyses Hall?"

"Oh no," said Robert. "It's not the Hall I'm watching. It's... it's..." Robert stammered to a halt.

"It's what?" demanded the Reeve. "If you are not watching the merchant's house what are you doing here? It is certain sure you are not considering what purchases to make at the market for, even if there were any wares for sale on a Sunday, you could see little of them from the corner around which you were hiding."

Robert looked this way and that, wondering what he could say to satisfy the man without giving away too much.

"Oh, I was just interested in seeing the manners of the foreign nobles who are within our walls for this great occasion," he said finally.

Durand barked with laughter. "Master Robert," he said. "I may look to be a man without any great wisdom, but a puling infant could put the lie to that tale. It is just as well that you are destined for a career as worthy as that of your father, for you would be a very poor man indeed were you to choose to make your fortune from deceit!"

Robert blushed, fingering his cap in embarrassment.

"Try again," instructed the Reeve severely.

"I was following William de Vere." The words seemed to burst out of his mouth unbidden and, once said, could not be taken back.

Eyebrows rising into his hair, the Reeve took the young man by the arm and started guiding him away from the market and Moyses Hall.

"We cannot discuss this in the middle of the street. What I have to say is not for the ears of all who pass by this place. Come with me."

The Reeve said nothing further as they walked down Churchgate hill. Glancing at his face, Robert could see Durand's grim expression. Not sure whether they were going to the Reeve's house or if he was being taken home in disgrace, Robert was greatly relieved when they entered Durand's house. Pausing only to tell his servant to fetch his horse from the stable, the Reeve directed Robert to sit at the kitchen table, placed a mug of small ale in front of him and said: "Talk!"

CHAPTER ELEVEN

He treated as a dear and close relative one man
of middling status, who had loyally preserved his
inheritance and served him devotedly when he was young.

"SEWARD," SAID AILEEN TO THE knight's groom, having found him in the stable tending to Raven, "Do you know the Lady de Vere and her son?"

Seward stopped brushing Raven's glossy coat and looked hard at Aileen.

"Why do you want to know? What business is it of yours?"

Well, that wasn't exactly a good start, thought Aileen. I'd better think of something quickly.

"Oh, it's just that I had to repair the young lord's cloak when it was damaged," she said. "It was such a beautiful cloak and it made me curious about the family."

"You seem to be curious about a lot of things," Seward said, turning back to continue his work on the Crusader's horse.

"It's just as you said the other day," said Aileen, wide-eyed. "Nothing much happens in our little town, and I really love hearing about all the noble families who are visiting the Abbey." He'll never know what it cost me to sound that silly, but if it gets me the answers I need, it will be well worth it!

Seward put down his brush and stood up straight, turning to Aileen with what she could only describe as a superior expression on his face.

"I can understand that," he said. "And yes, I know something of the de Vere family. They and my lord's family were close for generations. Their lands in France were not far distant from each other. In times gone by they would hunt together, and they attended festivals and court in each other's company. Why, even their children were betrothed."

"William de Vere was betrothed to a daughter of Sir Henri's family?" asked Aileen.

"No, Sir Henri was betrothed to Isabelle de Vere," responded Seward.

This was unexpected. Aileen found it difficult to contain her excitement.

"But they never married?"

"No," said Seward, thoughtfully. "I don't know what occurred, but of a sudden the two families were no longer friendly. I was but a babe at the time, and my father never would tell me anything, but I have heard since that there was a great rift between the two lords and that, had the king not intervened, there would have been violence between them."

111

"The king," breathed Aileen. "Is that when Sir Henri's family was banished from court?"

"I do believe it to be so," said Seward.

"And Sir Henri and the Lady Isabelle have not seen each other since?"

"I would not know that," said Seward. "I'm merely a groom and have no knowledge of great families and their affairs. All I know about the family of Isabelle de Vere in present times I have learned but recently from Agnes."

"Agnes? The Lady Alyse's maidservant?" Aileen asked in surprise.

Seward looked as though he wished he had not spoken.

"Yes, but you must not speak of this to any of the household. Agnes and I ... well, we have become friends this last week in the Abbey, but we know that this would not be pleasing to the noble lords we serve."

"I promise I will say nothing, Seward," said Aileen. "But do you think Agnes might be willing to talk to me?"

"About what? I don't understand why you are so eager to learn of the affairs of those better than you. All that it will bring you is grief, should Sir Henri or Lady Alyse hear of your questions."

Aileen realized she had gone too far in her eagerness. "Seward, you are right. I beg your forgiveness," she said. "I am but a silly girl, with stars in my eyes to hear of such a great romance." Oh Ruth, what I do for you!

112

"This is why great affairs of state are the duty of men," said Seward, standing tall as if a sword and shield should magically appear in his hands. With difficulty, Aileen forced her face into an admiring expression.

Seward relented. "Agnes and I will meet in the herbarium of an evening, if our duties permit. I will ask if she will speak with you. I do admit that she is over-fond of talking of romance and such silly matters, so perhaps tomorrow you may speak."

This seemed too long to wait, but Aileen wasn't sure that she could push Seward any harder.

As she bade farewell to Seward and turned away, she spied a maidservant crossing the courtyard toward them. The girl looked a little put out to see Seward talking to Aileen.

"Is that Agnes now?" asked Aileen, a possible reason for the girl's expression occurring to her.

"Yes," said Seward. "She is early today." He appeared not to see the frown on the maid's face as she approached.

"Good morrow to you," said Aileen as the young woman reached them. "I was just talking to the knight's groom here about the noble families you both serve. My father is a cloth and dye merchant, but I think I have never seen such fine fabrics and such beautiful embroidery as that I have seen in these few days we have been visited by such high-born lords and ladies."

The maid's expression softened as she listened to Aileen babble on. "Oh, this is but their traveling clothes" she said. "If you should see the finery that

113

adorns them when they attend court you would think that what you have seen here is but a poor sample."

"Truly I can scarce believe it," said Aileen. "It must be very grand, where you work?"

"I work hard to keep my lady's wardrobe so beautiful. From morning to night, I have but little time to admire the magnificence of castle or gardens. Howsoever that may be, my mistress is a kind woman most of the time, and I think that my family is blessed to be in the household of the Lord de Vere. I do hear that service in other households is sometimes less pleasant."

Seward rolled his eyes, and said he must return to his work, for his master wished to ride out that afternoon and he had to get his own mount ready to accompany him. Agnes and Aileen barely heard him leave.

"What about Sir Henri du Lac's family," said Aileen. "I have heard that the two families were close at one time, but that there was a great falling out between them and now they do scarcely speak."

"They do not speak at all," declared Agnes. She saw before her a young woman of the town who seemed so eager to hear about her life, poor though it might seem to Agnes herself. There were few girls of her age with whom she could speak freely. She would never meet this stranger again once her lady returned home. Surely there could be no harm in showing off her knowledge and enjoying a good gossip on such a rare occasion.

"Let us go to the herb garden," said Agnes. "It is quiet at this time of day, and we can enjoy our talk more."

114

The two young women walked to the herbarium in silence, each surreptitiously eyeing the other as if to see if this was someone in whom it was safe to confide.

Seated in the fragrant garden, Agnes took up the tale once more, her decision made.

"My father has been of the de Vere household his entire life," Agnes said. "My mother told me that Lady de Vere and Lady de Clare were once the best of friends, for they both grew up in this part of your land. Dame Alyse was the daughter of the lord of the manor of Lavenham. Lady de Clare's father was lord of the manor of Clare, which I believe is not far from here."

"Yes, it is but a half day's journey, close by the way to Cavendish, and Lavenham too is not so very far distant."

"I would that I could see it, but I am not sure my lady will wish to travel that way on this journey, especially given the events of the past few days."

"It may be that the desire to see her childhood home will be too strong to resist," said Aileen.

"That may be," replied Agnes. "In any event, their friendship is the reason behind my mother coming to be of the same household as my father."

"I have heard that there was violence between the families, but none seems to know any details." Aileen encouraged the maidservant.

"Oh, let me tell you all about it," said Agnes happily.

"It was told to me that, when Lady de Clare traveled to France to marry, she took my mother and several other servants with her. She became the closest

115

of friends with the Lady Alyse, and when my lady's old maid died suddenly Lady de Clare offered to send her my mother as a maidservant, so that there would be no need to train an inexperienced young girl as her maid. My mother told me she was sad to leave the only household she had ever known, but she met my father soon after arriving at her new manor and soon forgot to be sad."

Aileen couldn't imagine being torn away from her family and being sent somewhere she had never seen before, but she knew that it happened in noble families. She was so glad that her father was a free man and a well-respected craftsman of the Liberty of St. Edmund's Bury.

"I'm glad your mother and father found each other," said Aileen. "But what happened to turn these two great families against each other?"

"I was but a babe in arms at the time," continued Agnes. "But my father told me that it happened at the time the Lionheart and King Philip led the Crusaders against the Sultan Saladin, seeking to recapture Jerusalem.

"It so happened that Sir Henri du Lac's father and my lady's husband were in the retinue of the King of France. My father told me that they first traveled to the City of Acre to help those laying siege to the city. King Richard arrived a few months after they did, and it was soon after his arrival that the two kings and the two lords fell out."

"Why should it be so?" asked Aileen.

116

"I do not understand the affairs of kings and nobles," answered Agnes. "But my father told me that Philip and Richard had been great friends in their youth. The English prince was even betrothed to King Philip's sister. But when Richard became king it seems he became very proud and, in his arrogance, he decided to marry someone else."

"Yes," Aileen said. "Queen Berengaria. I did not know that he had been betrothed to another."

"Mayhap it is because I live in France that I know of this account," responded Agnes. "I think that such high affairs are not of great interest to most of us in our daily lives, but what we do hear will be something that affects our own land, rather than a foreign one."

To Aileen this seemed as good an explanation as any. "Please, go on with your tale."

Picking a mint leaf from the bed beside her and crushing it between her fingers to release the fragrance, Agnes continued: "It seems that the French king had to wait upon Richard longer than he expected. While he waited his men brought him reports of the Lionheart's heroic conquest of Cyprus and of his marriage to the princess of Navarre, Berengaria.

"All the talk in the camp was of the coming of the English king. It was as if all were convinced that the arrival of Richard would mean the end of their long wait for victory over the forces of Saladin."

"And did this not please King Philip?" asked Aileen.

"My mother told me that 'great men do not like to be made small by another'," quoted Agnes.

"I think perhaps that this does not apply only to great men," laughed Aileen, and the two young women paused a moment to share their amusement.

"Well," Agnes returned to her story. "Richard finally reached Acre, and not long after that the city fell to the Crusaders. It was about that time that the long friendship of the French and English kings failed. Philip returned to France, and Richard the Lionheart remained in the Holy Land to lead the Crusade."

"But what about the two lords who had taken the Cross with King Philip?" Aileen was fascinated by the tale of the two kings, but she had a greater interest in the tale of the two knights.

"No one knows for sure what occurred," said Agnes. "But it is rumored that they fell out over a matter of loyalty."

"Loyalty?" queried Aileen. "To the King of France?"

"Yes," said Agnes. "You would not know this, but the lands over which these two lords held power are close by the lands of the Norman dukes who now rule your country. In those times, fealty was owed to the Dukes of Normandy."

"So, many years ago, both families owed their allegiance to Duke William of Normandy, he who is called the Conqueror, and who became our king?"

"Yes. Of course, when disputes broke out between the sons of the Conqueror loyalties on both sides of the South Sea did not lie easy. Both sons of the houses of de Vere and du Lac swore allegiance to the Capetian kings of France, and thus it had been since that time."

Agnes paused, looking around to make sure they were still alone.

Aileen thought she might know what was to come. "But it did not so remain?"

"I do hear that it did not," said Agnes. "Once, many years ago, I heard my mother and my father speaking. They thought I was asleep, but I had had a bad dream so crept out of bed and thought to go for comfort to my mother.

"It was then I heard them talking about the lord Aillard du Lac, he who was Sir Henri's father. My father said that it was a great shame on the house of du Lac that Sir Aillard should bow to his lord the King while, at the same time, stab him the back."

"No!" exclaimed Aileen. "Sir Henri's father stabbed the King of France!"

"No, I did not mean he actually stabbed him," said Agnes. "My father was not talking thus. I confess I thought so myself at the time, but I cried out in fear and my parents heard me. My mother took me back to bed and told me that my father did not mean Sir Henri actually offered violence to the king and that I should go back to sleep and not worry about it.

"The next morning, when I asked my mother what my father had meant, she told me I had had a bad dream and that I did misremember the conversation. I pretended that I believed her, but I always knew that I had heard those words."

"Did you ever find out what your father meant?" asked Aileen.

"Yes. About two years ago, I asked my mother again. We were sitting in the Great Hall edging kerchiefs for Dame Alyse and Lady Isabelle, and I told her I still remembered that night. My mother told me I was now old enough to know the truth."

"What did she tell you?" asked Aileen.

"My mother said that my father had been in that same Great Hall when the lord de Vere had entered along with some of his household of knights. He was very angry and did not seem to notice my father's presence. He declared that, while he was besieging Acre, King Philip had discovered that Sir Aillard had fallen under the spell of King Richard of England. A spy in the court of the English king had seen Sir Aillard passing letters to the king's chamberlain. He found out that he had been acting as an ambassador to the court of the King of Navarre, negotiating for the hand of his daughter in marriage to King Richard."

"The king must have been very angry," said Aileen

"He must have been so, for it was at that time that he banished Sir Aillard du Lac and his entire family."

"Seward told me that, whatever the crime of which Sir Henri's father was accused, it was God's blessing that the King of France had merely banished the family and had not executed them," Aileen said.

"I do not know why it was so," replied Agnes. "Mayhap it was due to the long friendship and the great service offered the king's family over many generations."

"I think you may be right," said Aileen. "Howsoever it may be, it would seem that Sir Henri is seeking to

120

redress the sins of his father and regain the esteem in which his family name was once held."

"Yes." Agnes stood up and dusted off the shreds of leaves that had fallen on her skirts as they talked. "Now I must return to my mistress. She will be calling for me soon. In the mood in which I have found her these last days I do not wish to risk a beating."

"Thank you, Agnes," said Aileen. "Yours is a tale such as I have never heard before."

"I was glad to spend some time with you, Aileen. It is not often I have a chance to sit in the peace of a garden and spin tales of romance. God be with you," she finished, and ran off toward the guest hall.

CHAPTER TWELVE

The sacrist was referred to as the father and patron of the Jews, for they enjoyed his protection.

EVEN AS AILEEN WAS TALKING to Agnes and learning of the mighty families and their quarrels, Ruth and Avi were walking through the forest.

"Ruth," said Avi. "I am not sure that we should be doing this. I do not wish to anger your father by putting you at risk."

"Please do not fret, Avi," replied Ruth. "I promise that we will not leave the shelter of the forest and we will turn around immediately if you sense any danger. I just need to know."

Sighing, Avi gave in to the slight girl beside him, just as he had since they were small children together. Ruth has always been able to twist me around her little finger, he thought. I think perhaps that will never change.

Eventually, the pair could see the sun shining brightly ahead of them, and they slowed as they approached the edge of the woods. Kneeling down behind some bushes, they peered out at the wrecks of the houses before them. Fences were torn down, and the plants in the gardens were broken and trampled. They could see one of the homes was a burned-out shell, and there was damage to the walls and doors of the others.

"Oh, Avi, I'm so sorry," said Ruth, for they were looking at the damage wrought by the men of St. Edmund's Bury when they could find none of the Fornham families at home. All the houses were badly damaged, but nothing was left of Avi's home.

"It matters not, Ruth," Avi said. "It is as you said to Robert. We all escaped with our lives. Wood and wattle do not matter, though I confess that it saddens me to see all our hard work brought to naught."

Ruth laid her hand over that of her friend in sympathy. "Shall we see if we can recover anything?" she asked.

Before Avi could reply, they heard the sound of hooves upon the road. Shrinking back behind a group of trees some yards further into the forest, the pair tried to be as still as possible. When Ruth would say a word about leaving, Avi put his finger to his lips and shook his head gently.

Into their sight rode a knight and someone who surely was his groom. The knight was upon a black horse, its coat gleaming with health and the harness glinting in the sun. The groom rode just behind the knight, calmly surveying his surroundings.

Coming to a halt in front of the ruined houses, the knight dismounted. His groom hastily did the same, taking the reins of his master's horse and waiting for instruction. His face bespoke his puzzlement, but he was too good a servant to question the actions of the knight.

For the space of a minute, the knight stood still, turning his head this way and that, an expression of sorrow on his face. Then he started toward the burned-out house, passing through the broken-down gate and walking around the wrecked garden. Entering the shell of the home, he picked over pieces of burned cloth and broken plates. Coming out of the doorway holding what seemed to be a charred doll, he walked over to look at the damage sustained by the other homes.

"Master," said his groom, hesitantly. "Why are we here? What is it that you are seeking in these ruins?"

The knight started, as though the words of his servant had broken in upon thoughts that were too deep to acknowledge the presence of any other. Sighing, he indicated to the groom that they should sit on a bench that was close by the gate of one of the houses.

"Seward," he said. "Do you know where we are?"

"No, sire," responded the groom. "I have not been outside the gates of the Abbey since we arrived, and for certain this is not the way we rode when we approached St. Edmund's Bury."

"We are in the village of Fornham," said the knight.

124

Seward remembered hearing about Fornham. "Is this then where the Jews lived?" he asked, looking around him with interest.

"Yes, and it was from here that they fled the day after the relic was stolen," replied his master.

"They do say that that proves their guilt," said Seward. "Is that why we are here today, then, sire? Do you believe that you may see a sign that will lead you to the holy relic, and so to the end of your long journey to fulfil your vow?"

"It has been a long journey, hasn't it?" said the knight. "And you have traveled all the way with me. You are a good and faithful servant, Seward."

The groom blushed, his pleasure at the words of his master clear. "It has been my honor to serve you, sire," he said.

The knight's face darkened, and he stood up abruptly. Confused, Seward stood in turn. "What is it, sire?" he asked. "Did you hear something?"

Ruth and Avi, standing still as statues behind their tree, caught their breath in fear of being discovered.

"No, Seward," said the knight. "I heard nothing but the sounds of birds and crickets. But even those sounds, normal as the rising of the sun with each new day, taunt me with memories of fear and loathing."

Seward said nothing, for he could see his master was thinking of something deep in the past. Mayhap it was memories of the blackest days of the Crusade, but, whatever the cause of the knight's dark mood, this was no time to be asking more questions.

125

"Sometimes I think," continued the knight, "that there can be no end to the penance which must be offered for sin. Truly it has been said that the iniquity of the fathers shall be visited upon the children, and upon the children's children, unto the third and fourth generation."

"The priests tell us that the Jews put our Savior to death," responded Seward. "Truly their sin is great, and the priests tell us penance is still due."

The knight looked at his servant. "Do you think it is of this sin that I speak?" he said. "Well, perhaps it is. Yet there are none who are blameless, and the sins of the fathers continue, as do the sins of the sons."

Seeing that his groom's confusion was not lessened by his words, the knight turned back to the ruined houses and swept his arm around the scene. "If this is the price for the sins of a generation long since dead and in their graves, then so much greater must the price be for the sins of this generation. If the holy treasure were not stolen by the Jews, how then do they deserve to be so hounded, and what is due to the true thief?"

"But surely there can be no doubt that the Jews stole the relic, sire," said the groom. "As is said, no Christian man would dare lay his hand upon the sacred relic with evil intent. Why, the folk of St. Edmund's town do tell me that an Abbot of this very Abbey was paralyzed in his hands when he dared to touch the head of the blessed St. Edmund just to test whether or not the head of the martyr had miraculously been put back on his neck. Certain it is that no Christian would risk the wrath of the Son of God Himself by violently taking away a piece of the True Cross."

The Crusader studied his groom with compassion written across his face. "Perhaps you are right, Seward," he said. "You are a good man, and there is little guile in you. It may be written in the history of my family that sorrow and mistrust are to be our legacy. Mayhap I should allow the folk of St. Edmund's Bury to follow the obvious way and not suggest to them that there is any other path."

So saying, the knight led the way to their horses. Turning to take one final look at the houses, he spoke one last thought under his breath. "And yet, can it be that a man of honor would permit the hounding of any man who was not proven to be a traitor to any King?"

Seward understood only that his master was distraught. He has always felt the shame of his family's fall from grace deeply, he thought, but it has been a long time since he has been filled with this much sorrow.

"Enough!" said the knight, mounting his horse. "Let us return to St. Edmund's Bury. The Abbot will be expecting me at his table tonight, and I cannot be late."

The two men rode away, the sound of the hooves of their horses gradually fading into the quiet of the late afternoon.

Avi and Ruth waited for some minutes before leaving the safety of their hiding place.

"What do you think that was all about?" asked Ruth when they were once again standing at the edge of the

127

trees looking upon the ruins of the homes that had once been filled with laughter and peace.

"I do not know," responded Avi. "I could not tell whether the knight truly believed us to be innocent of this theft or if he believed that, whether or not we actually stole their relic, we were receiving only what is due those who put to death the Christian Messiah."

"It was confusing," said Ruth. "Yet he looked upon the ruin of our homes with such sad eyes, and I cannot but believe he was really filled with sadness at our plight."

Avi smiled upon his friend. "Ruth, you are ever the one to think the best of people. I fear for one as gentle as you, and yet I would not change you for anything."

Ruth looked down at her feet with embarrassment. "Well, that's just as well," she said. "My father says that men do not change, and I doubt not that that applies to women as well."

Laughing, the two of them left behind all thoughts of the Crusader knight and his sorrows and turned to walk home. The arrival of the knight and his groom had only strengthened Avraham's resolve to keep Ruth away from Fornham and the danger in which they all stood. Ruth, however, thought only of how this evening they might be able to meet Aileen and Robert, and this adventure at least would be something worth telling.

128

CHAPTER THIRTEEN

*And now sheets of gold and silver resound
between the hammer and the anvil, and
craftsmen handle craftsmen's tools.*

ROBERT'S DAY WAS BUSY, AND he had little time to think about the search for the relic. His father had need of him in the workshop all day and set him to the task of parting silver from gold in sheets of metal. John Palgrave, who never suffered anything but the best work, seemed to be an even more exacting taskmaster on this occasion.

"No, Robert," he told his son early in the day. "That is not how I taught you to work the sheets of metal to obtain the best gold. You have not put enough crushed brick and salt in the vessel. When you heat it, there will not be enough salt to separate the silver from the gold. I cannot use adulterated gold for such delicate work as the ring brooch for the wife of the High Sheriff of Suffolk."

"That's better," he said at noon. "You can begin working on hammering the lip of the chalice now."

"Robert," he called halfway through the afternoon, "Bring the seal for Master Winchester. He has come to fetch it."

Thus it was that by the time he heard someone enter the door toward the end of the day, Robert was tired and a little irritable.

Walking into the front room, wiping his hands on his apron, he stopped short. "Brother Sampson," he said in surprise. "How may I be of assistance to you today?"

"Good even, Master Robert," replied the subsacrist of the Abbey. "I have come to talk with your father, if that be possible."

"I am sorry, brother," said Robert. "He is not here. He was called to see a client."

"Ah, that is a pity. I should perhaps have sent word that I wished to see him," the monk said.

"I doubt not he will return soon," said Robert. "Is there something I can do to help you, or would you prefer that I ask him to call upon you on the morrow?"

The monk hesitated. "I believe you are now apprenticed to your father?" he asked.

"Yes, brother. I have been so honored these past several months."

"Then perhaps you may be able to answer a few questions for me," said Brother Sampson.

"Willingly, brother," responded Robert.

"Please come through here," he continued, holding aside a curtain for the monk. "May I fetch you a cup of hippocras?"

The monk, seating himself upon a chair, declined the offer and signed that Robert too should sit.

"As you know," he began, "your father has been commissioned to make a golden shrine in which the holy relic, whose theft is the cause of our current troubles, may rest."

Robert nodded in assent.

"Such work takes many months, or even years, so your father has fashioned a temporary housing of gold bars through which the blessed relic may be seen."

"Yes, brother," said Robert, wondering where this was going. "I can assure you that my father carried out his task with great reverence. Nothing but the finest gold and the best tools were used in the making of these bars and the door that will permit the passage of the casket containing the relic."

"Oh, I do not doubt it," said Brother Sampson. "It is not the quality of the work about which I have come. It is about its security."

"Security?" asked Robert. "I am not sure that I understand."

"The Abbot has sent me to ask if there is a way that the shrine which will hold the blessed relic may be made more secure," said the subsacrist. "We are, of course, confident that our Lord will return to us His holy treasure and, when He does, we wish to ensure that no one will ever deprive us of this gift of Christ again."

The monk sighed and shook his head in sorrow.

"Once it would have been unthinkable that any should dare to commit such sacrilege as has been done within the walls of our Abbey. All within the Liberty know of the great punishments meted out to those who have so dared. Yet now our confidence has been shaken, and Father Abbot wishes to protect our treasures from further outrage."

"Now I understand, brother," said Robert. "I am sure that my father will be able to fashion something that will add to the barrier without taking away from the beauty of the shrine. I would also suggest that, since my father works often with the blacksmith, he can ensure that a cunning lock is designed that will help protect the holy relic from thieving hands. We can also work with the smith to find a way of fastening the golden cage to the stone upon which it will stand. If you will, I shall tell my father of your concerns this evening so that he may call upon you tomorrow."

"Thank you," said the monk, rising from his seat. "I know Father Abbot will be pleased. We have been troubled by the thought that some felon escaped the bounds of our Abbey with our precious treasure, though none can tell us how. Regrettably, we must now turn our minds to close protection of such treasures."

The subsacrist's words started a train of thought in Robert's mind. "Brother Sampson, may I ask you a question?" he said, as the monk moved toward the door.

"Of course," responded the monk. "How may I help you, my son?"

"You said just now that you could not tell how the thief had left the Abbey grounds with his prize. Could he not just have walked out with it?"

132

"If he had walked all through the grounds of the Abbey as far as the River, he might perhaps have waded through the water and thus reached the vineyard on the other side," said Brother Sampson. "However, as the Lord Abbot so wisely propounded as we sat in the chapter house only the other day, that would have posed a great risk for any thief. Surely someone who has just committed such sacrilege would not wish to remain close to the site of his dark deed for any great period of time."

"But the Abbey is quiet at night, is it not? There is no one abroad within the walls?"

"It is true that the brothers rest after the last office of the day," said the monk. "But there are only a very few hours when there is no one abroad in the Abbey. Even then, there are times when brother infirmarer must attend to his patients and thus is abroad in the hours between Matins and Lauds. As Abbot Samson opined in chapter, the sacred relic must have been stolen during that period of time because, once dawn has broken, both monks and servants are astir, and no one could pass across the Abbey grounds unnoticed."

"Could the thief not have found a much shorter route out of the Abbey grounds by going out through the Abbot's gate onto Mustow St. or the South Gate by St. Mary's church, rather than going all the way through the courtyards and the vineyard?" asked Robert. "I know the gate to the Great Court is barred at night, but are not any other gates open to those who must come and go?"

"No, my son," said Brother Sampson. "It has been the practice since long before I became a monk of the Abbey for all gates to be barred at night. That is why all Abbey workers must enter by the Great Gate. Sergeant Ralph opens that gate at dawn and thus admits all who need enter the Abbey.

"I doubt not that there may be ways of entering and leaving the grounds of our Abbey without passing through any gate," continued the monk. "But all such ways would involve time or the need to climb over obstacles. I pray that a thief carrying such precious treasure would not risk causing damage to that for which he has risked so much."

"I can see why you are so sure of the time during which the theft must have taken place," said Robert. "Yet, if not by these means, how was this man able to escape with the relic?"

The subsacrist smiled. "You have touched upon the question that has been the cause of much discussion among the brothers," he said. Sitting back down, he rubbed his forehead as if in frustration.

"Perhaps I should not be talking to you about this," he said. "But we have spent so much time discussing it among ourselves and yet reached no conclusion. I know not whether speaking it out loud to another will be of any avail, but it is certain that it cannot hurt. There is nothing secret in our thoughts, for all of St. Edmund's Bury knows all there is to know about the sacrilege offered to our Abbey"

Robert fetched a cup of hippocras for the subsacrist, and the monk gratefully drank from the cup before proceeding.

"Until Father Abbot spoke of the difficulty of exiting the Abbey grounds, I truly believe that none of us within the cloister had given thought to much beyond the terrible loss of the sacred relic. Of course, once he raised the issue we could talk of little else."

The monk fell silent for a moment, apparently gathering his thoughts.

"Brother subsacrist," prompted Robert. "There are none who know the hidden places and the paths within the walls of the Abbey better than those who live within. Yet you have not found a solution to this riddle?"

"No, we have not," sighed the monk. "Some suggested that the thief must have climbed over one of the same gates as you mentioned. Others declared that would have been too risky for a man carrying the golden casket containing the holy relic. Others wondered, as did you, if he had gone through the monks' cemetery and past the infirmary, passing into the meadow and thus to the river and the vineyard."

"You did say that that would have been risky, even in the hours between Matins and Lauds," said Robert.

"Yes, even on a night without interruption that would have been the case. On that night, however, there was interruption, as we learned in the course of the discussion in the chapter house."

"Interruption?" asked Robert, eagerly. "What occurred on the night of the theft to disturb the monks' rest?"

"Only the rest of brother infirmarer," responded Brother Sampson. "Brother Peter, who has served the Lord faithfully within our walls for these past 30 years, was sick unto death with his breathing and his coughing. Brother infirmarer spent much of the night preparing medicine of liquorice and comfrey and soothing the cough with the juice of horehound. He told us that there was no single hour that night when he was not walking back and forth to the infirmary or gathering more herbs to help our ailing brother."

"Then the thief would likely not have risked taking that route to escape from the Abbey," said Robert.

"That is the conclusion to which we came," said the monk. "But beyond that we have not traveled far."

"Brother subsacrist," Robert asked, remembering a conversation he had had with Aileen days before, "is it possible that the holy relic is still within the walls of the Abbey, hidden in some secret place by the thief?"

"Master Robert," responded the subsacrist. "You are quick in thought, as well as in the learning of your craft. Your father must be proud of his apprentice."

Will I never rid myself of this habit of blushing, thought Robert. It is most unbecoming!

"Such a solution was in fact proposed by Prior Herbert," continued Brother Sampson. "We determined to make a search of all possible places, both inside and outside. It has taken us more than two days to

136

search in every nook and cranny. We even searched the guest hall, although naturally we could not search the personal belongings of our visitors. If one of our guests has secreted the blessed treasure, I cannot see what it is that they can hope to gain, and, in any event, it is unlikely that any of them would have had sufficient knowledge of the knight's vigil and the place in which the casket was to be found prior to the celebratory mass to plan such sacrilege."

"Yes, I can see that would be true," said Robert. "I did assume that the holy relic would be placed in a position of honor within the Abbey church, but I doubt many from beyond the bounds of the Liberty would know enough about the church to be sure of exactly where that might be."

"And who among them would have known of the knight's intent to hold his vigil alone?" said the subsacrist. "It was not proclaimed to all within the town. It is certain that few even of the cloistered brothers knew of that intent, and so I much doubt that others within the walls of the Abbey would have been able to plan the theft with such knowledge.

"So, it would seem that we have returned to the beginning," said Brother Sampson. "How did the thief leave the Abbey?"

To this question neither man could posit an answer.

"I can tarry no longer," said the monk, rising once again. "I will leave in your hands both the commission to your father and this seemingly unsolvable riddle. I should be most glad if your quick mind can shine a light on that which we have been unable to explain."

So saying, the subsacrist made his farewells and left Robert to his work and his thoughts.

CHAPTER FOURTEEN

He knowingly sustained the damage and loss his servants
caused to his possessions, and admitted that he did so.

"RUTH!" CRIED AILEEN, HUGGING HER friend. "I am so glad to see you. I feared so for your safety and that of your family."

True to his word given, it seemed, so long ago, Robert had returned to meet with Ruth and Avraham close by the holly bush, this time with Aileen beside him. Telling Aileen about his conversation with the subsacrist on the way, the two friends had arrived at the rendezvous full of hope that bringing the friends together again might produce at least some solutions to unanswerable questions.

"Were it not for you and Robert we would not be safe," said Ruth. "My father sends you his greetings and his gratitude. He also asks that I warn you to take care for yourselves. The people of the Liberty are angry and reckless in their distress, and we would not have you suffer because you have aided us."

Aileen clasped Ruth's hand. "We will take care, I promise you. But we have news to share, so let's sit down and talk."

Eagerly, Aileen told them all she had learned about the betrayal of Sir Aillard du Lac and the anger of the French king. She could not complain of a lack of attention on the part of her listeners, nor of the response as she brought her tale to an end. Robert sat open-mouthed, astonishment on his face. Ruth seemed quietly impressed, her expression thoughtful.

"I do wonder if this explains what happened to Avi and I only a few hours ago," she said.

"What happened?" demanded Aileen. "You were not discovered, were you?"

"Oh, no," said Ruth. "I am sorry. I did not mean to scare you. No, it is just that Avi and I ... well, we wanted to see ..."

"You wanted to see what?" asked Robert.

"What Ruth means is that we wanted to see whose house had been burned down in Fornham." Avi was usually so quiet that the others almost jumped at the sound of his voice.

"Oh," said Robert. "I understand. I would probably feel the same way."

"So you went back to Fornham," said Aileen. "Was that not dangerous?"

"Yes," replied Avi. "I do not believe that Isaac of Cordoba would have approved, but truth be told I can never deny a request of Ruth's."

Ruth looked somewhat shame-faced, but quickly turned to an account of their near encounter with the knight and his groom.

"And he called the groom 'Seward'?" asked Aileen. Ruth and Avi both nodded. "Then that must have been Sir Henri du Lac himself."

"I wonder why he would ride to Fornham," said Robert. "It is passing strange that a man hunting the relic that was so violently taken from him would go there."

"Perhaps it is as his servant said," Ruth said. "It may be that he was seeking a sign that would lead him to the thief."

"That is possible but, from what you have told us, it seems he found little but bad memories in riding to your homes."

"I think his memories must have been about the feud between his family and that of William de Vere," said Aileen. "When he was talking about children doing penance for the sins of their fathers he must have been thinking about the betrayal of the French king by his father. Truly his father's sins are being visited upon him. Or perhaps he was thinking about the betrayal of our Lord Jesus by his own people."

Suddenly realizing in whose company they were, Aileen offered a stammering apology to Ruth and Avi.

"Do not be distressed, Aileen," said Ruth. "We are well used to hearing such words. We know that you do not utter them with hatred, unlike many who use

141

them, but merely as a fact you have been taught since the cradle."

Aileen squeezed her friend's hand in gratitude.

"So, let us return to the subject at hand," said Ruth, making her friends smile at her tone of command.

"I think you have solved the riddle, Aileen," said Robert. "There is such enmity between the two noble French families that it must be that the Lady Alyse and her son traveled to the Abbey to ensure that Sir Henri gains no privilege from his vow."

"Perhaps," said Aileen. "But if it is the young heir to the lands of de Vere who is responsible for this terrible theft, where has he hidden the relic, and why is it that his mother is so angry and talks of his conduct besmirching the name of his noble house?"

"It may be that I can tell you some part of that," responded Robert, glad to have something really important to contribute to the conversation.

He told them how he had followed young William de Vere on the Sunday morning, and of his suspicious entry to the house of the merchant of Moyses Hall. "Then, just as I passed the Hall and sought to see inside, Master Durand stopped me."

"Master Durand," exclaimed Aileen. "The Reeve?"

"It is perhaps encouraging to those of us who have been hiding in the forest this past week," said Ruth, quietly, "to know that the Reeve is seeking suspects in this matter other than us."

"I would that I could offer you such encouragement, Ruth," said Robert. "But I must tell you that he was

142

outside Moyses Hall for quite another reason. It was pure chance that our two interests coincided."

Aileen smiled at Ruth. "Never mind," she said. "It will take many threads of this mystery to complete the picture, and mayhap this is one of those threads."

Turning to Robert, she asked "What happened next?"

"Master Durand took me to his house," said Robert. "I did not know what I was going to tell him. I knew he would not be pleased to find out that we are asking questions and following suspects.

"In the end I really did not have much choice but to tell him the truth," Robert said, apologetically. "The Reeve did not believe me when I told him I was just following the young lordling to learn his manners, and I could not explain why I was spying upon him outside the Hall."

"So you told him all about what we have been doing?"

"Yes, Aileen, I did. I'm sorry."

"No matter," Aileen said with determination. "We have not been doing anything wrong, merely seeking to help a friend in distress. I cannot see why we should be ashamed of that."

"Well, as you may imagine," said Robert, "the Reeve did not quite see things that way. In fact, he was most displeased. He gave me a firm lecture on the dangers of poking sleeping dogs and said we are foolish and headstrong."

Aileen sat up straight at these words. "Indeed we are not 'foolish and headstrong'," she said. "We at least have the sense to realize that someone is not automatically evil because he is different from us!"

"Aileen," said Ruth. "Be calm. Our people are well used to such suspicions. For many centuries, since even before the birth of your Christ, we have been hated and exiled. We are not permitted to be apprenticed to master craftsmen or join guilds, and many nations have forbidden us sanctuary merely because of our faith. You well know that even your Lord Abbot expelled our fellow believers from this town only a few years ago when anger arose over the death of a young boy. We were blamed for that death then, though none could give evidence that any Jew had caused the poor boy's death. Surely you are not surprised by the reaction of your neighbors on the occasion of this great theft?"

Aileen thought she had never heard so long a speech from Ruth before. Quiet as she was, it was a sign of the great emotion that dwelt within her that she should so share her thoughts out loud.

Avraham reached over and took Ruth's hand. "These are our friends, Ruth," he said. "They do understand."

"Forgive me," said Ruth. "I did not mean to complain. I doubt that anyone, of whatever faith, has ever had friends more true than the two of you. I meant only to explain that it is rare for any of our faith to be treated without suspicion by those around us. Do not fret because the Reeve is convinced that what you do is not right."

"Very well," said Aileen. "But I still do not like what he said."

She sounded so indignant they all laughed. Aileen gave her friend a quick hug, and then urged Robert to continue with his account.

"Well, once the Reeve had completed his scolding, he told me that I should stop concerning myself with Master William de Vere. He assured me that, whatever the young man was about, it had nothing to do with the theft of the relic or the Crusader."

"How could he know that?" asked Aileen.

Robert smiled. "That was my exact question to him," he said. "I asked him why he would be following Master William himself at such a desperate time for the town if he believed him innocent of any involvement in the theft."

"And what did he answer?"

"He sighed, and then said that he would tell me something of the situation if I would promise on my honor not to reveal what he said to anyone and not to ask any more questions of anyone about this matter."

"Did you so promise?" asked Aileen.

"Yes, but do not distress yourself," he said, seeing Aileen's alarm at his answer. "I told the Reeve that I could not give him my oath unless he gave permission for me to explain to my friends why we need not concern ourselves with William de Vere any longer."

"That was well done, Robert," laughed Ruth. "Your words did not promise that you would ask no more questions concerning any in the town, but merely of one man."

145

"It was perhaps not the most open way to speak," said Robert, somewhat shame-faced. "and I did fear to breathe for a moment until I saw that the Reeve was content with my promise."

"So what did he tell you, Robert?" said Aileen.

"He told me about Hazard."

"Hazard? What do you mean?" Aileen looked puzzled.

"I did not know what it was he meant either," said Robert. "Master Durand explained that it is a game on which men make wagers."

"It's a game?" Aileen wasn't sure what to make of this.

"A very serious game, apparently," said Robert. The Reeve told me that it was brought back from the Holy Land by the Crusaders. It's a game of dice. Players have to guess the numbers that will be thrown, or something like that. I'm not really sure what it's all about, but Master Durand told me many men have lost all they possessed making these wagers. He told me King Richard even put limits on how much his men were permitted to wager playing the game."

"But what does this have to do with William de Vere and the loss of the relic?" asked Aileen.

"Probably nothing," responded Robert. "At least, that was what the Reeve said. He told me that he has long suspected that Moyses Hall was no peaceful merchant's home, but rather a place where rich men are cheated out of their money. He has spent many quiet hours over many months watching the house. When he saw me there that morning, he was anxious that

146

those within did not see me, so he made sure to take me away."

"Would it not be hard in a town the size of ours to find many rich men to cheat?" Ruth asked.

"Were it not for the fame of our holy saint's shrine and the pilgrims who fill our town that would be so," said Robert. "But Master Durand told me that it is his belief that one of the gang that runs this game of Hazard is a high-born man. He believes him to be a younger son who has little hope of inheriting his father's lands. That man receives a reward from the leader of the gang to pass word of the wagering house to his friends. By that means the fame of Moyses Hall has spread. The Reeve told me that many of the visitors to the Abbey also visit Moyses Hall."

"So the Reeve believes that Dame Alyse's son is one of the young men who go to the Hall to place wagers," said Aileen.

"Or perhaps he believes him to be the high-born member of the gang," added Ruth.

"I do not believe he thinks him to be a part of the gang," said Robert. "He has a reputation for losing his money on dice, but he is foreign-born, and it is unlikely he has ever met anyone from our town before. It is more likely that he learned of Moyses Hall from a friend and took this opportunity to visit."

Aileen frowned in concentration as Robert spoke. "Was it at the Hall that William lost his cloak?" she asked.

"It would so seem," said Robert. "Master Durand was not able to enter the house until the night of the unholy theft. On that evening, he told me, the watchman alerted him to the sounds of shouting and screaming from within. He ran to the Hall and pounded on the door, demanding admittance. When the door was finally opened to him, all was quiet within."

"Was he able to find out what happened there?" Ruth asked.

"No. He could not see beyond the entry hall, and he was denied admittance. He was told friends had been drinking and had become a little too loud. Then the door was closed almost in his face."

"He did not leave, did he?" asked Aileen.

"He did not," said Robert. "He secreted himself very much where I stood Sunday morning, and waited. It was not long before the door opened again, and Master William de Vere and another young man were ejected quite forcefully from the Hall. They were indeed drunk, scarce able to stand on their own feet. The Reeve said they glared at each other for a moment, appeared to begin an argument in the street, but then went their separate ways when they realized they were in an open market square and like to be overheard.

"Remembering what you had told me at the gate, Aileen," said Robert, "I asked Master Durand whether the two men were clad in cloak and cap, so to keep out the chill of the night, and he said they were not, although the other young man did have a jaunty cap with a feather on his head. It was the Reeve's opinion

148

that the two men were warmed from within, but that they were like to take a chill by the morning."

"Do you think the argument between the two men was about the relic?" asked Ruth.

"It is possible," answered Robert. "The Reeve thinks it was concerning a wager. It is his belief that neither young man had a purse, either fat or thin, when he left the house. As I said, the Reeve is certain that this is a house where a rich young man may be easily separated from his purse."

"So it is his conduct in this that has displeased his mother," said Aileen. "Perhaps she fears that he will wager beyond his ability to pay and that he will bring down the name of the de Vere family. Or it may be that she fears he will be involved in some violence."

"If his conduct in this town is an indication of his habit, then mayhap he already has been involved in violence," Robert suggested.

"You may have the right of it," said Aileen, "There is another possibility, however. It may be that this young man, in hopes of regaining his standing before his father, determined to bring down the reputation of Sir Henri du Lac by stealing the relic."

"If that be the case," asked Ruth, "where would he secret it?"

"I do not know," Aileen said. "But I wonder about the timing of all this. The theft must have taken place after the excitement at the Hall. Is it possible that, in his cups, he was able to silently steal up behind the Crusader knight, render him unconscious, and take the relic? If so, and if Master Durand is correct that he did not have his cloak with him when he left Moyses Hall, then he cannot have carried it away from the Abbey wrapped in his cloak. In that case, the damage to the cloak has nothing to do with the theft of the relic, and we are back at the beginning of our enquiries. We cannot be sure that the young lord de Vere has anything to do with the theft at all and, even if he did, we do not know where he went or what steps he took to hide the relic!"

"From what you have told me of this young lord," said Ruth, "he does not sound to me to be the kind of bold, adventurous man that surely this thief must needs be. He seems to be weak and a little arrogant."

"That is certainly how he appears to many," said Aileen. "But people are not always as they seem on the surface, so perhaps he can be different when he sees a reason to be so."

"So, let us talk of what we know and what it means," said Robert. "Where do we go from here?"

"You have undertaken not to enquire any further into William de Vere," Aileen said. "But I can see if it is possible for me to learn anything further within the walls of the Abbey. I will be discreet," Aileen added, seeing Robert about to object. "We must decide, however, if he is as he appears or if he may be more cunning and determined that it seems."

"Well, all right," said Robert. "But take care."

"Yes, you both must take care," Ruth said. "This relic of yours was stolen by a man willing to do violence to obtain it. Mayhap it was even more than one man. Howsoever that may be, they will be angered and afraid if they discover you to be too close to the truth. You must promise me to risk no more for our sake. Promise me."

"Ruth," said Aileen gently, "we will be careful. We cannot promise that we will not work toward drawing near the truth, though. Since we do not know what that truth is at this moment to so promise would mean we must cease to ask questions."

"But we do promise to take care, Ruth," added Robert, seeing that Ruth was about to protest once again. "And should we believe we have found the answer to this riddle, we will seek the aid of others to bring the relic home to the Abbey and the thief to the tender mercies of the court."

With that Ruth had to be satisfied.

"And what of the other possibilities," asked Aileen of Robert. "Should we also look for someone who takes revenge on behalf of the French knight from whom Sir Henri du Lac took the holy relic, or someone who seeks personal gain from its theft?"

"Yes," said Robert. "I am still puzzled by what I learned on the road the other day. I am sure there is a connection with the theft from the Abbey. I just don't know what it may be, so I will make some more enquiries tomorrow."

"Good," Aileen said. "Then we have a plan."

"If it may be of help," said Ruth, "I can ask my father about these great families."

"Would he know of them?" asked Aileen, surprised.

"I do not know, but it is possible he has heard something of them," replied Ruth. "You would not know this, but my father is a close friend of Rabbi Maimonides, who is a great physician of our faith. They were both born in Cordoba and were children together. The Rabbi has lived for many years in Egypt, but he was a physician in the court of the Sultan Saladin."

Aileen and Robert stared at Ruth. "So he would have been in the Holy Land at the same time as King Richard and King Philip?" Aileen asked.

"I do not know," responded Ruth. "the Rabbi and my father have corresponded for many years. Indeed, my father tells me that he has learned much as a physician from the great man."

"Do you think this Rabbi may have told your father anything of the feud between these families?" asked Robert.

"I admit it is not likely, but I will ask," said Ruth. "You are trying to clear the name of our people in this matter. It is the least I can do."

"Time is passing, Ruth." Avraham had been so silent the three friends had almost forgotten he was there. "We must go."

"And so must we," said Aileen.

The friends hugged and said their farewells, with the hope that they would return to share their findings the very next evening.

"Is it not strange," said Robert as they walked toward the town. "We never thought that Ruth's father might be of help to us in this search?"

"I know," Aileen said. "Truly it is said that the many strands of a web are connected as one. Yet the more we find out the more complex this web seems to be. Sir Henri du Lac arrived at the Abbey only days ago, filled with a holy purpose. All the people, from near and far, were excited and ready to celebrate, yet confident of receiving holy blessings from God.

"Now here we are," she continued. "The relic has been stolen and we have discovered that there are many people who may wish ill on the Crusader knight, at least one of whom is present in the Abbey. And that doesn't even include those who may not care about the knight himself but who wish the power that possession of a piece of the True Cross may give them"

"It is indeed a web," said Robert. "Many strands that appear harmless, and yet trap those who innocently approach."

Aileen stopped in her tracks. Something ... a whisper of a thought ... something that had been said that evening ...

"What's wrong?" Robert had stopped a couple of yards ahead of her, suddenly finding himself alone.

"Nothing," she said. "I think perhaps a piece of what has been in the back of my mind for days just clicked into place."

"What?"

Aileen shook her head. "Let me think a moment. It's just a thread, but ..."

Tense with excitement, the pair stood silently for a moment.

"No," she said, finally. "It's gone now! Just for a moment I thought I had hold of a part of the solution, but now I'm not sure it was anything but a stray thought."

"There must have been something," said Robert, eagerly. "Let's go over what we were saying again and see if that jogs your memory."

"No, whatever it was it's gone out of my head now. And if we tarry any longer we will be late home. We can talk again tomorrow."

Robert wasn't sure this was the best plan. "You know we promised Ruth that we would not risk anything alone. You won't go off investigating on your own if you remember whatever it was again, will you?"

Aileen smiled. "No, Robert, I promise," she said. "But even if I can pick up the thread again I think it was such a thin thread that I will have to sort it out in my own mind before I can put it into words. If I don't it won't make sense when I talk about it. I know that sounds strange ..."

"I'd agree with that!" said Robert, trying to lighten the mood.

Aileen smiled. "But it's just the way I feel. Don't be cross with me, Robert," she said, sensing his disappointment. She laid her hand on his forearm. "It's not that I don't trust you. Really it isn't."

Recognizing defeat when he saw it, Robert gave way graciously. They walked home in companionable silence, both of them thinking furiously about what had just passed.

CHAPTER FIFTEEN

The abbot jumped up and said that he was prepared to search for his lord the king, either in secret or otherwise, until he found him.

IT WAS LATER THAN HE could have wished before Robert could pursue his enquiries the next day. John Palgrave had spent the morning showing his son how to form the handles of a chalice in wax, complete with decorations of flowers and leaves. It was delicate work, and Robert knew that it had to be perfectly done if the clay that was then molded around the work was to fill in all the hollows without damaging the sculpture.

Robert had scarcely dared to breathe as molten gold was poured into the mold, but the warm clay didn't crack. Now all he had to do was wait until the evening, when his father would break open the cooled mold and the handles inside would be revealed.

Being an apprentice to my father is all I have ever wanted to be, he thought, but I have to admit it is hard to be attentive and learn all that he must teach me while

I'm also trying to find time to help Aileen. I am glad that my father thought not to ask any questions of me today, for I would not wish to deceive him, and telling him of our plans would certainly have been unwise.

Sighing, Robert turned his cart on to the Cottishall road once again. As he traveled slowly along the road, he came across a peasant driving a cartload of grain to St. Edmund's town to be sold in the market and stopped to ask him if he had come this way the week before.

"Nay," said the farmer. "Last week I was too busy with the threshing to think about making a journey to market."

Well, thought Robert, I could scarce expect any other answer. It was worth a try, though.

In the same spirit, he asked everyone whom he met upon the road if they had seen anything unusual over the past week. Most people just looked puzzled and said no. Some told him it was none of his business, and others thought about it and said with regret that they could not help him.

One woman resting her feet by the road told him she had seen a rider on a fine horse riding hard along the road one day but couldn't quite remember when. "Come to think of it," she said finally, "It must have been that same day I saw all those other riders. They were behind him, and he stopped to wait for them. I heard them talking about looking for a thief."

Disappointed, Robert thanked the woman. "I wish I could help you," she said kindly. "I thought for a moment it was a different day I saw him, but it can't have been. So many people have been on the road in the last week, asking questions and searching bushes and just poking their noses where they aren't wanted, that I just got muddled in my mind."

Robert moved on, turning over in his mind all that they had discovered in the past few days. Thus engaged, it did not seem long before he arrived at his destination. Descending from the cart, Robert began walking slowly toward the pond which lay beyond the trees, looking around him carefully as he walked.

As he neared the pond, Robert spied a boy sitting on the bank, a rough pole in his hands.

"Good morrow," said Robert as he drew close to the boy.

"And to you," said the boy, looking at Robert with bright, inquisitive eyes. "Are you come to fish?"

"No, not today," Robert replied, sitting down beside the boy. "But you look as though you are well used to catching fish at this spot."

"We live close by," said the child. "Right over there." He pointed toward the other side of the pond. Robert could just see a hovel through the trees, broken down thatch on its roof and no sign of great activity around it. He recognized it as the charcoal burner's home he had walked around the other day.

"Do you come here every day?" asked Robert.

"No, not when my father needs me to help him collect wood or build the charcoal kiln," responded the boy. "But when it's lit and he's just sitting there watching to make sure it doesn't burn up, then I come here so I can dig worms and fish."

"Do you catch many fish in this pond?" asked Robert.

"After it rains is the best time," the boy said. "There's a stream that runs into the pond, and the rain stirs up the water."

"Have you seen anyone else out here in the past few days?" Robert wasn't sure whether this boy knew anything, but it was worth a try.

"No," the child said. "It's a small pond and only a few people know how good the fishing is. But someone must have been out here a few days ago."

"Why do you say so?" Robert said.

The boy looked as though he was sorry he'd spoken. "Someone left something, that's all, and I found it."

"What did he leave?"

"Oh, it were nothing." The boy pretended to focus hard on the end of his line.

"I'm sure it wasn't anything important," said Robert, encouragingly. "But you seem like a clever boy, so I'm sure it was something that a boy with less keen eyes than yours would have missed."

"I told my father it must have been left deliberately," the boy cried suddenly. "He said no man would leave such a thing and not return, but I didn't see how anyone would leave it behind unless he meant to leave it forever!"

"What was it you found?" Robert tried again.

"It was an old sack," said the boy. "I found it underneath a bush over there." The boy pointed toward the trees that stood to the left of them, close by the pond. The underbrush was thick there, well fed by the stream that flowed into the pond.

"Was there anything in the sack?" asked Robert.

"Yes," admitted the boy. "That was why my father was angry when I took it home. He said no one would leave such a nice fish trap and just walk away. He told me the man must have meant to come back for it. He said we are not thieves, and he made me put it back where I found it."

A fish trap! This must be the trap the gamekeeper had missed. But what was it doing here, hidden under a pile of brush?

"When was it that you found the fish trap?" Robert asked the boy, trying not to sound too eager.

The child pursed his lips in concentration.

"It must have been the day before there was all that fuss at the Abbey," he said finally. "I only know that because some men rode out from Bury and talked to my father. Then he came inside and told me all over again how we aren't thieves and how I should let things alone if they don't belong to me. But it wasn't as though I stole anything," the boy wailed. "All I did was find a sack!"

"I know," said Robert. "I'm sure your father was just worried that someone might accuse you of stealing if they found you with the fish trap. You must know that small account is taken of age when a judge imposes his punishment for stealing, and your mother would

160

no doubt cry for a long time if you were judged to be a thief."

The boy sniffed. "I could catch a lot more fish if I had a trap like that. Mayhap I'll make one when I get older." With that, the boy turned back to his fishing, leaving Robert to smile at the ability of children to switch moods in an instant.

Saying farewell to the boy, Robert wandered over to the trees beside the pond. He thought that if someone had placed the sack under the bushes there might be other traces of him to be found. If he could see any sign of anyone having made his way through the forest, avoiding the well-frequented paths, that might tell him the direction from which the stranger had come.

For an hour, Robert walked through the trees, following any faint path that seemed to him to be a possible way, but he found nothing. At times he heard the sounds of small animals making their way through the undergrowth, and once he thought he heard the crashing of a boar as it pushed through the woods, but he came across neither beast nor fowl.

The day was on the wane, so Robert retraced his steps until once again he came to the pond. The boy was gone.

Thinking to at least see where the sack had been hidden, Robert crossed to the trees indicated by the young fisherman. The undergrowth is really thick here, he thought. It would of a certain be a good place to hide something from any but the most curious eyes. It was unfortunate for this man, whoever he may have been, that the eyes of a child are among the most curious.

Robert slowly worked his way through the bushes, finding nothing other than a piece of frayed rope. I wonder if this was used to tie the sack, he thought, but he could see nothing special about the rope that would aid him in identifying whether the thief of the fish trap and the relic were one and the same. It's just a piece of old rope. It could have come from anywhere.

As he stood to return to his cart, Robert caught a glimpse of something glinting in the late afternoon sun. Going over to the bush, he parted the leaves and pulled out a small piece of metal. Well, it's not gold, thought the goldsmith's son to himself. Thinking that it looked as though it was a small piece that had broken off something larger, Robert touched the smooth edge.

"Ow!" he said out loud. "That's sharp!"

Just then Robert thought he heard a noise. Turning quickly toward the deeper part of the forest he thought he caught a glimpse of something large moving through the woods. The shadows were too deep for him to be able to tell if it was human or animal, but the hairs on the back of his neck stood up and Robert felt his breathing quicken.

"Time to go," he muttered, turning to return to his cart.

As he walked along the path, Robert heard the sound of twigs cracking and leaves rustling in the undergrowth not far behind him. Something's following

162

me, he thought. Fear lent speed to Robert's steps, and he began to run.

Faster and faster he ran, but yet he could hear the sounds gaining on him. Swerving off the path back into the woods, Robert thought to find a way to evade his pursuer.

Just as he began to believe his breath would fail him completely, Robert lost the sound of the pursuit. He stopped, gasping for breath, and slowly turned in a circle. He could neither hear nor see anything.

For the space of a minute, Robert stayed perfectly still. Then, just as he began to think he was safe, he heard the startled cry of birds and saw them rise above the branches not more than 20 yards from him. Robert fled.

Running through the dense trees, he risked a quick look behind him. He saw branches waving as though hands were pushing them aside, but he could not see who it was who was chasing him. Sweeping aside a large branch that hung in his way, he had no time to avoid the fallen limb lying across his path.

Robert tripped hard over the limb and started rolling head over heels down the steep slope that lay just beyond. Striking stones and smaller branches on the way, Robert came to a sudden, jarring halt at the base of the slope, his head spinning and the air knocked out of him.

Fear bringing him to himself, he looked up toward the top of the slope, but he could see nothing.

I must get away, he thought, trying to sit up. A sharp pain tore through his arm, making him feel sick. Looking down, Robert saw that his arm was hanging at an unnatural angle by his side.

As Robert sat on the ground, trying to stop himself from passing out and wondering how he could get out of there and evade his pursuer, the sun set.

CHAPTER SIXTEEN

We naturally thought he would make a sizeabledonation, but he gave only a silk cloth which his servants had on loan from our sacrist — and still they have not paid for it.

"BY GOD'S BONES!" EXCLAIMED THE voice. Aileen, shocked, rounded the corner and came across William de Vere hopping on one foot, holding the other in both hands.

"My pardon," said William de Vere, seeing the look on Aileen's face. Putting his foot back on the ground, he hobbled to a barrel and sat down. "I did not realize anyone was there to hear me."

"Sir," Aileen admonished the young man. "If I betray my feelings, it is because such words tear apart the body of our Savior!" A member of a noble family he may be, but she had been taught that no Christian would make such an oath.

The young man, still rubbing his sore foot, considered the young woman before him. "You are a brazen one to speak so to such as I."

"My pardon, my lord," Aileen said, bobbing a curtsy to the young man as she belatedly realized she had spoken out of turn. "I did allow my shock to overcome my good sense."

"Methinks you did," responded William without heat. "But in truth, my words were such that these sacred walls might cry out in protest, were you not there to do so!" He smiled at Aileen, who could not stop herself smiling in return.

"Are you injured, sir?" she asked.

William stopped rubbing his foot and placed it back on the ground. "Naught but my pride, I do believe," he responded ruefully. "Had I been watching where I was stepping, I may not have walked past the barrel so close and seemingly forgotten to leave space for my small toe to pass!" He took a few careful steps, and then sat back down, looking at the young woman before him.

"Shall I fetch the brother infirmarer to tend to you?" asked Aileen.

"No," said William. "The throbbing will go away, and, as you see, I can walk without a problem. I doubt that my reputation would be aided by rumors of drunken falls spreading around the town."

Aileen blushed. "I am sure that none of the brothers would impute such cause to a mere accident," she said. "And it is certain that I would spread no such tale."

William laughed. "You are a most serious young woman," he said. "But you have quite taken me out of my bad mood.

"Come," he said. "Walk with me to the guest hall. Mayhap you can steady me should my foot fail me." So saying, William stood and began to walk slowly toward the courtyard.

This was not the haughty lordling Aileen had expected, she thought to herself as she turned to walk with him. He seemed much as any other young man. His humor even brought thoughts of Robert to mind.

Forcing her thoughts back to the opportunity before her, Aileen turned to William de Vere. "Would you care to lean on my arm, sir?" she asked.

"No, thank you," he said. "It is more for the company of one who seeks nothing from me that I asked you to walk with me. I can walk unaided."

Seeing Aileen's puzzled face, he continued: "Your dress is of this town, but you do not carry yourself as a peasant. What brings you to the abbey this day?"

"Sir," she replied, stung by his assumption that she was the daughter of a peasant. "I am the daughter of a well-respected cloth merchant. My mother's skill in embroidery is known far abroad. Since I was but a small child, I have been taught the skills of my parents."

It was clear that her words conveyed nothing to the young French lord.

"Now, being of age, I am come to the abbey to bring glory to God through the use of my needle," she continued. "I was on my way to the linen room to begin my day when I heard your oath. I am sure that Mistress Taylor will be most offended should I delay much longer, for it is no small honor to be permitted to work with the Lord's linen."

Seeing the pride on the face of the girl walking beside him, William stopped. "In the chapel in my mother's home, there is an altar cloth most beautifully embroidered with gold thread and precious stones," he said. "I did never think of how such work may be accomplished. All I knew was that the work was of great skill and great cost. You are most assuredly not a peasant."

Aileen remained a little offended that anyone might think for a moment that she was the child of a serf, but she realized that taking offense would gain her no advantage when talking to the son of a high noble.

"You speak of your mother's house," she said. "May I ask where that may be, sir?" If she could get him talking, perhaps she might learn something of importance in her quest.

"My mother's family is of this area," William said. "She is the Lady Alyse de Vere, and her father is lord of the manor of Lavenham."

"And the cloth of which you speak is in the chapel here in England, or does it lie in the Lord de Vere's lands in France?" asked Aileen.

William did not appear to notice that, in talking of his father's manor in France, Aileen had betrayed a knowledge of his family that was unlikely to be of interest to those residing in St. Edmund's town. Resolving not to make such a mistake again, she decided that perhaps the young man merely assumed that the

168

lineage of families of such nobility as his would be known to all.

"It is in the chapel in France," William said. "My mother has not seen her home since she was married to my father. I have met her family only once in my life, and that was when they traveled to our manor in France."

William's brow creased as a thought crossed his mind. "Tomorrow my mother and I will be traveling to her father's house and I doubt not that I will spend my share of time praying in another well-adorned chapel." He sounded none too happy at the prospect of spending his time thus, thought Aileen.

"You will be praying for the return of the lost relic, no doubt," she said.

"No doubt," said William brusquely.

"My pardon, sir," said Aileen. "I have offended you in some way."

"Indeed no," responded William. "It is merely that this has been a trying time for all who came to see the holy relic installed in the abbey church. My mother, naturally, is greatly distressed at the theft. Until such time as the relic is restored to the abbey, I believe her devotion will require of her that she spend her days kneeling before the altar in prayer. It is possibly a source of sorrow to my mother that I would find other occupations for my knees were I to be offered the choice."

A little unsure what to say in response to this, Aileen decided to take the opportunity presented to her by William.

"The theft of this holy relic has disturbed the whole town," she said. "All around me I hear rumors of how it came to be stolen. You have so much wider an experience than I. Do you have any thoughts as to what may have happened and where the relic may be found?"

"Not I," said William. "If I am honest, I have had more concerns of my own to be giving so much thought to a search that others seem to be more fitted to conduct."

Well, this is disappointing. If appealing to his vanity will not work, I will just have to try something else, Aileen thought.

"I am sorry if the people of St. Edmund's have not welcomed you as is your due," she said. "In the midst of our shame and distress over the loss of the relic, mayhap we have caused our visitors distress of another nature. Is there a way I can help you that may restore our favor in your eyes?"

"Oh, the people of St. Edmund's Bury have not been unwelcoming," said William. "Well, one or two of them may not have been, but that is not a matter for your ears. And I should not have spoken thus, for my concerns are beyond your ability to address."

"If you say so, sir," said Aileen demurely.

William laughed. "Methinks your nature is not to be so coy. I would not suggest you take your vows as a nun."

170

"Sir!" said Aileen. "It is not my intent to do so but, should that be the life for which I was chosen, I would have you know I would make an excellent nun!"

"Oh, you are a ray of sunshine in a day of darkness," said William, tears of laughter streaming down his face. "Would that there were more like you of my acquaintance."

"Am I so different, then, from those around you?" Aileen asked, genuinely interested in hearing his answer.

"In my world, most of the young women I know are interested only in showing themselves to be the perfect candidate for the wife of the future lord of my father's lands. I doubt I have had a real conversation with any girl since I was five years old."

"That's sad," said Aileen. "I have many friends, both male and female, and we would never think to hide our thoughts or keep our fears within ourselves. We help each other in need and celebrate our joys together."

"I have few friends in whom I could place such trust," said William, wistfully.

"Well," Aileen said. "Perhaps, while you are here, you could find some other friends who would be worthy of your trust and with whom you could discuss what it is that so concerns you."

"As I said, tomorrow we leave St. Edmund's town, and I doubt that we will ever return. So you see there is little chance now for me to befriend anyone." William paused. "But, perhaps, if you ... no, that would not be possible ..."

"What would not be possible?"

"I am the heir to the title of one of the noblest of families," said William, drawing himself up to his full height. "I cannot befriend the daughter of a merchant."

"Why not?" asked Aileen simply, trying to ignore the insult offered to her by this quixotic young lord.

"It would not be considered appropriate," said William. "And I am in more than sufficient dispute with my mother already."

Aileen raised an eyebrow, and the young man cleared his throat. "That is to say, in families such as mine, affairs that would seem of minor importance to such as you carry great weight."

"I am surprised that you would so lower yourself to speak to me, then, sir," responded Aileen, stung to words in spite of herself. She turned to leave.

"No, don't go," said the young man, catching her arm. "I should not have spoken so to someone who sought only to be kind to me." William let go of her arm and hung his head.

He really is very young, thought Aileen. One minute he behaves like a child, and the next he stands on his dignity as the son of a wealthy lord. Perhaps I should try one more time to see if he will tell me anything of help that could help us in this search.

"You are troubled, sir," she said. "May I not be of some assistance to you? You have told me yourself that tomorrow you quit St. Edmund's Bury. Your words to me will not reach the ears of any whom you know, for it is certain that we will never meet again unless you should return to the shrine of St. Edmund."

"You tempt me sorely," said William. "But I know not whether you would understand."

"You told me there was some dispute with your mother," Aileen said gently. "Mayhap, as another woman, I may be able to help you understand something of what grieves a woman's heart."

"Oh, I know what grieves her," William said. "But all the same it might lift a burden from my shoulders to talk about it with someone else."

Having made his decision, William walked over to a bench in a quiet corner of the court, courteously waiting for Aileen to sit before seating himself.

"I think you will not know much of my family," he began, little knowing just how much Aileen had learned of the affairs of his noble house. "We are an ancient family, close to the French crown, and of great wealth." He said this simply, as though there was nothing unusual about such circumstances.

Aileen nodded, encouraging him to continue.

"My father is a proud and upright man," William said. "He speaks much of duty and honor, and my mother is of the same mind."

"And are these things so bad?" asked Aileen.

"Oh no, not at all," William answered. "It is the responsibility of those of high rank to demonstrate valor, honor and loyalty to their king."

Seeing Aileen's expression, William laughed. "You are correct. I am quoting my father's words, but nonetheless they are wise words."

William paused and then turned to Aileen, his face more serious than she had yet seen it. "Though I may seem to you to be far from the ideal knight, I know my father speaks the truth. I intend to bring pride and honor to our family when I am become Lord de Vere. It is just that in this time . . ."

"Yes," prompted Aileen.

"I fear I disappoint," said William, miserably. "My father was lord of his lands when he was but my age, and he fought in a great Crusade. He is a man whom I have sought to emulate since I was a child and one in whose eyes I desire above all else to see pride. But I have not always conducted myself as he would wish. Now, even though I have done nothing with evil intent, I do not know if I can ever regain my regard in my father's eyes"

"Why would you fear so?" asked Aileen. "What is it that you have done that you believe your father would find so unforgiveable?"

William turned to Aileen eagerly. "I do not know if you will understand, for you are but a girl, but for a young man of high birth it is very important to be held in respect by those of your acquaintance."

"I believe that is important for all men ... and women," responded Aileen wryly.

"I said you would not understand!"

"My pardon, sir," said Aileen. "If you will but explain a little further, I will try."

"Yes, I believe you will." William leaned back, gathering his thoughts.

"I have known since I was a very small child that my destiny is to become lord of my father's lands. My whole life has been a preparation for that. I was schooled in Greek and Latin, philosophy, astrology, music, and of course in keeping accounts of revenues and in managing serfs. I have also spent countless hours training in weapons and horsemanship. It is expected of such as I that I will be a strong warrior and yet a man of chivalric learning."

"It is a great burden to place on a small child," said Aileen, thinking that this was a world of which she knew almost nothing. Richard and Henry, her two brothers, were still so little that their only duties were to play and do what their parents said. When they were a little older, she was sure her father would send them to the abbey's school where they would learn mathematics and Latin, since these were necessary for anyone who would aspire to be a merchant of the standing of her father. She wasn't sure what use a man would make of most of the rest of William's list, but it all sounded like a lot of hard work for a young child.

"It may seem so to you." William interrupted Aileen's thoughts. "It is what is expected in noble families, however, and my companions and I studied together from a young age.

"There came a time," he went on, "when we began to learn the joust. You will have seen knights fight in tournaments, I think?" he asked Aileen.

"Only once," she responded. "The king came to the Abbey five years ago, when I was but a young girl, and

I remember a great crowd of people from all around the Liberty coming to a fair to celebrate. There was a tournament then, with knights and their horses bedecked in fine cloth, and swords shining in the sun. But I was scared by all the clashing of weapons and feared for the safety of the knights who fell under the force of the lance."

William smiled slightly at the memories of the daughter of a cloth merchant, who remembered little of the tournament except for the apparel of man and horse.

"Well, then you will know that it is a thing of great import to the king and the nobles of the land," he said. "A knight who wins the tournament is held in high regard and earns a place of honor in the court of the king.

"My friends and I fought many mock battles as we grew taller and stronger. But I regret to say that I won few of those battles. My cousin, with whom I spent much time studying and training as a youth, grew broad and tall as we achieved our manhood, but I am as you see me, thin and only of medium height."

"There is nothing wrong with that," said Aileen. "I know many good men who are neither tall nor broad."

"Yet in the eyes of my father, I was a failure," William said sadly. "I tried, really I did, but I just could not attain the strength and the quick responses to be a success in the joust. My father hid his contempt, but I could see it on his face. I knew he was wishing my cousin were his son, and not I."

"I am so sorry," said Aileen. "Yet surely there is more to being a worthy lord than winning tournaments."

"Of course," he said. "And my father knows that I am a clever and conscientious student. Already he has turned over to me the accounts for some of his manors. Or, at least, he did so for a time." William fell silent.

"Did something happen?" asked Aileen.

"I wanted so much to earn my father's admiration." The words burst out of William's mouth as though he had contained them too long. "If I could not earn it in the tourney then I must find another way, I thought."

"And did you find a way?"

"I thought I had," responded the young man. "Even though we have many manors and much land, it is not always easy to afford the cost of attending the king at court, or of entertaining him and his large retinue when he honors us with a visit. Then there are times when the rains do not come and the land does not produce such rich crops as is their wont."

He looked at Aileen questioningly, and she nodded. Droughts and floods were a way of life in England as well. Her father had talked before of the decrease in orders for his fine cloth and for her mother's rich embroidery when crops were bad. The serfs, whose very existence depended on the harvesting of crops, suffered most in such times, but she knew that the effects were felt by all.

"So what was it you thought to do?" she asked.

"My father sent me to study in Paris, as is the wont of the noble families of our acquaintance. There was a

177

fellow student there who told me about a way in which clever young men could invest but a little money and earn a great deal in a short time. He told me that only men of good birth and good education would have such an opportunity, and that it would surely impress my father when I took him more gold coin than he could oft have seen before."

"It must have seemed an attractive suggestion," said Aileen.

"Yes, at the time I was so happy to think that I could offer my father more than a weakling for a son. But I was foolish, for, in truth, all I did was succumb to insincere flattery. The result was to lower my father's opinion of me even more."

"Oh no!" exclaimed Aileen. "But how could that be?"

"Have you ever heard of a game called Hazard?"

Almost Aileen spoke up and admitted to having heard of the game. But she knew that a young woman of her background would scarcely know of such games of chance, so she merely looked thoughtful.

"I do not remember playing such a game as a child," she said. "Perhaps it is known by another name in this country?"

William laughed. "I scarce think this is a game children would play," he said. "For it has brought many a better man than I to ruin."

He put up his hand as Aileen started to speak. "No, let me complete my tale, for it is one that should serve as a warning to any who may be tempted to fall for a soft story and a silken tongue."

Composing his thoughts, William picked up his account once again.

"My friend took me to a house in Paris where he said I would meet other investors. When I arrived I was offered a goblet of fine wine and a seat at a table where some young men were playing a friendly game of dice. It was not long before I realized that an understanding of how the dice fell according to the style adopted by each player could help one win the game, and I began to enjoy myself very much.

"Soon, one of the young men suggested we place small wagers on the game. I was not averse to this idea. Why would I not approve, since I was guaranteed to win more than I lost?"

"And did you win?"

"Yes, that night I took home to my lodgings a goodly sum of money," responded William. My friend told me on the way home that this was indeed what he had discussed with me. He said that a man with my skill at strategy could not fail to become rich at playing this game he called Hazard."

"And so you returned to play again with these young men?" asked Aileen.

"Yes, to my shame, I did," William said. "I returned to the house the next night, and the night after that, and for many more nights. My studies fell away, and I could think of nothing but the game.

"I won more gold in those first few nights, but then I began to lose more than I won. I could not understand why this should be, so I kept returning to the game

179

thinking that I had devised some new way of turning around my fortune."

"But you did not succeed?"

"No, I would win a small amount one night, and then lose even more the next. I became desperate, but I could not stop.

"I soon lost the money that my father had given me for my lodgings in Paris, and I was forced to borrow from other players. Yet I could not win enough to pay them back, and so I would borrow from my friends."

William sighed but, having made the decision to unburden himself of his cares, it seemed as though he could not stop.

"When my studies were complete, I returned to my father's home, in debt and afraid of his wrath. But my father had not learned of my conduct in Paris and thought to give me control of some of the lesser manors within his domain. It was time, he said, for me to start conducting myself as a man of the king and not a purposeless youth."

"Surely this was good news," said Aileen.

"Oh yes, I was very happy. I thought that at last I would be able to show my father that I was worthy of his respect and his love. I was determined to do well, and I believe I did indeed live up to my father's expectations. At least I did so for the first few months." William's voice tailed off with the last words.

"What happened?" asked Aileen, gently.

"It is a sad truth that one can run away from one's troubles, but that sooner or later they will find you out," replied William. "One day a man came to the manor and demanded payment on a debt I had yet to pay. It was my father with whom he spoke, for I was in the town that day.

"When I returned, my father informed me of the man's visit and told me that he had paid the debt. Then he demanded an explanation."

"Was he very angry?"

"I do not remember when I last saw him so angered," said William. "He did not rant or threaten violence, but the very softness of his voice and the intensity of his tone bode ill for me should I dissemble in any way. I told him all."

William brushed his hand across his eyes, and Aileen looked away, not wishing to let the young man know she had seen the tear in his eye.

"When I finished my tale, I could see the great disappointment in my father's face," said William. "He told me this was not what he expected of his son and that he had no choice but to take away the authority he had given me over some of his lands and to forbid any journeys beyond the bounds of our lands. It was useless to contend that I had managed my manors well. He would brook no such argument."

"Yet he must have relented," encouraged Aileen. "For you are here now."

"With my mother," William responded. "It is a hard thing for a grown man to be permitted only such as his mother will allow."

Aileen hid her smile at the petulance of his words, but she had to admit that she was beginning to feel sorry for this young lordling who had seemed to her thus far merely arrogant. Indeed, men are not always what they appear to be. The memory of those words having been spoken in another context recently tickled at the back of her brain. What was it that kept worrying away at her thoughts this way?

William seemed unaware of Aileen's distracted thoughts. "When my father permitted this journey, I thought that this might be my last chance to show him that I am worthy of the name of de Vere, and that he can trust me once again."

"Yet it appears that you no longer believe your father will do so?"

"No," William said. "It was my intent to show myself to be a man of wisdom and restraint but, not long after we arrived in St. Edmund's town, I fell into an altercation with the knight who has delivered the holy relic to the Abbey. His family is well known to mine, and there is some ill-feeling between us that has lasted many years.

"In truth, I did not plan such a confrontation. But, nevertheless, there were many witnesses to the scene, and I have once again earned my mother's ire. She is a woman of great character and control and disapproved of such a public display of emotion."

Aileen nodded sympathetically, but said nothing, not wishing to interrupt the flow of the young man's remembrances.

"I was miserable," said William. "Then, almost immediately, I realized that a once-in-a-lifetime opportunity had been presented to me. I determined that I would recover for my family something that should never have been held by another. Were the plan I devised to succeed, then my father would have to recognize me for the man that I am!"

CHAPTER SEVENTEEN

*At that time, wheresoever the abbot went, there
came about him Jews as well as Christians,
demanding debts, and worrying and
importuning him so that he could not sleep.*

"Avi," said Ruth softly. "I'm worried about Aileen and Robert." The friends were walking back to the group's hiding place deep in the forest, baskets of freshly gathered mushrooms and herbs in their hands. They were treading carefully, pausing to listen when they heard shuffling in the trees or birds sounding alarms in the branches.

I'm more worried about you, thought Avi. Life has always been a cruel struggle for our people and yet you always see the best in everyone. I worry that one day you may suffer for that trust. I worry that one day I will not be there to protect you.

"Do you worry about them as you do about all those whom you love or is there something in particular that causes you concern?"

"I worry that, in their great desire to help us, they are interfering in the affairs of kings and princes," responded Ruth. "They have no experience of such a world, and I fear for them."

"Let us sit down for a minute, Ruth," Avi said. Placing their baskets carefully beside them, the pair sat down in the shade of an ancient oak tree.

"Ruth," said Avi, holding Ruth's hands in his and looking intently into her eyes. "I understand your fear and I share it. I would that we could seek answers for ourselves and have our friends remain as they have always been, free of fear and safe within the bosom of their families. But Ruth, that is not the way of life.

"No, let me finish," Avi said as Ruth opened her mouth to protest. "I do not say that freedom from fear and safety is unattainable. I merely say that men ... and women ... of honor," he added, glad to see a small, responsive smile on her face, "do not shy away from the pursuit of truth and the defense of those whom they love."

"But Avi," insisted Ruth. "This is our battle, not theirs. Already their families have told them they should not involve themselves any more in this matter. It is plain to see that neither of them wishes to break their word that they will not place themselves at any further risk, and yet they continue to pursue the real felons. They do this only for our sakes, and I would that they not risk either injury or loss of favor any longer."

Unconsciously stroking the hands he held, Avi thought for a moment before speaking.

"I understand, Ruth," he said. "Your heart near breaks when you see a rabbit desperately trying to escape the attack of a hawk. You could scarce bear to see your friends hurt or in disgrace." Ruth nodded, her face a picture of misery.

It near breaks my heart to see her so, thought Avi. "Tuva, look at me," he said. Ruth looked up, startled to hear him use such a term of endearment.

"None of us are children anymore," he said. "You know this." Ruth nodded.

"Once we are full grown, we have to find our own way and make our own decisions," Avi went on. "It is the same for Aileen and Robert. They are generous and strong, and they do honor to their fathers by being so. Is this not so?" Again, Ruth nodded.

"I fear they may be at risk, just as you do, Ruth," said Avi. "But they have promised to do all they can do, and it is not our part to dissuade them from fulfilling that promise. We will pray for their safety and success, but we can do no more."

For a moment there was silence between them. In the background the forest itself seemed to fall still and not even did a leaf fall from the canopy above them.

"I know you are right, Avi," Ruth finally said. "I know it with my mind, but my heart is reluctant to follow." Gently she removed her hands from Avi's grasp and then, as though to indicate that she was not displeased with his hold, she lightly brushed a piece of grass off his tunic.

"If we cannot prevent their pursuit," she went on. "Let us talk while we return to our encampment and see if there is anything further we may be able to discern that will help them."

"That is a good idea," said Avi. "But it is fast approaching dusk, and we must hurry else your father will think me a poor escort for his daughter."

"I did promise that I would ask my father about the Rabbi Maimonides' sojourn in the court of the Sultan Saladin," said Ruth as they wended their way through the darkening trees at a faster pace than before. "I confess I am nervous that he will demand to know why of a sudden I am so curious about this, but I am determined that I will ask him tonight. It is the least I can do to help our friends in their quest."

"I think this is a good idea," said Avi. "But I think we should also tell him something of the tale told us by Aileen and Robert."

Ruth came to a sudden halt, forcing Avi to stop midstride and almost stumble. "But think you not that father may be so angry he will forbid us to meet again with Aileen and Robert?"

"I think that is a risk we must take, Ruth," said Avi. "Your father is a wise and knowledgeable man. If we are to help Aileen and Robert, I think we must seek out whatever aid we can. Something tells me that your father may be of assistance in this."

It was full dark now and Avi could not quite read the expression in Ruth's eyes. "Do you agree?" he asked.

Ruth sighed. "I think you are right," she said. "Let us hurry home and we will talk to father as soon as we can."

So saying, the pair started on their way. They had little distance yet to travel but, without a light and in fear of striking a flint lest it give away their presence, they did not wish to tarry.

They had gone but a short way when they heard a sudden crashing in the undergrowth nearby. Avi put a finger to his lips, and they rapidly hid behind a tree.

Taking out his knife, Avi peered around the trunk. It is probably just a boar, he thought. Yet such a creature could be dangerous and Avi was prepared to fight it if need be. Taking a deep breath, Avi moved a little further around the tree, signing Ruth to get down.

It was hard to make anything out in the dark of the forest but suddenly the glow of the rising moon cast a gleam of light into the small glade between the friends and the sounds of heavy movement. In this ghostly ray a figure appeared, limping and lurching, falling and rising again.

Startled, Avi took one step toward the figure. Behind him, Ruth screamed.

CHAPTER EIGHTEEN

Someone was heard to say, "Curses on the court of that abbot, where neither gold nor silver is of any use to me in defeating my adversary!"

WILLIAM'S EYES WERE ALIGHT WITH the strength of his desire to regain his father's respect, and he failed to notice Aileen's shocked expression.

"Truly?" she finally said. "What was it that you determined to do?" Aileen held her breath. Was the solution to this mystery, after all, a young man merely trying to impress his father?

But William seemed unaware of her eagerness or her fears. "Let me go back a little to when I was such a foolish young student in Paris," he said. "When I borrowed money from my friends to pay my debts, I was forced to give as security for one of these loans a signet ring that I had from my father."

"Was it very valuable?" asked Aileen.

"It is a most beautiful ring, set with rubies," responded William. "And it was a ring that had come down through many generations of our family. Thus, to our family, it had great personal value, apart from its value in coin. More than that, even though my father possesses a seal die, it was the ring my father had used to seal many legal documents, and thus it would be seen as the mark of our family name were it to be used."

Aileen had seen the mark of her father's seal in wax on documents before and knew that one would not lightly part with such a thing.

"Did your father not know that the ring was no longer in your possession when you returned from Paris?" she asked.

"Yes, but I told him that it had been lost in a boating accident on the river and that it lay at the bottom of the Seine. At the time he was more concerned about reckless young men almost drowning than about the whereabouts of the ring."

"Did your father recover the ring when he paid your debts?" she asked William.

"No, and thereby lay one of the reasons for my father's great anger. He was forced to make it known abroad that the ring was no longer in our possession. He made it known that in the future, all binding documents would be not only sealed with a slightly altered crest on the die, but that they would be accompanied by a separate attestation of authenticity."

"It must have been a matter of great inconvenience to you and your family," said Aileen sympathetically. "But I am not sure that I understand the reason for your telling me of this now."

190

"I do not think I have explained myself very well," responded William. "You see, when my mother and I arrived at the Abbey, one of the first people I saw in the Great Court was the friend to whom I had given the ring. In that instant, I realized that this might be a God-given opportunity for me to recover it."

"What did you do?" asked Aileen, beginning to realize that this tale William was recounting was very far from an account of the theft of a holy relic.

"I could do nothing immediately, for my mother had many instructions for me to ensure that her sojourn at the abbey was comfortable.

"As you may imagine, I was somewhat impatient to escape my mother's presence and find my old friend," William continued. "Thus, late in the afternoon I began to seek him out. As I passed again through the Great Court, I spied him leaving the Abbey. He appeared to be in a hurry."

"Did you follow him?"

"I could not then. But, the next day, after my confrontation with Sir Henri du Lac, I saw him leaving the Abbey again, and this time I decided to follow. He walked up Abbeygate and through the market and was admitted to a house close by the hog market." Moyses Hall, thought Aileen. So this is how William came to know of the gambling house. Master Durand had been right about word spreading through word of mouth among the young nobles, but not about how William de Vere had learned of it.

191

"When I saw how he was admitted to the house, by a big, surly man, I realized that this house was a gambling house, just like the one in Paris," said William. "I hesitated then, for I had vowed to my father that I would never again darken the doors of such a place."

Aileen said not a word. She did not want to break into William's thoughts and risk him deciding against completing his story.

"I stood outside the house for some time trying to decide whether to wait until my friend returned to the abbey or to confront him in the house. In the end I determined to enter, for I could not tell who might overhear my conversation with him should I wait until the next day, and I did not wish my mother to know of our meeting at all."

"So you gained admittance to the house?"

"Yes," said William. "It was not hard, for I know of the game and I am clearly one of wealth and position." The old William is back again, thought Aileen, hiding a smile.

"Louis, my friend, was surprised to see me," William continued. "He feigned delight, but I do not think he was truly pleased.

"I greeted him courteously enough, but it was soon apparent that I was not interested in playing Hazard. I said that I wished only to watch this night, but would no doubt return to play the next.

"The proprietor was not best pleased when I declined to play, but the promise of future purses ensured that I was not summarily thrown out. However,

Louis suspected that I was there only to speak with him, and he began to play badly, constantly looking to see where I was in the room and paying little attention to the game."

"Did he lose much money?" asked Aileen.

"Yes, he did, and then he became angry. He confronted me, demanding to know why I was following him and what it was that I wanted. I was very calm, which seemed only to anger him more. When I told him I wanted the return of my ring, and that I would undertake to pay this night's losses in return, his anger only grew. He declared that the ring was now his, and, to prove it, he removed it from his purse and said he was going to play another game and offer the ring as his wager."

"He actually had the ring with him?" Aileen asked in surprise.

"Yes. I was not certain he would carry it with him on this journey, but it is a fine ring, notwithstanding it is a signet ring. Any man would wear it with pride."

"What did you do when he said he was going to gamble with your father's ring?"

"I snatched it out of his hand and declared he would never gamble it away. Louis swore and struck me a blow with his fist. The punch took me by surprise and, in falling back, I tripped over a stool and fell to the floor. The ring went flying into a corner, and Louis dove after it. I swung around and tripped him, and we ended up clawing and striking each other, rolling all around the floor.

"There was a great shouting and hallooing in the room, until the man who guards the door came over and picked us both up off the floor like a pair of young pups. The owner threw us both out of there without allowing us to say a word. We might have continued our fight out in the street, but the sight of curious men staring at us as we erupted out of the door of the Hall brought us to our senses. We each went our way, and, I have to say, the cold walk home without my cloak to keep me warm was enough to ensure I was sober and quiet upon my return to the guest hall."

Aileen knew what had happened to William's cloak, but there was something else in the story about which she could not help but ask.

"What happened to your father's ring?"

"That was strange," returned William. "As I was being dragged to the door by the guard, a man, cloaked as though he too was about to leave, quietly placed something in the palm of my hand and closed my fingers over it. He said not a word, and I did not look at what he had given me until I was on my way back to the Abbey. Then I realized he had handed me back my ring."

"That is strange," said Aileen. "You have no idea who this man may have been?"

"No, and I doubt I ever will discover his identity, although I confess, I made the attempt to find out. In spite of my aversion to the gambling house and my determination to never again enter such an establishment, I was forced to return to retrieve my

194

cloak. I admit I returned yet again yesterday to see if perhaps the stranger was within, but he was not, and, since we are to depart on the morrow, I will have no further opportunity to seek him out.

"I cannot tell how this stranger could have known the ring was so important to me, but I will forever be grateful to him," William declared.

"I can well understand that," said Aileen. "I think you are wise to not make further enquiries, though, especially if continuing to do so would require you to return to that place."

"I cannot yet say what explanation I will give my father for the ring's return," William said. "You will easily understand that it is my hope he will look with some favor upon me when I place it back in his hand."

"And this is all the adventures you have had while in St. Edmund's town?" asked Aileen.

William laughed. "Do you not think this is sufficient? What else could you want to hear?"

"Oh, nothing," said Aileen. She was silent for a moment.

"And yet, you are not happy," she said. "If you have recovered this treasure and will be able to please your father, why are you so troubled?"

"It is but a small thing to accomplish," said William. "Although I now have the ring back, the story of how it came into my possession does me no honor, and still I do not know how to regain my father's trust."

"I have no great wisdom to share," said Aileen. "But do you not think that each small action that shows your father you are worthy of trust is one more stone in a building that may take a lifetime to erect? My advice is to be steadfast and honorable. Mayhap that is all your father is looking to see in his son. I know it is what my father seeks in his children, and I cannot see that great lords would be any different from any other men of good heart and will in this."

William stared at the girl beside him for a long moment. Then a smile slowly spread across his face. "I did not think to hear such ideas from a merchant's daughter," he said. Then, seeing her expression, he hurriedly continued. "Please do not be insulted. I merely meant that I am sure that I would have laughed had someone suggested I would bare my soul to a young woman and that she would offer me advice that I would consider the best I have yet heard."

"The best advice?"

"Yes," he answered. "And I thank you from the bottom of my heart."

William rose, and offered his hand to Aileen. "Now, come, I think we must both be about our business. Let me accompany you, so that I may explain to your Mistress Taylor why you have been detained overlong. I am sure that you will not be punished too severely if the excuse is offered by a noble visitor to your magnificent abbey."

Aileen smiled. "Indeed, I believe Mistress Taylor will be quite charmed by your explanation, and I thank you kindly, sir."

So saying, the two went on their way, each deep in thought and glad of the chance meeting.

CHAPTER NINETEEN

The abbot was agitated, and said:
"'I am beset with trouble on every side' [Dan. 13:22];
Either I shall offend God or I shall offend the king."

"ROBERT!" CRIED RUTH. "HELP HIM, Avi!" Ruth's companion came swiftly toward the pale youth whose limping form had just come out of the trees. Taking Robert's good arm around his shoulders, he half-carried him over to the base of a tree and gently laid him down. Taking a small flask from his belt, he held it to Robert's lips.

"It's merely water from the stream in the forest," said Avi, when Robert pulled away. "Sip slowly, for it will not be good for you to drink too deeply when you are hurt."

Robert did as he was told, taking a few sips from the proffered flask. As Avi replaced the flask in his belt and stood up, Ruth took his place, kneeling beside Robert and looking anxiously into his eyes. She took a kerchief and wiped his brow, asking him gently how he came to be so injured and how it was that he had come to their meeting place.

"I did not know if I could make it as far as our secret meeting place," said Robert, weakly. "It seemed a long way to go, but it was not as far as St. Edmund's town, and I did fear to go back the way I had come." He leaned against the tree, eyes closed and his breath coming in short, painful gasps.

Ruth put her hand against his forehead. "I do not understand what you are saying, Robert," she said. "But you are fevered, and your arm must be tended. We will take you to my father."

"I must get back home," Robert said as he struggled to rise. "My parents will be worried that I am gone so long. They will fear I have been waylaid. They must know that I'm not lying somewhere, lost and hurt."

Robert's voice faded with the effort of such a long speech, and Avraham pushed him back down. "Do not take care for such matters," he said. "I will go to your parents and let them know you are found as soon as we have taken you to Isaac of Cordoba. The good townsfolk of St. Edmund's Bury will soon be in their beds, and then I can travel safely to your house."

"But …"

"No, Robert," said Ruth, firmly. "I do not know what has happened, but if you were in fear of returning home alone in daylight, we can scarce allow you to move along the lanes at nightt, especially when you are sore wounded. It is not safe, and I will not permit it."

Had his pain been less, Robert might have smiled at the unanswerable tone in Ruth's voice. Avi had no such qualms, and he laughed outright.

"My childhood friend is all grown up," he said. "But Ruth is right, Robert. You came to us because you dared not return home along the road. Until we know what it is that has happened to you and why you are in fear, we cannot allow you to return to St. Edmund's town alone, and we dare not accompany you in case we be recognized. We will take you to Ruth's father. Better decisions may be made when your wounds have been tended and your pain is less."

So saying, Avraham bent down and picked up Robert as though he were but a child, making sure that he did not further injure the damaged arm. Robert was too tired and in too much pain to care.

Ruth led the way through the forest, stopping every now and then to listen to the sounds of the forest around them.

"Do not wonder if we are lost," said Ruth. "If it seems to you that we are walking in circles it is just that we must be very careful that we are not followed. It would not do for our hiding place to be discovered."

Robert had been only dimly aware of their passage through the forest, and had noted nothing of their route, but he nodded his understanding of the explanation offered by his friend.

Eventually the party came to a clearing.

"Papa," Ruth called, softly. "It is Ruth and Avraham. We are not followed."

Out of the dark shelter of the trees came a group of people, led by Ruth's father and mother. At sight of the youth in Avraham's arms, they halted.

"Papa," said Ruth. "It is Robert. He is hurt."

Isaac came forward then and, seeing the pale young man clearly for the first time, told Avraham to carry him to their shelter. "Do not fret, my young friend," said Isaac. "As you care for us, so we will care for you."

Under cover of the trees, Robert realized that there were several shelters cunningly made out of branches and leaves, so well disguised that only when one was in among them were they discernible as living quarters. Ruth spoke truly when she had told him they were prepared, he thought, as Avraham laid him gently down.

The physician laid his hand on his young patient's forehead, noting its warmth and seeing the flushed face damp with perspiration.

"Robert," said Isaac. "Lie still. I must see your wounds if I am to make you whole. I will be as gentle as possible."

Gentle and skilled as the physician was, Robert could not hold back a groan as Isaac cut away the sleeve of his tunic and then felt around the bone in his arm.

"I doubt not that you realize the bone is broken," said Isaac. "It is a clean break, however, and I believe that I will be able to set your arm without risk of permanent harm."

"Thank you, sir," Robert said. "I am sure there is no one I would rather have tend my wounds than you."

Isaac smiled at the young man. "You may not feel as kindly disposed toward me after I have set the arm," he said. "This will hurt a great deal, but it must be done."

With this, Isaac gave Robert a stick to place between his teeth. Robert winced, realizing what was to come but did as he was told. Isaac grasped Robert's arm, one hand above the break, one at Robert's wrist. Then, with a sharp twist the physician aligned the bones of the arm, ignoring the cry of pain from the young man and the gasp of horror from his daughter.

Pale sweat started from Robert's brow, but the young man said nothing, merely lying back against the pillow.

Isaac wiped the sweat away with a cloth dipped in cool water. "You have courage, young Master Robert," he said. "My daughter has chosen her friends well."

"Thank you, sir," Robert said, his voice weak and his face grimacing as he tried to hold down the waves of nausea from the pain coursing through his body.

"Ruth," said Isaac. "Bring me a cup of water with the ground fennel and yarrow root."

Concern etched on her face, Ruth was swift to obey. She returned in just a short time, carefully handing her father a small cup. Taking it in his hand, Isaac raised Robert's head and instructed him, "Drink this. It will help you sleep. When you wake, we will talk."

Robert drank. The concoction tasted terrible, but as he lay back down with a sigh, he wondered that he should feel so safe in such a situation. His friends were in danger, he had been injured fleeing from an

202

unknown enemy, and the relic was still missing. Yet he was among friends, and even the pain seemed less. Perhaps he could rest for just a little while. After all, Avraham had promised to tell his parents.

He should have told him to let Aileen know as well. Robert started up, gasping as the pain burned through his arm again.

"Master Isaac," he said. "Please, I need to let Aileen know where I am and that I am all right. She will be worried if I do not come to the riverbank to meet her this evening."

"Calm yourself, Robert," said Isaac.

"Papa," Ruth said. "Avi has promised to tell Master Palgrave this evening that Robert is safe with us. Should he also visit Aileen's house?"

"No, Ruth," said her father. "I would prefer that Avraham spend as little time as possible in St. Edmund's town. He would have to cross the town to reach Aileen's parents, and that is too great a risk."

"Master Robert," he continued, turning to his patient. "Fret not. I am sure that your father will carry the news of your being safe with us to Aileen and her parents. She will worry about your health, but not about your absence."

With that Robert had to be content. He tried to think of a response or even to plan what he would say to Aileen next time he saw her. But really, he was so tired. He could hear the physician moving around the shelter, and there were whispered words between

Ruth and her father. The pain was fading, and he was pleasantly warm.

Sighing, he thought that he could talk to Isaac and Ruth about what had happened and what Aileen needed to know once he had had just a little rest. It would all be better if he could sleep for a short while.

CHAPTER TWENTY

King Richard commanded all the English bishops and abbots to arrange for one knight to represent every ten in their baronies, and to join him immediately in Normandy.

AILEEN WAS WORRIED. OTHER THAN William, whom she had met purely by chance early that morning, she had been unable to take the time to ask questions of any within the walls of the Abbey. Mistress Taylor was determined to permit no further disruptions to the routine of the day. She scarce allowed her ladies to pause from their labors to eat. Aileen could do no more than try to gather the scattered strands of her thoughts and decide on how she may be able to proceed.

Going to the riverbank in the evening, Aileen had been disturbed to find that Robert did not join her. Thinking that, once again, his father had required his services, she returned home, only to be told by her father that John Palgrave had just left.

"Robert fell in the forest," said Jude. "It would appear that he has broken his arm."

"Oh no!" exclaimed Aileen. "What happened?"

"Master Palgrave does not know," said her father. "A young man of Fornham brought him the news, but he did not know many details."

"Fornham," said Aileen. "Was he of Ruth's family then?"

"No, but he is a friend of hers."

"Avraham!" said Aileen, earning herself a sharp look from her father. "If he came to Master Palgrave's with the news, then it must mean that Robert did not accompany him?" This was becoming more concerning by the minute, thought Aileen.

"No. It would seem that Ruth's father is tending his wounds." Jude's expression was grave.

Aileen caught her breath. "Father, Robert is not sore hurt, is he? He will recover?"

"Your mother asked Master Palgrave the same question, Aileen," responded her father. "Isaac did send the message that he believed Robert would heal, but that he wished him to rest this night."

"Thanks be to God," sighed Aileen.

"Praise His name indeed," said Jude. There was something about his tone that made Aileen look up. It was clear that her father had something more to say.

"Master Palgrave came this evening not just to tell us about Robert's accident," he began. "He came to discuss with me how it could be that his son was wandering through the forest in the first place when he was on his father's business to Long Melford. He was expected back before darkness fell."

206

Jude paused, but Aileen had no reply.

Sighing, Jude continued: "Aileen, I believe that Master Palgrave and I made our wishes very clear. We instructed you and Robert to interfere no more in the matter of the theft of the relic and the Jews of Fornham."

Jude of Arundel was not a man who often lost his temper, but Aileen recognized the signs of exasperation in his voice. Truly it is said that the calm comes before the storm.

"You said we should not put ourselves in danger, father," said Aileen. "And truly we have not interfered in the Reeve's investigation. We have only asked such questions as anyone might ask."

"Enough!" roared Jude. Richard and Henry, playing with a spinning top in front of the fireplace, looked up in surprise. Mabel, who had been totally focused on hemming a kerchief with tiny, delicate stitches, jumped, pricking her finger. Aileen's mother stopped what she was doing and started toward them. Jude put up his hand to stop her and turned back to Aileen.

"You do sore try my patience today, Aileen," he said, more calmly. "Can I not trust you to follow my orders?"

"I beg your forgiveness, father," Aileen said, eyes to the ground. "It was not my intent, nor that of Robert, to disobey you. We thought merely to see if we could solve this mystery."

"And had you done so, what would you have done with your solution?"

"Bring it to you or Master Durand, or someone who could do something about it," said Aileen. "I know you think we are but young and inexperienced, but we did not see the harm in making the attempt."

"Do you now see the harm?" asked her father. "Do you see how your interference may well have placed Robert in peril, and how Master Palgrave and I fear for you since no one knows the identity of this thief or where he may be?"

"But, father," said Aileen. "Is it so certain that Robert's fall was no mere accident? What is it that you are not telling me?"

"I have nothing further to tell you of his fall," responded Jude. "Master Palgrave knew nothing other than that his arm was broken and that he was being tended in the forest. However — and you will hear me in this, Aileen — it is clear that he was where he should not have been. Mayhap we will find out that he just tripped and fell. I will pray that such is the case. It does not signify anything, however, except that the result is an injury that has cost many a man his strength, even his life."

"But you said he would recover!" exclaimed Aileen.

"That is what Master Isaac says," responded Jude. "And we will pray that his skill as a physician is as great as we have always believed. But you well know that men have died from injuries such as these. The humors of the body do fight against each other and some are not strong enough to resist. When I marched behind

King Richard all those years ago, I saw many men who took less injury and yet died."

Seeing the look on his daughter's face, Jude relented.

"But I doubt not that Isaac the physician is a skilled healer. He has ever been truthful in his assessments of his patients' conditions. That he keeps Robert by him now may be a cause for concern in a mother who wishes to tend her son, but I believe is a favorable sign for his recovery."

"I will pray so, father," said Aileen, still shaken by this development.

"So will we all," her father said. "Now, Aileen, you will tell me why it is that you have disobeyed me in this matter and what it is that you have done. My fear now is that you have placed yourself in peril, and I needs must know what may be done to ensure your safety and that of your friends."

It took a long time, and her young siblings had long since been put to bed by the time Aileen finished her tale. She held nothing back, for her father's trust was something she did not lightly abuse, and she knew her only chance of regaining it was total honesty.

"That," said Jude as silence fell between them, "is a story I would scarce believe had I heard it in a tavern. But it brings back many memories of those dark days in lands far away."

"Father," said Aileen, "you have never spoken of the time you fought for King Richard. Is it those days of which you speak?"

"Yes, and I have never spoken of it because I would not wish to bring such remembrances into my home," said Jude. Anne, seeing the look on her husband's face, came over and sat beside him, taking his hand in hers.

Jude sighed. "Perhaps it is time I told you something of this Crusade," he said. "You are of age now and must put aside childish things. Already you have learned some of the tale from others. Mayhap my tale may help you understand my anger, and my concern."

Settling on his stool, Jude began to talk, his words soft and sad.

"It was a time of great emotion," he said. "The Pope had declared that the loss of Jerusalem was punishment for the sins of Christians. He called for a Crusade to recapture the City, and old King Henry started collecting what he called a Saladin Tithe so he could take the Cross in answer to the call. Then he died."

"But King Richard took the Cross in his place?" Aileen asked.

"He did," said Jude.

"And you followed him?" pressed Aileen.

"Yes, Aileen, I did. I was but a young man and had been married to your mother for less than a year." He smiled at his wife, sitting quietly beside him. She squeezed his hand, encouraging him to continue.

"The tithe was a burden to a young man who had barely completed his apprenticeship and was a new landholder. Those who took the Cross were exempt from the tithe. It seemed to me that this was a great adventure that would both absolve me of the stain of the sin that led to the loss of the Holy City and would save me from the loss of my land by taxation. So I armed myself with what poor weapons I could afford and left for Dartmouth to join the king."

"I feared so for his safety," Anne said as Jude paused. "We were young, you were but a babe, and it was hard to set aside our hopes for the future to send him to war even though it was a holy mission."

Aileen could only imagine how she would have felt had it been her. Home always seemed to have been there. She had never given thought to her parents' lives before she was born. Impulsively, she stood and reached over to hug both of them before sitting back down to hear the rest of her father's tale.

"We crossed the South Sea to France," he said. "Our army joined with that of King Philip, at least at the beginning. I do not know why, but there came a day when the two forces separated and our army turned south, marching for many days. We made camp in Marseille and waited for word to come that we should set sail for the Holy Land.

"It was high summer before we left France, but the days were cooling by the time we arrived in Sicily. Even then we could not proceed with our mission to free Jerusalem, for the Lionheart was greatly angered to find that his sister had been imprisoned by the King of Sicily. He ordered us to capture the city of Messina, and so we fought against fellow Christians before we ever saw the Holy Land."

"And did you free the princess?" asked Aileen, never having heard of these events before.

"Yes, but it was yet many months before we left Sicily. Even then, we were delayed by a great storm at sea and were forced to limp into Cyprus.

"Is that not where the king married Queen Berengaria?" Aileen remembered.

"Yes, and that at least was a happy day. We ate and sang and toasted the royal couple in wine, which tasted strange to lips that were more used to small ale."

"To think that you were there when the marriage took place," exclaimed Aileen. "I have heard accounts of this time in these past days, but never thought my own father could tell me as much."

"I doubt that I can tell you much that will solve this mystery," said her father. "I was but a foot soldier, and great affairs of state are not decided within the hearing of such as me. Yet perhaps the mood of the times may help us understand better the twisted roots of what we now see before us."

Jude paused a moment and then picked up his tale once again.

"We had been far from our homes for more than a year before we finally reached Acre," he said. "It was a source of pride to us that our king took the City in only a month when the other kings had been unable to break the siege for two years. And yet it was not the victory of which I had dreamed."

"What do you mean, father?" said Aileen.

"As I said before," replied Jude. "I had thought this would be a great adventure. Through all those long months of marching, suffering in the heat with little food or water to sustain us, and then waiting endlessly for action, I had comforted myself with the thought that it would be a magnificent thing to defeat the enemy and recapture lands so cruelly taken from us. I was sure that it was God's will that we triumph in this just fight."

"And what you saw made you doubt this?" asked Aileen, puzzled.

"I do not doubt that God's will is that we triumph against those who deny Him," said Jude. "And there are times when we must fight for a just cause. But what I saw, both in Acre and in the battles we fought as we advanced toward Jerusalem, is what troubles my memories to this day. There was so much horror, and such great suffering. Yet the kings and princes who led us in these battles did seem to spend as much time arguing with each other and seeking more favorable positions amongst themselves as they did in battling the enemy. I am not a learned man, but I could not help but wonder if there are times when Man's interpretation of God's will is not more about his own desires than about God's."

Aileen had never heard her father talk like this. Jude was a devout man, who raised his children to be strong in their faith. He must have seen terrible things, she thought, to so wonder about the wisdom of both earthly rulers and those representatives of our Lord Himself who had preached the Crusade throughout Christendom.

"Howsoever that may be," said Jude, bringing his thoughts back to the present and looking somewhat disturbed at having spoken out loud his own doubt, "you may imagine how very happy I was when I finally returned home to you and my beautiful wife."

"And how my joy could not be contained," added Anne. "I had scarce heard from your father in two years. I feared he had been injured or even died, but little news was carried back to our town concerning our men. Word of great battles or the weddings of kings perhaps, but there was little news for the women of England who had sent their men so far."

"Yet we took pride in our victories," said Jude. "Even as we wondered at the motives of some of those who led us into battle."

"Father," said Aileen. "You speak of the motives of the nobles. Did you then hear rumor of any particular discontent among them?"

"I regret I must disappoint you, Aileen," said her father. "I did hear nothing of a dispute between two lords of France. But you must remember, not only was I a lowly foot soldier, but those who served under the French king were not of our number. In the dark of night, around our fires, we were more like to talk of the deeds of King Richard and whether we would live to tell of his exploits against Saladin. We cared little for disputes between French lords."

"Of course, father," Aileen said. "Indeed it would have been surprising had you heard anything about something that was of so little moment in the course of the Crusade."

"Yes, those were times of great affairs in the lives of kings and nobles, but for the common soldier the most important thing was often how to stay cool in the day and warm in the night."

Turning to his wife, Jude kissed her hand. "I believe most men would say that I am not someone given to much talk," he said. "I think that even you have not heard such a great speech from me in many a long day."

Anne laughed. "Indeed, for I do remember that my father told me he thought it might take you all night to ask for my hand, you were so reluctant to put together the words."

Jude laughed with her, but then became once again serious.

"My words may not be fine, Aileen, but it is important to me that you understand that those were times when men's emotions sometimes overcame their senses. We were weary and hurt, hungry and hot. No one, not even noble lords who were better used to living at ease, could escape the dust, the storms, the battles. Small disputes could turn into conflicts likely to last a lifetime. It would not greatly surprise me if such a dispute arose in the court of the French king then, and mayhap the sons of those lords have neither forgotten nor forgiven the insult offered by each to the other."

"I think I understand, father," said Aileen.

215

"Do you?" her father said. "Such feuds can destroy not only those who keep them alive, but any who stand in the way of revenge, one upon the other. This is why I am concerned, and this is why I must now find a way to protect you and those around you. But hear me well in this, Aileen. I admire your faithfulness to your friends. I am proud to have raised a daughter of such character. But I am equally disappointed in your disobedience.

"No," Jude raised his hand as Aileen started to speak. "You have said enough. You may twist my words to justify your conduct, but you understood well what I was saying. Now you have risked not only yourself, but your friends and even your family. You will do nothing further without my sanction and my involvement. Is that clear?"

"Yes, father." Aileen knew when there was to be no further argument. "And I'm glad."

"You are?" responded her father in surprise.

"Yes, father. I never meant to disobey you. Truly, I didn't. It seemed as though we got caught up in something and then, of a sudden, we realized we were too far involved to turn around. I have felt such guilt that my conduct should so deceive you, and I know Robert feels the same way. I am indeed glad that you know everything. I will work hard to regain your trust. This I promise."

Jude was not an unjust man. "I will take you at your word, Aileen," he said.

A smile lit Jude's face as he continued: "I well remember that, as a young man, my father would oft disapprove of my adventures. However," and he looked hard at his daughter, "the adventures of a young man about to set out in life are one thing. A young woman such as yourself must take more care not to find herself outside the bounds of accepted conduct. See that I have no reason to speak thus to you again."

"Yes, father," said Aileen.

"So now," Jude said, "we must decide how to proceed. I think it best to wait until the morrow and see if we can find out from young Robert how it came to pass that he was in the woods and how he became injured. Mayhap his answers will help us bring an end to this matter and restore peace to our town."

"I can seek out Ruth tomorrow, if you will," said Aileen. "She will be able to tell me how Robert fares, and may perhaps know something of how it came about that he was sore injured."

"No," her father said firmly. "You will remain within excepting only when I escort you to the Abbey in the morning. There you will remain, speaking to none except the women with whom you work until I arrive to escort you at the end of the day."

"I will abide by your will, father," said Aileen, not wanting to push things too far. "May I ask your permission, though, to speak with one person not of my company?"

"With whom do you wish to speak, Aileen?" asked Jude.

"You will remember," said Aileen, feeling her way carefully, "that it was the young groom in the stable who

217

first gave me knowledge of the long history of trouble between the great families of du Lac and de Vere?"

"Yes," her father said. "Do you not know enough of that tale now?"

"Yes, father," said Aileen. "But he was also the one who told me about the discovery of the loss of the relic and the unconscious knight. With your permission, father, I would like to ask him more about that morning."

"I do not see what you can hope to gain by asking more of him, Aileen," sternly responded her father.

"It is only that there is some small detail about that morning that has escaped me," Aileen frowned. "If I can tease it out into the open then, perhaps, we will know the answers to the greater question and can bring this to closure."

Jude thought for a moment. "Very well," he said. "I do not see how talking to this young man can do harm. He is a servant who would have nothing to gain by disgracing his master and who had no part in what happened so many years ago. I can conceive of no way in which he could be involved in these evil deeds.

"You may talk to this young man, Aileen," Jude continued. "It seems unlikely that he can know of anything that will be of value, but you have my permission to ask your questions."

"Thank you, father."

"But," Jude went on in as stern a tone as Aileen had ever heard from him, "do not leave the Abbey and do not attempt to do anything further until we have had a chance to talk to Robert and put together all the information that has been gathered. Only then will we consider what must be done, and, when we have arrived at a conclusion, you will abide by my decision as to the proper course of action to be taken. Do you understand?"

"Yes, father," said Aileen. "It shall be as you say."

CHAPTER TWENTY-ONE

That man is almost the wisest among us in
both secular and ecclesiastical matters.

ROBERT WOKE TO SOFT RAYS of sunlight sparkling through the branches of the leafy roof of Isaac's shelter. Sitting up with a start, he cried out in pain.

"Softly now," said the voice of Isaac at his side. "You must not undo all my good work." Isaac smiled at Robert as he pushed him back down on the bed. "See, you have so ill-used my medicine that you have thrown aside the cloths of soothing chickweed I placed on your bruises."

"Master Isaac," Robert said. "Forgive me. I am indeed grateful for your tending. I did forget where I was when I awoke."

"There is nothing to forgive," said the physician, mixing some ground herbs into a cup of water. "I am pleased that you are once again yourself after such a night. But come, let me help you sit up more slowly."

Taking more care this time, Robert sat up. Looking at his injured arm, he saw that Isaac had bandaged it and applied a splint covered with bandages that were stiff with some kind of coating. He touched it carefully but felt no pain.

"If you will take care not to move so unguardedly as you did upon waking, I believe the bone will knit well," said Isaac. "The splint is covered with cloths soaked in lime and egg white. Not only does the mixture soothe the injured limb, but it will keep the arm straight until the bone heals."

"I thank you, Master Isaac," said Robert. "I will do as you say, sir. Were I to do otherwise, I am sure my father would say that I am the most ungrateful of wretches."

Isaac smiled at the poor attempt at humor of his patient. "As the son of a goldsmith I know that you must have a strong arm," he said, gently checking the bruises on Robert's face. "Your father is renowned throughout the Liberty for his great skill, and I would not deprive him of the help of his apprentice and heir."

The physician smiled at the young man. "Now, drink this tonic of sanicle," he continued. "I will prepare more for you to take with you when you return home. You must drink it at least twice a day if you wish your wound to heal completely."

Robert drank from the cup, and Isaac expressed his satisfaction at both the state of the young man's injuries and his cool forehead. Then, having satisfied his medical duties, Isaac called to his daughter to come. Robert smiled when he saw his friend. She came into the shelter so quickly he was sure she must have been hovering just outside these past several minutes.

"Robert," Ruth said. "How are you feeling this morning? I have been so worried about you."

"I am sorry to have so startled you," said Robert. "I did not know where else to turn."

"Your decision to find Ruth and Avraham was well made," said Isaac. "And we are honored that you would think to come to us in your distress."

"It is I who should thank you," Robert said. "But I need to know the answer to one question. Was Avraham able to safely reach my father's house and tell him where I am?"

"Yes," responded Ruth, reaching out and taking Robert's hand. "It was as he said. In the dark even a Jew may walk the road and not be recognized. He met no one and was able to give your father news of you."

"Was my father very angry?"

"Avraham said your mother and father were both much distressed and asked many questions. There was little he could do to satisfy them, though, since he knew nothing more than that you were hurt and that my father was tending you."

"That would seem to bring us to the matter of how you came to be hurt," said Isaac. "Do you feel able to tell us about last night?"

"I think so," Robert said. "I only hope that the account does not make me seem foolish, for in the light of day, there seems little enough to tell."

So Robert recounted his adventures of the day before, leaving nothing out from the scorn of a young boy for anyone who would leave such a prize as a new fish trap under bushes to the pricking of his skin at the sounds in the forest and his subsequent headlong flight to disaster.

"This is quite a tale," said Isaac when Robert fell into silence. "You are correct that there is little fact upon which to build a complete history, but lack of substance does not mean that your suspicions were unwarranted. I do believe that you were right to flee from the walker in the woods. You may well have fared worse had you stayed to see who it was who followed you."

This was a chilling thought, and Robert paled to think of it.

"Papa," said Ruth. "Do not frighten us so."

"It is as well that I frighten you now," responded her father sternly, "than that any of you risk further harm to yourselves. I know that your parents, and those of Aileen also, will have said much the same to you as this." Isaac raised his eyebrows in enquiry as he looked at Robert.

Robert hung his head. "Yes, sir, that is so. But truly we did not believe ourselves to be in any danger just for asking simple questions."

"It does not appear that your questions are as simple as you believe," said Isaac. Sighing, he drew his robe closer around him, and then looked at both young people as if trying to make up his mind about something.

"Very well," he said. "I believe that this has gone too far for any of us to leave to others the matter of the loss of this relic and the identity of the thief responsible. We need to discover that truth as quickly as possible, else I fear we all will face more danger."

"Does that mean you will help us, Papa?" asked Ruth.

"There is no 'us' to help, Ruth," responded her father, fixing his daughter with a look that would not be contradicted. "You have asked me about the court of the Sultan Saladin and Rabbi Maimonides. I will tell you what I know, and mayhap we will find something in the tale that will assist the officials of the Liberty to identify and apprehend the thief.

"Neither you, Ruth, nor you and Aileen, Robert, are to place yourselves in any further danger without seeking the assistance of those officials. Do I make myself clear?"

Robert and Ruth had little choice but to agree.

"It is hard to know where I should begin," said the physician, composing himself. "I do not know that I have anything to tell you that will help, but I have a long correspondence with the Rabbi over many years, and perhaps there is some hint of controversy and corruption that may be relevant to these recent sad events."

"Master Isaac," said Robert. "From what Ruth has told me, you appear to hold this Rabbi in great respect. Is he so well-known as this to all of your faith?"

"Yes, he is," Isaac said, simply. "And not only to those of our faith. He is consulted by many of your faith and has spent many years among the followers of Mohammed. To me, though, he will always be my childhood friend, Moses ben Maimon."

Isaac's eyes looked far into the past, and he smiled. "We were both born in Cordoba, and our families were close. Rabbi Maimon, his father, was the leader of our Jewish community, the seventh generation of his family to be so, and Moses and I played together as children."

"Our people have found security in few places since we were exiled from our land many centuries before the birth of your Christ," the physician continued. "Yet we spent many generations living in relative peace and prosperity in Iberia. But power does not always remain long in the hands of one line, and such was the case in Cordoba. In the time of my father, the people began to realize that our happiness could not last. Indeed, it was not long before that fear was realized, for the Jews were exiled from Cordoba.

"When the time came for us to leave, my family and that of Moses chose different paths, and for many years I heard no more of the adventures of my childhood friend. In due time I was honored to study under the skilled physicians from the medical school at Salerno, and then it was that I found that my friend was already a revered philosopher and physician."

"Did you study together?" asked Robert.

"No," said Isaac. "We remained separated by many miles. We have not seen each other since childhood, but we do correspond faithfully. His letters are very precious to me, filled as they are with discussions of his medical theories and practices, as well as news of our people in their travels."

Isaac looked at the two young people before him and sighed. Memories of his youth must be put aside. The present must be cured if the future of his daughter was to be secured.

He picked up a bundle of letters that lay by his side and, untying them, said: "Used as we are to fleeing our homes, there is little of material substance that we consider necessary to carry with us. I consider these one of those necessities."

Opening up one of the well-thumbed letters, Isaac began to read.

"'Look well into a man's theory and his belief, just as you should do concerning the things which he declares that he has seen. Look into the matter without letting yourself be easily persuaded.'

"Those are the words of my friend when he wrote to me concerning a certain controversy that had arisen in the court of the French king during the time of the Sultan Saladin."

"Papa!" cried Ruth. "The Rabbi speaks of the dispute between the two kings?"

"Yes," responded her father. "But I know not if what I have to tell you is important to finding the thief who stole the relic from the Abbey."

Turning back to the letter in his hand, the physician began to read once again.

226

"'Do you remember, my friend?'" quoted Isaac. " 'How, as children, we would wonder at the ways in which men of good faith could so betray their code as to harm those whom they are sworn to protect, all for the sake of riches or position?'"

The physician paused. Robert realized he was holding his breath, and Ruth was holding on to his hand so hard he could feel his fingers tingling. "Oh, I'm sorry, Robert," Ruth said, as he wiggled his fingers. She let go of his hand, and they both turned their attention back to Isaac.

"'I am mindful of those talks of ours,' my friend said in his letter. 'For I have but lately seen an example of such betrayal and confusion of faith..'"

Isaac put the letter down. "I do not need to read the missive to you," he said. "I have my friend's letters by heart, I do believe.

"Moses told me that word had been brought to the noble Saladin of a great argument that had broken out in the camp of King Philip of France. A matter of honor did distract the French king to such an extent that the spies believed it might offer Saladin an opportunity to relieve the City of Acre from its siege."

"I did not think that such a close matter could so impact the plans of kings," exclaimed Ruth.

"The fate of kings and their realms can sometimes be decided by the obsessions of a few minds," said her father.

"It must be a great burden to bear, to have the fate of many people in your hands," Robert said. "I am glad that it is not mine to carry."

"Would that such wisdom was always in the minds of those whose burden it is," responded Isaac, smiling at the young man.

Glancing once more at the letter in his hand, the physician continued with his tale.

"As you have surmised, the affair that caused such disturbance in the court of the French King concerned the conduct of Sir Aillard du Lac. It would seem that, when the knowledge of his negotiations with the King of Navarre was reported to Philip, the king's anger was so great that he had Sir Aillard and his son placed in chains."

"His son?" said Robert. "Sir Henri was with him in the Holy Land?"

"So it would appear," Isaac said. "He was still but a young man, but old enough to accompany his father on the Crusade as a part of his retinue."

"It must have been terrifying for him to be treated thus," said Ruth.

"Terrifying, and humiliating," said her father. "He was the scion of one of the most influential families in France and was said to be a proud young man, impatient and disdainful of those of lesser rank. His father, it would appear, was of the same nature."

"Did the Rabbi then know of them, that he should give you so much detail of their characters?" asked Ruth.

"No, but this, at least, was the account offered by the spies who brought their report to Saladin," said Isaac.

"What happened next, sir?" asked Robert.

"It would seem that King Philip was of a mind to execute Sir Aillard for treason, but his long friendship with the family did cause him some pause. He also sought to find out what part in the affair was played by Sir Henri.

"Sir Aillard declared that no treason was intended and that his son had taken no part in the affair. He swore that he sought only to aid one whom he thought a great friend to his king. He said also that he believed that, by acting as ambassador to the English king and thus distracting King Richard from his mission in the Holy Land, the French king would be able to take the City of Acre alone and thus claim victory for himself. Sir Aillard took an oath that his actions were only to further his own lord's reputation, not to damage it. He said he was not pleased that King Richard's reputation preceded him and diminished that of King Philip."

"And did King Philip believe him?" asked Robert.

"He was unsure, but his anger was scarce abated. The king thought to put Sir Aillard, and possibly his son, to torture to obtain the answers he desired, but then Sir Giles de Vere asked the king to permit a Trial by Combat."

"And the king agreed?" asked Ruth.

"Yes," said Isaac. "It would seem that the king was seeking a way out of his dilemma. Sir Giles and Sir Aillard were both from families close to the throne for many generations and had been close to each other their whole lives. Indeed, their children were betrothed. According to rumor, the match between Sir Henri and Isabelle de Vere was one of love, a happenstance that is not to be found often in the houses of great nobles."

"Oh," breathed Ruth. "It was a great romance. How tragic that it should end in such sorrow."

Robert rolled his eyes, but Isaac smiled upon his daughter. "My child, it pleases me that you can still find it in your heart to sigh for love, and for sorrow. Never allow the deeds of bad men to harden the loving heart Yahweh has given you."

Ruth blushed. "Thank you, Papa," she said. "But I do beg your pardon for the interruption. Please continue."

Isaac, smiling, took up his tale once again.

"Whatever the reason, the King granted Sir Giles' request to engage in combat with Sir Aillard du Lac. The battle would decide the truth of what Sir Aillard du Lac had said, and thus the fate of his entire family.

"The battle between Sir Aillard and Sir Giles took place in the presence of the king and the men of the camp. According to the report made to the Sultan the men around the battle square were quiet, each one fearful of drawing the ire of the great lords among them. The spies told the Sultan that the mood of the entire camp was low and believed that this lack of morale could easily favor their forces should Saladin launch an attack."

"How would these spies have seen so much?" wondered Robert. "Were they hidden around the camp, or were they posing as members of the Crusaders' men?"

"This I do not know," responded Isaac. "My friend merely told me of their report, not of how they came to obtain their information. However, it would not surprise me if they had been posing as local traders, attempting to sell food or other exotic items to the many men in the camp.

"Howsoever that may have been, their report of the combat was apparently very complete. According to the spies Sir Aillard and Sir Giles entered the field after noon, as is required by the rules of combat. They made their obeisance to the king, and asked God to favor the innocent. Sir Giles' anger was clear, but the grief in the eyes of Sir Aillard soon turned to determination to clear his name and that of his family.

"The two combatants then faced each other in such a way that neither had the sun assaulting their eyes, and thus the battle began."

"Who won?" asked Robert, as the physician paused to take a drink from the cup by his side.

"It was a long battle," replied Isaac, not to be deterred from recounting the story in his own way. "The two men fought valiantly, each giving the other no quarter. But they grew tired, fighting in the great heat with their heads bare to the sun and their swords and shields growing more heavy the longer they held them.

"Eventually, Sir Giles drove Sir Aillard to the ground. All who watched gasped, thinking that they were about to see the death of the fallen knight."

The sounds of a robin singing in the sunshine and crickets clicking just outside the shelter could be heard, but there was only silence within.

"And did Sir Giles kill Sir Aillard?" asked Ruth, unable to bear the tension any longer.

"No," said Isaac. "He stood over the knight, the tip of his sword against his throat. 'Cry "Craven,"' he said. 'Admit that you are vanquished and guilty of the charge against you!' But Sir Aillard refused. 'I will not so besmirch the name of my family,' he said. 'I will die declaring my fealty to my lord the king and none other!' So saying, he threw his arms out and stretched his neck to receive the blade of the sword."

"Sir Giles stood over Sir Aillard for what seemed like a long time," continued Isaac. "Then, slowly, he lowered his sword. He turned to the king and said, 'My Lord, I have proven this man a traitor, and his life and those of his family, are forfeit. Is it your wish that I carry out this sentence?'

"King Philip looked long at Sir Giles, and then sighed. He stood up and declared that, though the lives of those who were of the house of du Lac were forfeit to the crown, yet he would have mercy on them for their long service to his family. Henceforth they would be banished from the presence of the court, their lands would be confiscated, and they must be exiled to a distant manor of little influence."

"And Sir Henri, Sir Aillard's son?" asked Ruth.

"He would share in the punishment of his entire family, and the betrothal between him and the Lady Isabelle was null and void."

"How sad," said Ruth. "But does it not seem strange that Sir Giles would fail to deliver the blow that would end the battle after he had fought so hard?"

"My child," said Isaac, "You ask for an answer to the mystery that is the mind of a man. Mayhap that was the reason the king became so thoughtful. Sir Giles was greatly angered at the news of his old friend's apparent betrayal, but perhaps he yet could not bring himself to take the life of his lifelong companion. He risked the ire of King Philip himself by holding his hand at the last, but it would seem that the king himself was of two minds. Perhaps that moment of mercy on the part of Sir Giles was what saved Sir Aillard and his family from death."

"Yes, but perhaps it is also what has brought us to our current troubles," said Robert.

Isaac laughed. "Master Robert, you are indeed a man of a practical turn of mind. Yet you may be right. The sons of the fathers can sometimes carry burdens of guilt or anger down through many generations. I cannot say whether that is the case here. I merely tell you of events as they were reported to me by my friend."

"Yet they do not seem to have so impacted the course of conduct by the kings," said Ruth. "For I do not believe that the sultan ever broke the siege."

"You are correct, my child," said Isaac. "Indeed, it was the two kings who broke the defenses of the City, and Saladin never did recapture it after the surrender. King Philip left the Holy Land soon after, but the friendship between him and the Lionheart was broken forever."

For a moment, all of them were silent, thinking of those distant battles amid the heat of the East.

"Sir" said Robert, shifting uneasily on his bed, "I am indebted to you twice over. What your friend has told you would make of a mere quarrel between two noble families a great affair of state. Mayhap the wrath of that time has not faded, but rather grown. If such be the case, then it is not impossible to believe that the feud has reached all the way from the Holy Land to our great Abbey."

"Perhaps," responded the physician. "And if what I have told you does aid in finding the thief of this relic, then I will be glad. But remember, men's hearts are not always easy to understand, and sometimes what appears to be obvious is not truth. Take care in ascribing events of today to those of many years past. You may find that the answer lies in simple thievery and not the business of nations."

If that be the case, thought Robert, then we would be no further along the road to discovery than we were yesterday. But he knew Isaac's words were wise, and he would never wish to offend him by rejecting his warning.

"I believe I am strong enough to return to my home now, sir," he said instead. "I am indeed grateful to you, but I cannot risk your safety by remaining any longer. If I do not return home soon there may be questions asked by those who would seek your hiding place."

"Mayhap you are correct," responded the physician. "However, I will not risk the return to health of my patient for the sake of such an argument. You will remain here with us one more night, and then we will see. If your wounds are knitting on the morrow then I will have Avraham take you home."

"But Master Isaac," said Robert, "Avraham would be in danger were he to approach Bury in the light of day. If you believe it is necessary for him to accompany me cannot it be this evening, while the moon shines just enough to light our way but no man may discover us?"

Isaac contemplated the determined young man, a smile wiping away the frown of concern. "Very well," he said. "But let me look at your wounds first. Your arm will take some time to knit, but it is well guarded. Most of your other hurts will also heal in good time. Your mind is perhaps too clear, so I fear no great lasting damage there other than a continuing streak of stubbornness."

Satisfied with his answer, Robert lay back and submitted himself to the ministrations of the physician.

235

CHAPTER TWENTY-TWO

He was a very serious-minded man and never idle.

"WHY WAS THE KNIGHT'S BODY servant not with him the night of the vigil?" asked Aileen of Seward. "I thought such noble lords were never without someone to tend to their needs."

"The master would allow no one with him," replied Seward. "He even forbade a servant from being within call. He said that his vow to God must be fulfilled alone and without comfort. A servant to attend to his needs would break that vow."

Aileen had come early to the Abbey again in order to seek out the young groom. She found him, as she had expected, in the stable, grooming Raven.

"Does anyone know how long after the attack it was before the theft was discovered?" Aileen asked.

Seward looked sideways at Aileen.

"What a strange question," he said. "Why should that be of interest to you?"

"Oh, I'm just curious," Aileen replied. "If we knew how long the thief had to get away before the cry was raised, perhaps we could work out how far he might have ridden."

"I'm sure the noble knight and the abbot have thought of that," Seward said. Then, seeing Aileen's expression, he softened. "But I don't suppose it would hurt to tell you.

"Sir Henri doesn't know exactly when the thief crept up behind him," Seward said. "But the last office for the night had been said by the monks in the church, and they had gone to their rest."

"So that means it must have been after midnight," said Aileen. "Was it one of the monks who found the knight unconscious?"

Seward smiled. "Do you ever reach the end of your questions? No, Sir Henri regained his senses before the monks returned to the church choir and raised the alarm. Are you satisfied now? For I have work to be done, and I can spend no more time lallygagging!"

Realizing that there was nothing more to be gained by asking more questions of Seward, and that she ran the risk of annoying him if she stayed longer, Aileen went to her work.

Mistress Taylor, pleased with Aileen's stitching and her reaction to the Abbot's chasuble, had assigned to her the task of working on a beautiful new white silk mitre. Care was needed in working the gold thread

237

on the silk ground, but Aileen was confident in her ability to couch the threads. She had soon left behind her early nervousness, and the embroidered surface was beginning to show the design of the martyrdom of the blessed saint for whose Feast Day the regalia was being made.

Managing to get herself seated next to the woman who had told them about the disturbance in the stable on the night of the theft, Aileen had no difficulty bringing the conversation around to those events.

"Could the stable boy tell what hour of the night he awoke?" asked Aileen, casually.

"No, but Will, for that's the boy's name, said that he had much trouble going back to sleep afterwards, and the hours were long. And when he finally did manage to get back to sleep, it seemed like no time before he was woken up again!"

"Truly?" said Aileen. "What aroused him that time?"

"The horses moving around again, I expect," said the woman, shrugging her shoulders. "The lad told me that it was only minutes later that he heard the first cock crow and had to rise for the day. The horses were just astir early, that's all."

With that, Aileen had to be content for the moment. She spent the rest of the morning working on the mitre under the close watch of Mistress Taylor.

At the luncheon rest, Aileen went in search of Will, the stable boy. He was sitting on a hay bale outside the main stable entrance, munching on a thick chunk of black bread and sipping a mug of weak ale.

"Good day," Aileen said as she sat down near him, putting her cloth-wrapped lunch down carefully beside her on the hay bale. "You must be Will, the stable boy."

"Aye, and you're Aileen, the one who's always asking questions," replied Will.

Somewhat put out to discover that she was earning a reputation for being nosy, Aileen decided the only thing to do if she were to find out anything from Will was just to laugh it off.

"Oh, well," she said. "You know how it is. Nothing this exciting has ever happened in St. Edmund's Bury before. You can't fault me for wanting to know what's going on. After all, I'm right here where it all happened."

"You're not the only one," said Will. If I have to answer any more questions from soldiers, and monks, and reeves, and all, I don't know what I'll do."

This is going to be tricky, thought Aileen. She sat silently for a moment, chewing her bread and cheese and watching the scene in the courtyard.

The Great Court of the Abbey was always busy, but with the large number of visitors staying in the guest hall, most of whom had come to see the installation of the relic and had then stayed to hear news of its recovery, the courtyard never seemed to be empty. Several of the visitors were standing around talking, and others were apparently just enjoying the warmth of the sun, deep in their own thoughts. Personal servants were crossing the courtyard, busy on errands for their masters, and Abbey servants were equally busy seeing to the needs of visitors and monks. Aileen could see squires cleaning weapons and polishing armor, and beggars slinking through the gates when nobody was looking, trying to take advantage of the increased opportunities for generosity. All these and more were constantly crossing the courtyard, the murmur of activity never still until night fell and law-abiding folk were gathered in front of their hearths.

As Aileen watched, thinking of how to approach the subject of the night of the theft with Will, she saw Sir Henri du Lac coming towards them across the courtyard, his brow furrowed. The knight seemed unaware of the bustle going on around him.

As he approached the stables, Sir Henri looked up and called out for Seward to saddle his horse. He came to an abrupt halt in front of Aileen and Will, looking hard at the pair sitting on the hay bale. Aileen quickly got to her feet and dropped a curtsy to the knight. Will, dipping his head briefly in a quick bow, scurried off to his duties, leaving the knight and the girl alone in a small pool of silence.

Sir Henri continued to look at the young girl before him and seemed about to say something. Just then, however, Seward led Raven out of the stable, and the moment was gone. The knight moved quickly to mount his horse, and Aileen returned to her lunch.

"Phew," said Will, coming out of the stable as soon as Sir Henri had moved away. "Did you see that look on his face? I'll wager he's heard about all your questions, too!"

Just what I was thinking, said Aileen to herself, watching as the knight walked his horse around the yard. I wonder what he was going to say, had Seward not come out of the stable just then. Perhaps he was going to tell me something that would prove of help in our quest. More likely, he was going to tell me to mind my own business, Aileen thought ruefully. A chill ran up her spine, but she knew she couldn't stop now. Too many people were depending on her.

"Will," she said, thinking that Will's comment opened the door for her to ask some questions. "Tell me about the night the relic was stolen. I heard that you were awoken by sounds in the stable below?"

"Yes, and before you ask, I haven't any idea who or what it was," said Will. "I was warm and comfortable, and I didn't stir. So it's no use asking me about it."

"But couldn't you tell if there was anyone in the stable with the horses?" Aileen was determined to get some answers, and a little lack of cooperation from Will wasn't going to stop her. "Would you have woken up if it was just the normal noises you hear every night?"

Will started to answer, but then stopped, looking thoughtful. "I hadn't thought about it like that," he said. "Come to think of it, you could be right. But if there was something different, I don't know what it was. I was deep asleep, and by the time I came to my senses, all I could hear was the sound of the horses moving around."

Sir Henri had dismounted and was examining one of Raven's hooves.

"And that was after the bell sounded, calling the monks to the church for the last service of the night?" asked Aileen.

"I don't remember hearing the bells at all, so it must have been," replied Will. "I lay awake a long time that night and wasn't best pleased when I was disturbed yet again just as I got back to sleep!"

The knight was leading his horse around the yard now, looking concerned.

"What disturbed you then?" asked Aileen.

"Horses," said Will, shortly. "But I could have sworn I heard something jingle as it moved. I told the Reeve that I thought that was what woke me up the second time, but he just told me I was imagining things. So don't you go asking any more questions, and then disbelieving me."

"Really, I *do* believe you," said Aileen. "I think it's very interesting, what you have to say. Please go on."

Will was pleased. He had told his story again and again to the Reeve and the soldiers and even the monks, and most of them looked as though they thought he had made up most of it. Now here was this pretty girl, all ears, paying attention to every word he had to say. Perhaps he should tell her the rest of it, after all.

"Well, there's one thing I've told no one," he said.

Aileen sat up straight, all attention.

"They were all so proud," said Will. "They didn't think much of what a lowly stable lad had to tell them. So when they didn't ask me about later, I just didn't tell them!"

242

"Later?" asked Aileen. "What happened later?"

"It wasn't what happened, so much as what I found," said Will. "You see, one of my first jobs each morning is to feed and water the horses in the abbot's stable. It's one of those jobs you always get stuck with when you're the youngest in the stable."

Aileen nodded her understanding.

"That morning, after all the fuss had died down, I took around the water as usual. I had almost finished when I noticed something strange about one of the horses. It looked as though. . ."

"Will," cried the senior stable lad, coming out of the stable door. "You're supposed to be cleaning out the stalls. Get to it right away. You've spent enough time lazing around in the sun!"

Will jumped to his feet and started for the door.

"Please," Aileen said, catching his arm as he went past. "Can't you tell me what you saw?"

"Not now," said Will, snatching his arm away from her. "I'm in enough trouble already. I'll earn myself a beating if I stay another moment."

Seeing Aileen's disappointment, he relented. "Come back at the end of the day," said Will. "I'll tell you then." With that, he was gone, pausing at the door only long enough to allow Sir Henri to pass through first.

"Boy," said the knight. "Run and fetch the blacksmith. My horse has thrown a shoe, and I need it replaced straight away." As Will turned to obey the Crusader's order, Aileen slipped away, and back to her work.

Aileen was impatient for the day to come to a close. Will's story had re-awakened the feeling she had had when talking to Robert that she was missing some connection between the events. Somehow she was sure that whatever he had left to tell her would help her make that connection and find the solution to the mystery. She could barely wait to find out what he had to say.

Finally, after endless hours of crawling time, Mistress Taylor told everyone to tidy up and go home. Aileen had done her best to concentrate on undercouching the mitre, and her work did not show any lack of attention to detail. But she was very glad that Mistress Taylor chose to focus her attention on the work of her other workers that afternoon rather than continuing to look over Aileen's shoulder and commenting on every stitch.

There was a chill in the air as Aileen crossed the courtyard. She drew her cloak closer about her and tucked her hands in its folds. The bustle of the day had died down, and there were few people around.

She could see no one as she entered the stables. The only sounds were the rustle of hay as the horses moved and the occasional snort from one of the animals.

"Will," she called. "Are you here?"

Silence. Aileen sat down on a hay bale to wait. He's probably over in the other stables tending to his chores, she thought.

Several minutes passed, and Aileen grew impatient. She had just decided to go and see where the stable lad might be, when she heard a groan from one of the stalls. Startled, Aileen jumped up and cried, "Who's there?"

The only answer was a low moan.

Someone's hurt, she said to herself. Crossing over to the stall, Aileen saw Will lying, half-buried, in the hay. He was holding his head, trying to sit up, and groaning.

"Will! What happened? Can you sit up?" She bent down and put her arm around his shoulders, helping him.

"What hit me?" exclaimed the boy. "Ooh, my head!" He touched his head gingerly, flinching as his fingers touched a swelling on the right side.

"Let's have a look at that," said Aileen, gently parting the hair and examining his head. "The skin isn't broken, but you're going to have a giant headache in the morning."

"I've got one now," grumbled Will.

"Do you remember what happened?" asked Aileen after a pause to allow Will to gather his wits about him.

"I was mucking out this stall," he said. "I seem to remember hearing something just behind me, but that's the last thing I remember."

"It's all right," said Aileen. "Don't worry over it. Someone obviously hit you over the head, but at least there isn't any serious damage done."

"No serious damage?" Will said, indignantly. "What about my head?"

"Get one of the brothers to look at it," Aileen said in a practical, if somewhat unsympathetic, tone. "But I think your thick skull saved you."

Will scowled at the girl by his side, and struggled to his feet, hanging on to Aileen's arm as he rose.

"Why would anyone want to hit me over the head?" he said. "I've harmed no one."

Aileen guided the boy over to the bale upon which she had been sitting when she heard him moan.

"It's because you were talking to me," she said. "Someone didn't want me to find out what you have to say."

"Then I'd better shut up," said Will. "I don't want another of these heads."

"You can't do that!" Aileen said. "Think about it. As long as whoever it is thinks you know something that can harm him, you'll be at risk. Remaining silent won't help. The only way you can make sure you're out of danger is to tell all that you know."

Will thought about that for a moment but could find no fault with Aileen's logic.

"Oh, very well," he said. "I don't know what's so important about it anyway. All I was going to say was that I found one of the horses all sweated up and streaked with dirt on the morning after the theft. What's so dangerous about that, I'd like to know?"

"You mean that it looked as though the horse had been ridden during the night?" asked Aileen.

246

"Yes, that's what I mean," said Will. The pain in his head was not making his temper any sweeter, but Aileen chose to ignore it. "I don't look after all the horses in this stable. The knight's horses are taken care of by his own men. But afore I went to bed myself I looked at all the horses in the stable, including the Crusader's." The stable lad looked as though he were admitting to a crime.

"I would have done the same thing," said Aileen.

Thus encouraged, Will went on. "His mounts are something special, and I couldn't resist running my hand over Raven's glossy coat. He was as clean and dry as could be."

"Was it Raven you found dirty and tired in the morning?" asked Aileen.

"Yes," said Will.

"Why didn't you tell the Reeve that when he questioned you?" Aileen asked.

"I told you," Will said. "He didn't believe the rest of my tale. Why should he have believed me about this? After all, we all know that the knight could not have ridden Raven that night. He was lying unconscious in front of St. Edmund's shrine.

"It must have been someone else who took him out," the boy said. "Besides, I don't need anyone accusing me of telling lies or, worse, messing around with the knight's horses. So I decided to just keep my peace and let them think what they may."

Aileen did not reply. She was busy thinking about this latest piece of information. Yes, finally it all made sense. She really thought she knew what had happened now, but one question remained. Why? Why had the relic been stolen?

Frustrated that the information she thought would complete the whole picture had only created more questions, Aileen turned to Will.

"Will, ..."

Just then, Aileen heard a sound in the loft above their heads. It was so slight she might have missed it altogether, except that the Abbey seemed unnaturally quiet at this time of day, and all sounds are louder in the midst of silence.

The hair on the back of Aileen's neck stood up, and she turned her head sharply to look up at the loft. As she raised her eyes, she saw a bale of hay fall off the edge of the loft, right above where she and Will sat.

Before she had time to react, Aileen felt something hit her hard from the side, pushing her into Will. The stable lad, crying out in alarm, fell to the floor with Aileen on top of him, just as the falling bale smashed into the bale upon which they had been sitting.

CHAPTER TWENTY-THREE

Now let our philosophers understand the consequences of their philosophizing!

"ARE YOU SURE YOU'RE ALL right?" asked Robert.

"Yes, I'm fine," said Aileen. "And you can hardly complain of my being too careless of my own safety when you have fared much worse than I." Aileen's concern, so obvious in her face, belied the stern tone.

"Aileen," Ruth, ever the mediator, said softly. "Robert has told you how it came about that he was injured, and he has already suffered many words of warning and instruction from his father and mine. I do believe that he would prefer no more remonstrance from us."

Robert threw Ruth a grateful glance. "Indeed, it is a wonder that my father permitted me to see you at all today," he said to Aileen, "Even if it meant you had to bring Ruth and Avraham here." Ruth's protector had insisted on accompanying the young women when Aileen asked that they meet Robert in the meadow behind his house once darkness had fallen and, truth be told, Aileen and Ruth had both felt happier to have him with them.

"My mother, of course, was most interested in fussing over me and treating me as though I were still a small child," Robert continued. "My father's reaction was to send his servant to retrieve the horse from where I had left it grazing in the grass near the pond, and then to make sure I knew exactly how angry he was to find out that I had disobeyed his instructions to leave this matter alone. It was useless to protest that I had done nothing more than ask simple questions such as any curious person might."

"I know exactly what you mean," said Aileen, with feeling.

"How was it that you obtained his permission to meet with us, then?" asked Ruth.

"My mother would suffer nothing but that I bring this gift of a golden plate as a sign of gratitude and friendship to one who saved the life of her only son," said Robert. "She pleaded with my father to attend upon your father herself, but I said that I had already risked your discovery by coming to the forest and that I should be the one to offer my remorse and my gratitude by offering your father this gift."

"What did your father say?" Aileen asked.

"My father agreed with me. He said that it was the duty of a man to make restitution for his errors, and that only a child would allow his mother to stand in his stead. His only condition was that any meeting to offer our gift of gratitude would have to take place here and not in the forest. He said that, since Avraham had been able to travel safely to St. Edmund's town in order to let him know my whereabouts, he hoped that perhaps he would be able to again make the journey."

"And if Ruth's father had forbidden the journey?"

"Then, according to my father, my apology must wait upon my healing and a less angry time in the lives of the good people of the town. My mother could argue nothing in return."

The plate that Robert held out to Ruth was beautiful, simple in its decoration, but worthy of a lord's house. The friends all crowded around to admire it, knowing it was wrought by a master goldsmith whose work was sought after throughout the Liberty and beyond.

"It is very beautiful, Robert," she said. "But I know my father will say that we cannot accept such a gift. We did merely what was right, and your recovery is all that we could ask. Your friendship is a gift more valuable than any worldly prize."

"Please take it to your father," Robert said. "It is as my parents wish, and they would be sad to think their gift rejected."

Reluctantly, Ruth took the plate from Robert's hands. "Besides," said Robert, "you don't want me to try to hold on to it anymore. You know I can barely stop myself from tripping over my big feet in the best of circumstances. Add a broken arm and I'm sore afraid I may be a danger to myself!"

His joke worked to break the tension, if not to ease all their anxieties. "We had better talk quickly now," said Robert. "My father will not be patient if he believes me to be taking too long in presenting you with our gift of gratitude, and my mother will start worrying about my being out in the night air too long should we tarry."

Turning to Aileen, he repeated his original question: "Are you sure you're all right?"

"I'm still finding shreds of hay in my hair and clothes," Aileen said, thinking to make Robert smile again, "but neither Will nor I were hurt at all."

"You think the falling bale was no accident, don't you?" said Robert.

"When the stranger looked in the loft he saw no one, but it must have been the thief, or else an accomplice, who pushed that bale off the edge." Aileen picked a stubborn stray piece of straw out of her sleeve.

"So who is this stranger?" demanded Robert. "I mean, I'm really glad he was there to save you, but who is he?"

"Before I tell you about him, I need to tell you about my conversation with William de Vere," Aileen said.

"You spoke to him! When?"

"While you were being chased in the woods," said Aileen, smiling at her friend.

"What did he have to say?"

As quickly as she could, Aileen gave her friends the details of William de Vere's sad tale.

"He does seem to have put himself in some difficulty," said Ruth, sympathetically.

"Yes, he does," responded Aileen. "I'm not sure it was wise of him to pursue the matter of the ring by going to Moyses Hall, but his account of what happened there would appear to clear him of the suspicion of stealing the holy relic."

"His cloak was torn during the struggle with the other man, I assume?" asked Robert.

"So it would seem," Ruth said. "But didn't you find it interesting that this stranger would give him back the ring as he was being thrown out of the Hall?"

"Yes, that does seem strange," agreed Robert. "I wonder who it was who would do such a deed."

"I can tell you that!" declared Aileen, smiling at the look of surprise on the faces of her companions.

"Don't keep us waiting," said Robert. Who is he?"

"He is Edward Gaunt, and he is in the service of the Lord de Vere."

"The Lord de Vere!" exclaimed Robert. "But that would mean ... but ... but ..."

"I think perhaps this is the first time I have ever seen your speechless, Robert," laughed Aileen. Ruth, hiding her mouth with her hand, could be heard softly giggling.

"Well, you must admit that this is a startling piece of news!" Robert said defensively.

"Yes, Aileen," said Ruth. "This is unexpected. How did he come to be right there at Moyses Hall at just the right moment?"

"To answer that," said Aileen, "I must tell you that the stranger who saved Will and I did introduce himself to me as Master Gaunt."

Seeing the eager looks on the faces of her friends, Aileen continued. "As soon as he had set both Will and I on our feet and been assured of our taking no harm," said Aileen. "I asked him if he was the same stranger who had so mysteriously returned to William de Vere the ring which had been thought lost."

Pausing to make sure that a rustling in the grass was nothing more than a simple rustle in the breeze, Aileen returned to her tale. "Before the stranger would answer he made sure that there was no one remaining in the loft from which the bale had fallen. Then he said he would wait with me by the gate until my father arrived to escort me home. I will admit I was shaken enough by the events of the evening that I was glad of his company.

"Thus it was that we left Will in the stable and walked together to the gate. Once there, we found a quiet corner and he told me that his master had sent him to ensure that the lord's son did not return to his old ways and risk again the family's honor and wealth," Aileen told her companions.

"I wonder that this servant would be so free with such information when talking with a young woman of the town who is unknown to him," said Ruth.

254

"I think he would not have been so," Aileen said, "had he not already seen me talking to the young lord and heard me asking questions about the night the relic was stolen. He was as curious about me as I was about him, but when he realized that I was a target of mischief and not the one creating it, he decided to trust me. He said it was a matter of protecting the innocent and helping assure that only the guilty took harm."

"I think you need to start at the beginning and tell us what he was doing at Moyses Hall when William de Vere went there to try and get back the ring," suggested Robert.

"Ah, the ring," said Aileen. "It would seem that the ring was the reason for much of the false trail we have followed."

She settled a little more comfortably on the grass before continuing.

"Master Gaunt told me that the Lord de Vere had never quite believed the story of the ring being lost in the river. He was afraid, after learning of his son's gambling, that the ring had indeed been lost in a wager. He did not believe he would ever recover the ring, but he did hope that perhaps he might find out who had possession of that family treasure.

"When he gave permission for William to attend upon his mother during the journey to the Abbey, he instructed Master Gaunt to travel to St. Edmund's Bury separately and to keep an eye on his son and see with whom he associated. Sir Giles, unfortunately, had no doubt that William would find bad company, and he thought that he might gain more insight into his companions and their habits if his son should again fall into the hands of false friends. It seemed to him a slight chance, but one worth taking, if he could thereby discover the whereabouts of his ring."

"But surely those he met in St. Edmund's town would not be the same men with whom he had associated in Paris?" asked Robert.

"Master Gaunt told me that the circle of such acquaintances as would be known to the young lord is not so large, and the arrival of the relic in our town was widely known. As we have seen, visitors from near and far have come to see the holy relic. It seemed not unlikely that, among our pilgrims, would be families of others of his son's friends.

"The Lord de Vere, of course, knew many of the families of those with whom William had associated in Paris, but he had heard no word of the ring and thus sought merely to cast a wider net in search of his treasure."

"So the young lord was wrong when he thought his father might be starting to trust him once again," said Ruth sadly.

"I don't know about that," Aileen said. "I doubt he would have allowed him to come at all if he was not softening in his attitude toward his son. It would have been too great a risk. But he certainly didn't trust him as completely as I'm sure William would like.

"Master Gaunt traveled alone and without the baggage that Lady de Vere required as befitting her position, so he reached the Abbey first. He immediately made enquiries regarding a possible gambling establishment in St. Edmund's Bury."

"He found out about Moyses Hall!" exclaimed Robert.

"Yes, he did," said Aileen. "Not only did he find out about it, but he gained entry on the ground that he was a traveling knight seeking distraction from the rigors of his duties. He has the bearing of a well-to-do man, and no doubt appeared to be worth their effort to strip him of his purse.

"It was perhaps as well that Lady de Vere and her retinue arrived only a day after Master Gaunt found Moyses Hall, else he might have been forced to wager more than he could afford to lose. Be that as it may, it was on the second night of Master Gaunt's attendance at the game that young Lord William did appear and became embroiled in the fight with his luckless friend."

"So it was Master Gaunt who returned the ring to William?" asked Avi, clearly intrigued by the whole account. He had been sitting so quietly that the friends had almost forgotten his presence.

"Yes, for he thought that the father would have been proud of his son's resisting the temptation offered to return to gambling and also of his efforts to retrieve the ring. Thus, though he could not reveal himself to William, it seemed to him that the return of the ring from the son himself would be most fitting."

"That was most kindly done," said Ruth.

Robert was not so easily impressed. "This tale does become more strange and more intricate by the day," he grumbled.

"Actually, I think this helps make some things more clear," said Aileen. "Even before the fall of the bale in the stable, I think we would have been able to exclude William completely from our search."

"Speaking of which," Robert said, "what happened in the stable, and how did Master Gaunt know you were there?"

"Apparently, after seeing me talk to William for so long the day before, he decided to keep an eye on me. He no longer needed to watch over his lord's son, for he had learned all that he needed to know about William's gambling habit and, of course, he had retrieved the ring. He was, however, concerned that I might be the cause of some trouble for the young lord."

"So he followed you?" asked Robert.

"Not exactly, but he was close by when I was talking to Will in the morning and heard us arranging to meet later. He decided to return and make sure that nothing was said that would pose a risk to the reputation or security of his master's family."

"But did you not see him?" asked Ruth. "Surely at that time there were not so many people around that you would not be aware of a stranger standing close by?"

"That would have been true, had he just stood by the door," answered Aileen. "Master Gaunt told me, though, that he secreted himself in a stall so that he could hear our conversation without difficulty. Had he chosen a different stall he might have come across Will lying unconscious earlier, and then I would never have learned of the key to the whole mystery."

"What do you mean: 'the key to the whole mystery'?" Robert demanded.

"That's what I want to talk to you about," said Aileen. "I think I may know who stole the relic, but I'm not sure why."

"You know?" exclaimed Robert. "Who?"

Aileen bent her head forward, forcing her friends to bend close until no one beyond their tight little circle could have heard a word. As she spoke of her theory, and how she had reached her conclusions, Robert's eyes widened, and surprise was stamped across his face.

When Aileen stopped speaking, there was silence.

"Phew!" said Robert, at last. "What you say all fits together, but I can scarce believe it!"

"I know," said Aileen. "I could scarce believe it myself, but I think it to be the only possible answer to the riddle."

"But *why*?" asked Ruth. "Why the theft?"

"That is the only thing for which I have no answer yet," replied Aileen. "What we need to do now, though, is talk about how we prove the thief's guilt."

"We must take care, Aileen," said Robert. "If you are right, then the shadow I saw the night I believed I was being followed was the thief, and the same person pursued me in the forest. What is worse is that he must be becoming desperate to dare so much by attacking you in the stable. We must act before the thief tries again to attack us. Yet, if we risk too much the true answer to the riddle may never become known, for we will be unable to speak!"

"We must have help, then," said Aileen. "If silence is danger to us, then speaking to another is safety."

"Who will believe us?" Robert said. "Who will aid us?"

Aileen thought for a moment.

"I must talk to my father, of course," she said, finally. "I have promised that I will bring to him any further discoveries. More importantly, I promised that we would not do anything without consulting him, and I believe that he may be able to help us in some way."

"That makes sense," said Robert. "Besides, we are in enough trouble with our parents already. We need no further warnings and punishments."

"We may need assistance from those in the Abbey as well," Aileen continued. "Brother Herbert, the Prior is a kindly man. I believe he may listen, and he may perhaps be able to help us."

The others were not so sure about this.

"He is an important and busy man, Aileen," he said. "And he does not know us. Do you think he will believe such a tale as ours?"

Robert's words warmed her heart and gave her courage. He believes my theory is correct, she thought.

"I am not sure," she admitted. "It may be that he will not listen, but I would like to try and talk to him. Does this plan seem worthwhile to you?" she added, knowing full well that her friends would be very unlikely to disagree with her suggestion.

"Oh yes," Robert said. "You must talk to the Prior if you believe he may be able to help. At the very least there will be another person who knows of our suspicions."

"He may even have some ideas for proving the guilt of this robber," said Aileen.

"Perchance he will," said Ruth. "But, in the meantime, I think I should tell my father of our suspicions. It may be that he will be able to recommend some way in which to trap the thief."

"That's a very good idea," said Aileen. "Perhaps he has some herbal potion that we may be able to use to force a confession!"

"That sounds more like magic than God's justice," said Robert. "I don't think that is what we seek."

"Of course, you are right," said Aileen, momentarily subdued. "But he is a man of skill and learning. I'm sure he will have some ideas that will help us bring this matter to a close and free all of you from your hiding place in the forest."

"I will ask him, you may be sure," Ruth said. "It is certain that he will wish to do all he can to help clear the name of our people, as long as he knows that we are not trying to do this without obtaining the permission and assistance of those in authority. Also, of course, he must be confident that we are right in our theory, for he would take no steps to place another in peril, even if by doing so it should free us from suspicion."

"Your father is a good man, Ruth," said Aileen. "I would feel even more sure we are right if he could find no fault in the theory."

"And what of me," said Robert. "What shall I do?"

"Nothing!" chorused his friends.

"You must regain your strength," said Avi.

Aileen nodded her agreement with Avi's words. "We shall make sure you are there at the end, but, for now, the plans are ours to make. You must return home and work only on healing."

Robert was hardly in a position to argue, so he had to satisfy himself with a low-voiced grumble and the extraction of a promise to report back to him as soon as the plans were finalized.

That done, Ruth and Avi returned to the forest, and Aileen accompanied Robert to his back door. Strange, she thought as she walked home, I am more used to being walked to my door by Robert than the other way around. Please Lord, she silently prayed, let all things, including that tradition, soon return to normal.

CHAPTER TWENTY-FOUR

I do not want anyone coming to me with an accusation against another that he is not prepared to make openly.

PRIOR HERBERT WAS SURPRISED TO be approached by a young woman he thought to be one of the Abbey workers the next day. It was rare that one such as she would dare speak to the powerful monk.

He was even more surprised when the girl requested a private audience with him and said that she must talk to him of the stolen relic. He looked into her eyes and read there no sign of gossiping or play. What he saw was determination and, yes, fear.

"Child," he said, leading the way to a bench in the great cemetery of the Abbey. "What is it that troubles you? Are you fearful that the town may be punished by God for the actions of this thief?"

"No, brother," said Aileen. "Or, at least, I might fear such a thing were I to think on it. But that is not why I have come to you today."

The monk waited patiently as Aileen tried to think of how to tell the Prior all that was on her heart.

"Brother Prior," said Aileen. "Since the holy relic was taken from this place I have been very worried that justice would not be done."

Was there to be no end to the surprises this girl had in store for him, wondered the monk? Justice was a large thing for someone so young to be concerned with. He raised his eyebrows in a questioning look and signed for Aileen to continue.

"My father has always taught us that God is a just God," Aileen began.

"Your father is correct," replied the monk, softly. "He who is guiltless will not be condemned by the Lord."

"Then why do all condemn the Jews?" asked Aileen. "Why do all the people of the town say the Jews are guilty of this crime, and burn their homes, and hunt them like animals, when there is none who can say they saw them commit the crime?"

Prior Herbert saw the passion in the young girl before him. He knew that his answer was important and that he could not lightly brush aside the question. He was a fair man, and the question demanded a fair answer.

"The people believe that no man who has accepted the Lord Jesus Christ as his Savior would dare steal such a sacred relic," said the Prior. "The Jews have not accepted Christ and do not stand guiltless before God, covered by the blood of our blessed Savior shed at Calvary on that day long ago. Indeed, it was the Jews who caused that blood to be shed."

The Prior looked to see if the girl was paying attention to his words. She looked at him with a clear-eyed gaze, waiting for him to go on.

"Since the Jews do not accept Christ, they do not fear that the theft of the True Cross will bring down God's wrath upon them. For many believers only the denial of our blessed Savior could lead to such a terrible crime."

"I understand that that is what the people believe," said Aileen. "But it seems to me that all Jews are hated because of what certain men did many, many years ago. That is wrong"

"Why do you care so much for these few people?" asked the monk.

"I know them," said Aileen. "I have played with Ruth, the daughter of Isaac of Cordoba, since we were children, and I know that none of them would have done anything like this. They are good people, and I fear that they will die because of hatred when it is someone else who has committed this crime"

She has courage, thought the Prior. There are not many who would so openly claim friendship with outcasts.

"My child," said Brother Herbert, trying to soothe the girl before him. "You are right to care for those you know, and you shame us by your willingness to see

265

the good in all men's hearts, even the hearts of non-believers. But why are you so convinced that another is responsible for this blasphemous act within the Abbey?"

"Because I think I know who stole the relic," said Aileen. She had not intended to come out with this quite so directly. But the words were said now, and she could not take them back.

The Prior's reaction was all that Aileen could have hoped for. He sat up straight, shock written on his face. His eyebrows rose until they almost disappeared into his clipped hair. His mouth fell open, and it was a moment before he could get out any words.

"How would you know what men skilled in the darkness of the human heart have not discovered?" The monk's tone was stern.

"Please do not be angered, Brother Prior," said Aileen. "I know that it is not greater wisdom that has led me to the answer. I knew, though, that my friends could not be guilty. If not they, then another it had to be."

Truth is often simple, thought Brother Herbert. Would that we could always see as clearly in times of doubt and uncertainty.

"My friends and I have been seeking the truth," Aileen went on. "We knew that God would honor our search for justice, and so we have asked questions of those both within and without the Abbey. I believe that God has indeed blessed our efforts and has led us to the one who did wrong. I believe also that He has led me to you."

"What is it that you want of me?" asked the Prior, feeling rather as though the ground were unsteady beneath his feet. It was difficult to believe he was having this conversation, but the steady gaze of the girl before him was hard to resist.

Aileen drew closer to the monk, certain now that God had indeed led her to one who would listen and who would assist them in bringing the thief of God's treasure to justice. As she talked, waves of emotion flooded over the Prior's face; disbelief, astonishment, anger, sorrow and, finally, acceptance.

Prior Herbert drew a long sigh as Aileen came to the end of her tale. Then, looking sightlessly into the distance, he gave voice to his grief.

"Truly it is said: 'The devil, as a roaring lion, walketh about, seeking whom he may devour..'"

The Prior sat in thought for a moment. Then, coming to a decision, he rose.

"Come, child," he said. "We must seek an audience with Abbot Samson.

The Abbot was seated at his desk, going over requests for excuses from service owed him as lord of the Liberty. He was puzzling over how to convey to the king that the knights in the Abbot's service, whom the king was demanding aid him in his latest campaign, were adamant that they did not owe service outside the kingdom. Perhaps, mused Samson, he could offer the king scutage in place of service, and thereby allow the knights to avoid the military service that was due without risking the anger of the king. After all, he had done as much only seven years ago, when the king demanded service of the knights for his campaign against the French king.

As he pondered, he heard a knock on the door.

"Enter," said the Abbot.

"God's blessings be upon you, Father Abbot," said Prior Herbert, entering quietly, followed by a young girl unknown to the abbot.

"And upon you," replied the Abbot, looking with interest at the visitor.

"This young girl sought my help, and I now beg an audience to seek yours," said Prior Herbert.

Intrigued, the Abbot signed for them to be seated.

"Child," he said, turning to Aileen, "what is it that you ask of us?"

Aileen had never been in the close presence of anyone as powerful as Abbot Samson, even though he hardly looked to be important. He was short, bald and his bushy eyebrows seemed to dance across his forehead as he spoke. His eyes, though, appeared to see right into the deepest part of Aileen's soul, and she was struck dumb.

"Child," prompted the Prior, "you were eloquent in explaining yourself to me. Speak now and be confident that there will be no harm to you in speaking of what you believe. You have persuaded me of the possibility

268

that you have happened upon the truth. Methinks you may persuade our Father Abbot of the same."

The Abbot's eyebrows rose high, and he turned to Aileen once again. "The truth of what?" he asked. He offered Aileen an encouraging smile, and suddenly the words started pouring out of her.

The tale that Aileen had to lay before the Abbot was one he could scarcely have imagined in his worst nightmare, but the girl's words carried the weight of conviction, and her account of the parts played by various players in this drama was persuasive. Her narrative, dismayed though he might be to hear it, hung together. He could find no holes in the fabric of her account.

As he listened to and questioned the girl, Abbot Samson remembered how he had bewailed the fall of the holy city of Jerusalem so many years before. The Pope's declaration that only sin could have resulted in such a tragedy had cut him to his heart. He thought of how he had chosen to offer penance by wearing a hair shirt and breeches of hair cloth, by eating no meat, and by praying ceaselessly for the Crusaders who had taken the Cross twice since then in an attempt to recapture the sacred city of Christ.

As Aileen spoke the Abbot began to pace back and forth, until finally the anger that had been growing as he listened burst forth.

"By my oath," he cried, "I will suffer no man to blaspheme this holy place or make a fool of the Abbot of St. Edmunds. We must devise a plan to either prove

269

this theory of yours and bring the thief to justice or to trace the real villain and release your accused from this most vile suspicion."

Thus decided, the Abbot sat back down and began to discuss with the Prior and this surprising young woman how they might bring this terrible episode in the history of the Abbey of St. Edmunds to a close.

Ruth's father experienced much the same feelings of disbelief and sorrow as the Abbot upon hearing the tale. Yet he had the advantage of knowing his daughter and understanding that she did not bring mere children's tales to him, asking that they be believed without any offer of proof.

"Are you sure of this?" he asked. "You know all too well how terrible a thing it is to be accused of a great crime when you are innocent. I could take no part in bringing such an accusation against anyone, subjecting that person to ridicule and great punishment, were I not certain of their guilt."

"Papa," responded Ruth, "I know that. I would not ask for your help if we were not certain. But Aileen is going to the Prior at the Abbey to lay the same facts before him. It may be that he will not believe her but, if he does, we are hopeful that he will have some suggestions as to how to catch the thief."

"And you are wondering if I have some ideas as well?" said Isaac.

"Yes, Papa," Ruth said. "You have so many skills, and it may also be …"

"It may also be … what?" asked her father.

"If we were to help capture the thief, Papa," said Ruth. "Perhaps the people the Liberty would not hate us so." Ruth looked down at her feet, tears pricking at her eyes.

Isaac took her chin in his hand and raised her face so that she looked into his eyes.

"My daughter," he said, "I would wish that I could tell you that it will be so. I fear, though, that the mistrust and hatred that so many have felt for us these many centuries are not so easily overcome. We must be content to serve Yahweh as He dictates, and to be glad in such friends as we have found in Aileen and Robert."

"Yes, Papa," murmured Ruth.

"That does not mean that we should avoid helping those who hate us do what is right," said her father with determination. "It is every man's duty to do that which is right, and we will not shirk that duty. In so doing we honor Yahweh and all those of our people who have sacrificed so much for so many years.

"Come," he said, patting the bench beside him. "Let us sit together and see what we may be able to do."

CHAPTER TWENTY-FIVE

*In arranging and settling these matters ... he put
complete trust in God's help and in his own commonsense.*

"Sir Henri," said Abbot Samson, rising to greet the knight. "Welcome to my humble quarters. Please be seated and let me offer you some refreshment."

The Abbot graciously seated his guest, served him a goblet of hippocras, and placed a plate of sweetmeats by his side.

"Ah, Prior Herbert," said the Abbot, as the Prior entered the room and quietly took a seat slightly apart from the pair seated either side of the fireplace. "Is all in readiness for the special mass?"

"Yes, Father Abbot," said the monk. "Everything is prepared."

"Special mass?" asked the knight.

"We will hold a mass today to pray for the safe return of the holy relic and for the soul of the thief who

272

desecrated God's holy house," said the Abbot. "Will you attend?"

"It is my deepest desire that the relic be returned to its rightful place in this ancient Abbey," replied Sir Henri. "I will gladly attend such a mass."

"We are honored by your presence," said the Abbot. "Several of those who are oft within the walls of the Abbey, hearing of the mass, have asked to attend. I granted their request and even thought to ask that your groom, who I understand has served you faithfully for many years, be in attendance. However, I wished to extend this invitation to the bringer of this most holy gift in person." The knight bowed his head in acknowledgement of the honor.

"But now," said the Abbot. "Let us talk for a moment of other things. Our hearts have been heavy for many days. It would perhaps ease our minds if you were to tell us of your adventures as a knight of the Cross, and of your time in the Holy Land."

"It shall be as you will, my Lord Abbot," said the knight. "I must confess, however, that my memories are filled with darkness and sorrow, and there is little that is uplifting to the soul of man in them."

The Abbot said nothing in return, but merely looked expectantly at the knight.

"As you know," continued Sir Henri, "I fought in the campaign which led to the capture of Constantinople. It is one of my great sorrows that I was not able to visit the Holy City of Jerusalem after the surrender of

Constantinople but must perforce return to England in completion of my vow."

"Your faithfulness does you credit," said the Abbot. "Tell us then of Constantinople. I have heard that it is a great city, filled with riches."

"It was indeed a golden city," said Sir Henri. "It shone with the glint of silver and gold, of precious jewels and the finest silks and furs. The very altar of the church of Saint Sophia was laid with gold and jewels. I have never seen the like." The knight's eyes looked into the past as he relived his time in the bright air of the East.

As the monks watched his eyes clouded over, dark memories overwhelming him.

"It was golden," said the knight. "But it was corrupt. And, like all corrupt things, it spread its evil to all around. The desire for gold and riches made thieves and murderers of men who had gone to the East to fight for Our Lord."

There was anger in the knight's voice as he spoke of the dark days of pillaging that followed the entry of the Crusaders into Constantinople. He spoke of the desecration of the churches of the East, of the stripping from the altar at Saint Sophia of all its precious gold and jewels. He spoke of the innocents who died at the hands of murderous soldiers and the greed which overtook the army.

"God forgive me," said Sir Henri, his face twisting in pain. "But it was hard to resist the temptation of riches and power. It is only now, as I see around me the

274

peace of this green land, that the fever of those days is slowly leaving me. It seems to me, as I sit here today, that it was a different man who took the Cross and went to Constantinople. I do not think I like this man I have become."

There was so much sorrow in the Crusader's voice that Prior Herbert was almost moved to lay his hand upon Sir Henri's shoulder. Even Abbot Samson, that proud and powerful man of the church, appeared moved by the Crusader's words.

Then the moment was broken. The knight shook himself slightly and the Abbot placed his goblet on the table.

"It is almost time for the mass," said the Abbot. "What say you, Sir Knight? Shall we go to the holy shrine of St. Edmund and pray a while? It may ease the torment of such dark memories."

Sir Henri hesitated for a moment. Then, rising from his chair, his smile betraying some secret sadness, he walked out of Abbot Samson's quarters ahead of the two monks.

The three men crossed the Great Court and moved toward the door of the Abbey church. They were silent, each wrapped in his own thoughts. Even the air seemed still, as though it held its breath waiting for some eagerly anticipated event.

As they entered through the great bronze doors of the west front, the three paused, dazzled by the sun streaming through the stained-glass windows, forming bursts of brilliant colored light along the nave of the church. Dust motes drifted in the air, emphasizing the sacred silence which reigned within the walls of this house of God.

Slowly the three men walked down the long nave of the great church, through the choir where the monks daily sang the offices of the day, past the high altar, until they reached the shrine of St. Edmund. It was a magnificent sight, the gold plate which overlay the tomb studded with colored stones. The canopy erected over the tomb by Abbot Samson had sheltered many in search of healing and shielded others in search of refuge.

Today, as Sir Henri and the two monks approached the shrine, they could see a small group already standing before it. Sir Henri knew well the town Reeve standing next to his groom, and he recognized the young woman who stood next to a young man with a broken arm as the girl who had been asking questions of Seward and the stable lad. He did not recognize the man who stood silently behind the girl with his hand on her shoulder, closely watching the knight and the monks walk down the echoing aisle.

As the three men approached, Seward shuffled forward half a step. "I'm sorry, Master," he said. "I was asked to attend by Brother Prior here. I have left none of my tasks undone," he added, as if to reassure his lord that he would never neglect his duties due to a request from anyone other than his master.

A slight smile lifted the tired expression of the knight's face. "Prayer is the duty of every Christian,

Seward," he said. "Do not fear my anger because you come to the shrine to offer your devotion to God."

Turning to speak to the Abbot, the knight saw a young girl accompanied by a tall man of around her own age and another, older man emerge from the shadow of one of the pillars into the light shed by the candles which illuminated the shrine. They seemed little at ease in this place, and stood in silence, gazing at the scene before them. Puzzlement at the appearance of these dark eyed strangers was clearly etched on the faces of knight and groom, but since none offered an explanation, the knight continued.

"Father Abbot," he said. "This blessed place seems unlikely to offer a haven of peace in which to offer our obedience to our Lord this day. Perhaps we should return after the mass?"

"The pure of heart never need fear that God is unable to hear them when they pray, whatever the circumstances," replied the abbot. "I am certain that prayer in the heat of battle always reaches God's ears, and that you must have felt His presence easing your pain and fear on many such an occasion?"

"Yes, of course," said the knight. "I merely felt that such a deeply personal moment as this was not for public view."

"Can there be anything more suitable for public prayer than a man declaring his purity of purpose before God and his deep desire to serve his Savior? Do you not think that our Lord will honor the prayers of such a man and his companions, and lead us to the place where the holy relic lies?"

"Let it be as you will, My Lord Abbot," said the knight. Sir Henri bowed his head in submission to the will of the Abbot.

Sir Henri walked slowly to the shrine and knelt. Seward, unsure of what was happening but aware of a tension in the air, came up close behind his master and went to his knees. The Reeve knelt beside Seward, with Prior Herbert and the others behind. The young girl and her companions bowed their heads but remained where they were and did not kneel.

Abbot Samson stood before the shrine and raised his hands.

"Lord God Almighty," he said in a deep voice. "We, your humble servants, come before you this day before the blessed shrine of your servant Edmund. We come to offer You our duty and our obedience. We humbly ask that You will hear our petition."

The Abbot's voice rose to the rafters as his plea to God gained in strength and power.

"Grant us Your wisdom and grace to seek out the desecrator of Your Holy House and return to its rightful place that most holy of relics, the very wood upon which Your Blessed Son, Jesus Christ, suffered so for our salvation."

The Abbot seemed to grow taller as he prayed, his voice echoing through the church in a rumbling wave of sound. Even the candles around them in the shrine

278

appeared to cow before the passion of his prayer, their flames beginning to flicker and splutter.

The Abbot turned to the group behind him.

"Let us all place our hands on the shrine of the saint," he said. "Let us declare here, at this time and in this holy place, our purity of heart. Let us ask the saint to aid us, that the thief might be punished in this world and his soul saved from the dark fires of eternal damnation."

Seeing uncertainty on the faces of a couple of those present, the Abbot drew himself up in all the majesty of his office.

"Come!" he commanded. "Why do you hesitate? It is only the guilty who need fear the wrath of the saint should they touch his shrine. None who come with honest purpose will be struck down."

At his words, they rose and stepped up to the shrine, most quickly and surely, some slowly and hesitantly. They knelt once more, and one by one placed their hands on the tomb.

"Most holy and powerful God," said the abbot. "You who have said that You will set no wicked thing before Your eyes, that the work of those that turn aside will not cleave unto You, that he who worketh deceit shall not dwell in Your House, nor he that telleth lies tarry in Your sight. Hear us as we pledge our oath to You this day!"

As the Abbot spoke, his voice filling the emptiness around them with impassioned sound, the sunlight was cut off from the church. Whether by cloud or hand of God none could tell. The candles began to flicker continuously, sparks shooting bright arrows into the gloom surrounding them. The silence hung heavy around them.

"Hear us, Oh God!" cried the Abbot, raising his arms to heaven. "We swear to You this day on the blessed shrine of Your servant Edmund, that we will never rest until the piece of your True Cross is restored to this Abbey and the thief brought to justice. If we violate this oath or swear faithlessly, may we be struck down in this very place!"

Placing his hand on the tomb, the Abbot said to all present: "Swear, swear!"

No sooner had he spoken these words and the mouths of those present opened to make their oath, then the candles around the tomb flared up in brilliant flame, casting ghastly shadows across the floor and across the faces of those kneeling in front of the tomb.

There was no time to note the expressions of those caught in the light, be they shock, excitement or terror, before the shrine was plunged into darkness. The candles, which only a moment before had illuminated the sacred place as day, now had their light cut off as suddenly as if a hand had come down and smothered them.

Into the tense stillness that followed, a sob was heard. It was rung from a broken heart and echoed around the pillars like the cry of the lost.

"Have mercy," cried out a voice. "Have mercy on me, Oh God. I am the vilest of sinners. I have defiled

Thy holy place and turned away from Thy light. Do not strike me dead, most holy God. Have mercy, have mercy upon me!"

CHAPTER TWENTY-SIX

May God be blessed for having given the
abbot the will to put these matters right.

NOTHING BUT THE SOBS OF the sinner could be heard in the black stillness that surrounded them. Then, slowly but surely, light returned to the Abbey church. First, sunlight filtered through the windows once again. Then, a spark was struck on the stone by the old man who had remained standing by the pillars, and one by one the candles were relit.

The scene disclosed by the light would never be forgotten by any who witnessed it. Aileen who, of all present, should have felt nothing but satisfaction, could only look with sadness on the wreck of greatness before her. Victory is not always sweet, she thought. Sometimes it is no real victory at all, except for the fact that truth has triumphed.

Seward, the faithful groom of an honored Crusader, stood before the tomb, horror and shock written on his face. He looked down upon his master, confusion and pity sweeping across his features.

Sir Henri du Lac, once a man of power and influence, a knight of the Cross, lay stretched out before the tomb of St. Edmund, his body wracked with sobs. As they watched, he shakingly reached his hands out to touch the tomb of the saint, as though fearful of instant retribution for his sins. From his lips issued the whisper of a man suddenly faced with the unbearable: "Have mercy upon me, have mercy upon me."

Aileen, overcome with compassion at the sight before her, went over to the Prior and gently touched his hand. He looked at her, and nodded slightly, as though understanding her unspoken message. Going over to the knight, he knelt down and took Sir Henri by the shoulders, urging him to rise.

Slowly, painfully, the knight responded. He stood but looked at none within the church.

"Sir Henri du Lac," Abbot Samson said. "You have dishonored the Cross under which you served, and the noble name of your house. Your sin is greater, though, in that you have defiled the House of God and sought to place blame for your heinous crime on others."

The knight stood before the Abbot, whitefaced and ashamed, saying nothing.

"Now you crave mercy of Him whom you have rejected. Justice may be tempered with mercy, but first you must confess your sin and receive the forgiveness of those whom you have offended." The Abbot's voice rose in righteous anger. "What say you now to God, whom you have most deeply wronged? What say you to the monks of this house, whose hospitality you have most vilely abused? What say you to the people of this town, who accepted you as one of their own?"

Sinking to his knees, the knight sought to reply.

But the Abbot had not finished yet. "What say you to this man, Isaac of Cordoba, and his companions, who stand here in God's house for the first time, though unbelievers they be?" The small party of outsiders came forward as Abbot Samson spoke. "With their people, they have been forced to hide from the anger of the people of this town, most unjustly kindled by your lies. Through your actions St. Edmund's Bury is shamed.

"And, Sir Knight, what say you to these two young people here?" The abbot gestured to Aileen and Robert. "Did you seek to harm them? Had God not worked His will through this young girl would you have sought your safety in their hurt?"

The knight finally raised his eyes from the ground and looked at Aileen. "It was not until I saw the bale falling towards you that day in the stable that I realized what it was I had become," he said. "Truly, I was struck with horror when I realized what I had done."

The knight gazed at Aileen, his eyes burning with his intense desire that she believe him. "I had thought to speak to you the morning of that day, but after I saw you fall in the stable I realized I could never carry out my plan," he went on. "God be praised that He still works within my conscience, for it is almost a relief that this moment has come."

The knight, still on his knees, bowed his head. "I humbly beg your forgiveness," he said to Aileen. "I

284

cannot expect that you will grant me such, but I must beg it of you."

Aileen was aware of the fact that everyone present was waiting to see how she would respond to the penitent knight. What she said now could affect what others might do. She also knew how hard it must be for a proud man of noble birth to ask forgiveness of a young girl from a merchant family.

"Sir knight," she said, bending down and touching one of his hands. "Sir knight, I do forgive you, as our Lord Jesus Christ forgives us all when we confess our sin and are truly repentant. How could I do otherwise?"

It was as though everyone present had been holding their breath. A sigh sounded on the air. The knight put his head in his hands and wept, and Robert and the others came forward to stand beside the Abbot and Aileen.

"I am not of your faith," said Isaac. "I do, however, speak for my people, and as their leader I speak with the authority of Yahweh, who is a just God yet merciful. Our law requires that those who ask forgiveness receive it. If you therefore seek forgiveness of the Jews of Fornham you will receive it, but you must atone as you can for the wrong you have done us. That is the Law." Isaac was stern, but the words were spoken without anger.

"The wrong I have done you and your people," said Sir Henri, "will be put right. What was destroyed I will make sure is made whole. May God be as merciful to me as you have been, who most assuredly have cause to hate me."

"God is more just and merciful than any man can be," said the Abbot sharply. "Yet to receive absolution you must be truly repentant, and if we are to believe in your remorse it is fitting that you should confess what you have done in front of these people whom you have wronged."

Sir Henri rose and walked over to the saint's shrine. Hesitantly, he touched his hand to the tomb, and then turned to the Abbot. "All my life I have placed honor and name before all things," he said. "I was shamed by the banishment of my family by the French King and saw no hope for redemption until the call to take the Cross came once again.

"My Lord Abbot," he continued, "I know not how much you know of the history of my family and of the great humiliation we have borne in the years since the siege of Acre."

"Of my own knowledge I have no great insight," responded the Abbot. "Yet this day I have heard a tale of the dispute between your family and that of the noble Lord de Vere."

"Then you can perhaps imagine the desire that has burned in my heart since my father was disgraced," said Sir Henri. "All my days and nights have been consumed by an overwhelming need to reclaim the honor of my family and return to the favor of our king."

"And this was why you answered the call to take the Cross?" The Abbot's voice was harsh.

"No, my lord. Not entirely," answered the Crusader. "I truly sought to respond to the Pope's edict as any

286

true Christian should. But I will admit freely that it seemed to me that the call to arms came at a propitious time. I had been but a young man, too young to fight, when I accompanied my father to Acre. Now I was full grown and strong. I believed that our Holy Father had granted me a last chance to expiate not only my sins but those of my father."

"How could you dare to hope that the theft of the Lord's Cross would bring you redemption?" The Abbot's voice was filled with anger.

"The vow I made in Constantinople was not made with any evil purpose," declared the knight. "I had no thought of theft or villainy when I came to your Abbey, and, even when this deed was done, it was never my intent that the holy relic should remain long away from this house.

"Please, My Lord Abbot, may I tell you how it came about that I did this terrible thing?"

The Abbot assenting to this, Sir Henri turned to face the group before him. "I have told some of you, I think, of the horrors that were done in Constantinople under the banner of the Cross?" he asked. Abbot Samson and Prior Herbert nodded their heads.

"In time of war men do things that they never would consider in a more sane time," continued Sir Henri, unconsciously expressing the same sentiment as Aileen's father only a few days earlier. Jude, standing behind his daughter, murmured in recognition of the concept, if not its application.

The knight continued, unaware of the reaction to his words from the cloth merchant. "But he who already has great pride may find himself tempted beyond measure when presented with a chance to achieve that which he has long desired."

"In the wilderness not so far from where you faced your trial, Christ faced greater temptations than man could ever dream," said the Prior.

"It was as you say," said the knight. "But he triumphed over Satan. I did not."

For a moment he was silent, but then he gathered his thoughts and found the strength to continue. "I saw in the holy relic my chance to achieve the power and riches that I felt was my due, as a son of the houses of du Lac and de Clare. I knew that there was no changing the mind of the French king, but it seemed to me that influence was mine for the taking in the land of my mother. Perhaps I could rise to power in England, if not in France."

Sir Henri looked around to see if he was making himself clear. Satisfied, he returned to his tale. "I schemed to obtain the relic, and perhaps it was my reason for seeking its possession that led me down this terrible path," he said. "But I swear to you all that when I began my journey to this great Abbey, it was not my intention to do anything other than present the holy relic to this House and to find favor in the eyes of my mother's family and, perchance, the king."

Aileen did not know if the Abbot believed this, but, to her, the voice of the knight, strained and tired

288

though it was, rang with the sound of truth. This was not an evil man, she thought. This was a man who had been made blind by his own ambition.

Realizing that her attention was wandering, she concentrated once again on what the knight was saying.

"When I arrived in England, I was treated as one who is of the royal house. The king received me, and the people of the countryside cheered as I passed by. By the time I rode through the gates of this Abbey I knew that it was indeed in England, and not France, that my future lay." The knight paused, remembering that day, little more than a week ago and yet seemingly a lifetime away.

"I do not understand," said Aileen. "Sir knight, if you were so full of hope for the future among the people of this land, why did you steal the relic?"

"Fatal ambition," said the knight simply. "It seemed to me that to be sure of my position among the noble lords of this land I must not only give this priceless gift to the Abbey but must be seen to be brave and true to the country of my mother's birth."

"Fatal ambition indeed," said the Abbot. "Did you not know that merely bringing this holy gift to the great Abbey of St. Edmund's was sufficient to guarantee you a place of honor in the hearts of the people of this land? Could you not see the pride and joy in the eyes of the people of England as you rode by, or tell by the reception you received from our noble King John that your standing in this country was assured?"

"Indeed you tell the truth," responded the knight. "Yet, in my heart, plagued as it was by memories of shame and by the sights of horror I had seen in the Holy Land, I could scarce believe that such honor would be offered me. And then, on my first morning in this holy place, I was faced by the realization that still I could not escape the ignominy of my family's past."

"The son of the house of de Vere did accuse your father again of treachery?" asked Aileen.

The knight nodded his head. "It was as you say, and I became convinced that ever greater deeds of faith and courage were required to assure myself of that place of honor and privilege which I had so desired and for which I had so schemed."

"You were blind to that which was before you and around you," said the Abbot. "You thought to steal the relic and then recover it by noble deeds seemingly guided by the Hand of God. When word of such devotion reached the ears of the king, your position would be assured."

"Yes, My Lord Abbot," said Sir Henri. "I cannot deny it. Only now do I see how the madness of greed has brought me so low."

"If you would be shriven, then you must confess all," said the Abbot, holding the gaze of the fallen knight. "Reveal to us now the way in which you did steal this most sacred relic. Withhold nothing, for only in this way can you hope to receive absolution for your mortal sins and avoid the fires of eternal damnation!"

CHAPTER TWENTY-SEVEN

We have sworn enough oaths.

HEARING THE COMMAND OF THE Abbot, the knight paused, seeming to falter in the strength of his purpose to lay all before those whom he had wronged. Then, whether it be virtue or fear of those fires of which the Abbot had spoken, his determination to make a full confession gave strength to his voice.

"I do not know this country," he said. "But on my first night here, as I broke the fast of my journey, I heard one of the abbey servants talk of the land to the east of this town. He was talking of his favorite fishing pond, hidden in the forest not very far from here. At the time I took no note of such gossip, but his words came back to me the next day as I rode upon the way east of St. Edmund's Bury.

"My spirit was troubled after the confrontation with William de Vere," the knight continued. "Father

291

Abbot, you had been very kind to me and had assured me of the regard of the people and of God. You told me something of your own life and bid me remember that the ways of the Lord are just. But still I could not quieten my thoughts, so I told my groom to saddle Raven. It has often been my way to seek solace in a solitary ride, for the quiet power of my horse's stride calms me. It is almost as though he senses my mood and seeks to comfort me."

"Rather you had taken note of my strictures regarding contemplation of the ways of the Lord," said the Abbot. "Did you not understand that the humble will be lifted up, but the proud will be brought down?"

The Crusader bowed his head. "My Lord Abbot," he said. "Would that I had taken that lesson from your words. But, I fear, pride still held sway in my spirit and, thus, was my downfall set in motion."

The Abbot sighed, then signed for the knight to continue.

"As I rode through the forest east of this town, I thought of how I might yet achieve the high honor for which I had so long schemed. I had delivered the holy relic into your hands and could not see what more it was within my power to do.

"As I rode, I came to a shadowed path that led off the road, and I remembered the servant's talk of the pond the night before. It seemed to me that I would rest for a while at the water's edge and that perhaps that might soothe my fevered soul.

"I turned off the road, but the path did not lead to a pond. It led rather to a worker's cottage. No one was there, but outside the door lay a fish trap."

Aileen started. Could it be that all that had happened in the past days had been the result of the chance discovery of a gamekeeper's fish trap?

"I think it was then that I conceived the idea of stealing the relic," said the Crusader. "Oh, not in any great detail, but it came to me that such a cage could safely hold more than fish, but also a treasure."

"Surely, you are not saying that a fisherman's tool caused you to stray from the path of the Lord?" asked the Abbot, aghast.

"No, my Lord Abbot, not at all," protested the knight. "Had I not had mischief already in the back of my mind, such a find could not have placed it there. But when I saw that trap I began to imagine the outline of a plan."

The knight looked around to see if all those present were following his reasoning. Hearing no further questions, he continued with his tale.

"I took the fish trap, together with a sack and some old rope I found lying there. Then I rode back to the road, and began to retrace my steps, for I had taken little note of the turnings from the road on my way out of St. Edmund's town and believed that I had therefore missed the path that led to the pond.

"It was not long before I saw that narrow way. When I followed the path I did indeed find a pond, surrounded by trees and out of sight of any who might be traveling along the road. There was no one to see me hide the fish trap in thick bushes close by the water.

"I remained by the pond for a short time, formulating my plan, and then I rode back to St. Edmund's Bury."

"That evening, before you began your vigil at the shrine, you broke bread with me," said the Abbot. "I saw nothing that would have led me to doubt your humility and devotion. Now I wonder how I could not!"

"My Lord Abbot," said the knight. "Do not take any fault upon yourself. I have spent many years hiding my thoughts from those around me. Those who know me well rarely know whether my spirit is calm or troubled. You, who have known me for only a matter of days, welcomed me into your hall but could not know what lay within me."

"Pray continue," said the Abbot, somewhat mollified.

"I knew, of course, that the gates of your great Abbey were barred at night, and that fact meant that I had to find a way to both leave and return to your grounds without being seen once the deed was done."

"Why did you not simply hide the holy relic within the walls of the Abbey?" asked the Prior.

"It would have been difficult to hide such a sacred object within the bounds of a place about which I knew nothing, Brother Prior," said the knight. "Had I found a place that seemed sufficiently hidden to me, I could not have known for sure that it was secure enough to avoid the discovery of the golden casket by a monk of the Abbey or a servant performing some task."

Seeing no further questions, he returned to his tale.

"I had made some small conversation with your gatekeeper on that first day. We spoke of campaigns and battles, and he offered me a cup of mead. He told me that it is his special brew and that he shares it with others only on very special occasions. I was not insensitive to the honor he did me by sharing his mead with me, I assure you. That I later abused that honor I will not deny."

Sir Henri's voice faded for the moment. Then he seemed to regain his resolve and spoke once again with assurance.

"In the hour before Vespers, I watched for a chance to enter the gatekeeper's shelter. That opportunity came when a cart, loaded with grain, overturned just outside the gate and the Sergeant went out to help right the cart and replace the load.

"I entered his shelter, found his mead and poured into it a small portion of henbane which I have carried with me since the campaign in the east, and which eases the pain in my joints. I knew it would increase the effect of the mead and make the sergeant sleep more deeply. Thus there would be no one to see me unbar the gate and pull it shut behind me, or again spy upon me upon my return."

Mistress Taylor was wrong, thought Aileen. The gatekeeper did not drink too much the night of the theft. It was the henbane in his mead. Such a small detail that I never connected with the theft. Perhaps I am not such a clever investigator as I thought!

295

"That night, I made sure that no one attended upon me," continued the knight. "When all was quiet within the walls of the enclosure, I took the holy relic in its golden box and wrapped it in some fine linen torn from church vestments. It seemed to me then, I do not know why, that such wrappings would not further desecrate the sacred Cross."

Aileen and Robert exchanged quick glances. They had not thought of such a reason for the destruction of the vestments!

"I stole as quietly as I could out to the stable and saddled my horse. I think it was then that the stable boy first awoke, for I almost dropped the bridle in my haste to be gone.

"I unbarred the gate as I told you and rode as fast as I could to the east. I knew it would take me some time to find the pond in the dark, and indeed it did. Eventually, however, I arrived at my destination. I placed the trap containing the box in the water by an old tree stump, with a length of rope securing it to a rock so that it would remain where I had placed it. None would see it. But the water is not deep, and I knew I could retrieve it when the time came. It was my intent to triumphantly return the relic to its rightful place in due time, for, in my mind, I saw myself, with divine guidance, leading the searchers to the pond and its holy treasure."

"But the relic will be destroyed!" Aileen blurted out. "The water will rot the wood!"

"It will not," said the knight. "The box in which the piece of the True Cross lies was made by a master craftsman in the East. It is safe against water and air. It was made so to ensure that the sacred wood upon which Our Savior gave his life would never be destroyed by any malice or accident of man."

Sir Henri paused for a moment.

"There is little more to tell," he finished quietly. "I rode hard back to the Abbey, for it had taken me far longer to find the pond again than I had expected. I was late and had barely time in which to return my horse to the stable and make my way to the Abbey church in time to raise the alarm. The rest you know, I think."

"Why did you begin to follow Robert and me, and why did you attack us?" asked Aileen, her desire to know how he had found out about their activities overcoming her interest in his sad story.

The knight looked at the slight girl in front of him. "The abbot said that God had worked His will through you," said Sir Henri. "Truly, I think that must be so.

"I heard about the questions you were asking," the knight went on. "My groom was full of his account of the pretty girl who was so interested in the adventures of a Crusader knight and his groom."

Seward colored up to the roots of his hair, and the knight spared a wry smile for him.

"It gave me no cause for concern," continued the knight, "until I was walking by the river a few nights later, seeking an inner calm that I found increasingly hard to attain. I heard you and your friend here talking about seeking out the truth and saving your friend. I realized that, should you continue with your plan, there

297

was a chance, however small, that you might draw near the truth."

He turned to Robert. "When you set out for your homes, I followed. I think you nearly saw me in the light from the tavern?"

"Yes," said Robert. "But I could not see who it was standing in the shadows, and I could not know if it was in truth someone following me or merely someone in his cups staggering home in the dark."

"I do not know what I would have done had those men not come out into the street," said Sir Henri, looking Robert straight in the eye. "But when I knew that I had been seen, I ran. Would that I had taken my warning there and not taken the evil way even further in the next days, when I realized that you were both asking questions of people both within and without the Abbey.

"You were not the only ones asking questions," he informed Aileen and Robert. "It was no difficult task to find out the identity of the young woman who had captured the attention of my groom, but it took several attempts to find out who the young man was with whom Mistress Aileen could so oft be seen talking intently."

With a shock, Aileen and Robert realized that they had given no real thought to the possibility that another could be observing them as they pursued their investigations. It was disquieting to think that, while they were hunting a thief, they were in turn being hunted by their unknown quarry.

298

"Three days ago," Sir Henri continued, "I followed Master Robert on his errands. It was no great feat, for it was clear that his mind was on the tasks before him and not on surveying his surroundings.

"I do not know whether to congratulate you on your seeming trust in your fellow man," said the knight to Robert gently. "It may be better as you go through life that you develop a little more awareness of what is happening around you."

Seeing Robert's embarrassment, Aileen touched his hand. "I never thought to look around me either," she whispered.

"I could not hear your conversation with the boy fishing in the pond," continued the Crusader. "But I saw you searching through the forest. When you began to make your way through the brush in which I had hidden the fish trap I became very concerned. Then, you picked up something too small for me to see from a distance. As you examined what it was you had discovered you cried out in pain, and I realized that you had found the tip of my dagger. You see, I had used the dagger to cut a length of rope to hold together the sack in which I had placed the box and did not see until the next day that a small piece had been broken off it.

"As soon as I knew what it was you held in your hand, I was overtaken with a sense of dread. All my hopes and plans were unraveled, and I think a madness came over me. I chased you through the forest and, fleet of foot though you may be, I think I would have

299

caught you had you not tripped over that log and tumbled down the hill."

Robert winced at the memory of that fall but the Crusader, holding out his hand to the broken arm, shook his head. "I regret that you were sore hurt but know now that it was that fall that gave me a moment of sanity and mayhap saved your life.

"When I beheld you at the bottom of the slope, scarce in your senses and clearly injured, I could not continue with the chase. I have done many things of which I am ashamed, but I am not a murderer. I returned to St. Edmund's town and waited to see the course of events unfold. I threw my dagger into the river so that it could not incriminate me, but I thought no more of pursuit."

"But it was you who struck the stable boy only the next day, was it not?" asked Aileen. "And then you threw the bale down upon us?"

"Yes," answered Sir Henri. "For the night of my vigil I heard the boy stir as I led my horse out of the stable and feared he had heard me moving about."

The knight turned to Aileen. "When I saw you talking to the boy my fear was renewed that he might have identified me and was about to betray my presence in the stable that night. Yet, as soon as I saw you both lying on the ground I think I finally and completely accepted what I had become, and I knew I could no longer hope for peace and privilege. I had forfeited my right to either and had become lower than the basest felon.

"I saw the stranger who had saved you from the falling bale and made my escape through the end of the barn as he helped you up. Aware of my wretched state as I was, yet still I was not ready to acknowledge my sin openly. I confess I do not know if I would have had the courage ever to do so, had you not prepared this trap for me."

The knight's story was ended. He stood quietly, awaiting the judgment of the Abbot, whose word was law in the Liberty of St. Edmund.

What a pitiable tale, thought Aileen as silence fell over the group. *That a man of such position and pride may be brought so low is hard to contemplate. Yet perhaps those very qualities were in fact the seed of his fall. Mayhap I should be glad to be a child of this town and not a lady of a manor.*

"This is neither the time nor the place to decide upon your fate," the Abbot said. "The Reeve will bring you before me in my court, and the whole town will know of your treachery and faithlessness. Your pride is overthrown, and you must pray now for the healing of your soul and for the mercy of God."

"I will do so, My Lord Abbot," said the knight. "But I would ask one thing of you, that I be allowed to make amends to this man here, and to his people."

Sir Henri gestured to Isaac as he spoke, then walked over to face him. "I rode to Fornham," he said. "I knew that the men of St. Edmund's Bury had damaged your homes in their anger and, even in the midst of my

301

madness, I felt that I had to see for myself what had been done.

"I think that in some way I felt as though, if there was not so very much damage, I could continue to allow the blame to lie with you and your people. After all, this is not the first time you have been forced to leave all behind and begin anew." Aileen was shocked at the emotionless tone of the Crusader's voice as he talked about people running and hiding from those who would destroy them. Isaac stood like stone, listening to the knight's explanation without interruption.

"When I arrived at Fornham I saw the homes of ordinary people, such as any in this Christian town. When I held a child's toy in my hand, I could no longer think of you as unworthy of life and respect.

"I think it was then that I felt my first qualm about what I had done." Sir Henri continued. "Yet I was not ready to acknowledge my full sin, and thus I continued on that false path which has led me to destruction."

"Truly, you speak that your path has led to destruction," replied the physician. "Yet do not go forth with the hatred of the people of Abraham. Yahweh is a fierce God, yet merciful to those who acknowledge their sin and seek to atone for the wrong they have done. Even David the king was close to the heart of Yahweh, though he showed himself unworthy and, thus, was denied the honor of building the temple in Jerusalem."

Tears pricked the eyes of the fallen knight, and he bowed his head to the Jewish physician. Then, turning back to the Abbot, he once again requested that some

302

part of his possessions, which must now be forfeit to the Abbey, be awarded to the people of Fornham.

"That is only fitting," replied Abbot Samson. "Though your possessions in this land will indeed be forfeit to this Abbey, according to the law, I will ensure that payment is made in compensation for their losses at Fornham."

The Abbot smiled slightly and turned to Isaac of Cordoba.

"Justice will be served, according to the law of both our peoples. And, Sir knight," he added, turning once again to Sir Henri, "you must know that it was the faith and loyalty of this girl and the skill of this man whom you have so gravely wronged that led to your undoing. For when she became sure that you were the thief, she sent to ask for his help in bringing you to account.

"When Master Isaac brought me candles he believed might provoke a confession from a Christian sinner, I confess I did doubt him." Abbot Samson turned to the Jewish physician. "I was wrong to do so. I should have placed more trust in your skill and your knowledge of men."

"The candles were not snuffed out by the hand of God?" asked the knight, catching his breath in surprise.

"There is a lesson here for all of us," replied the Abbot. "For, although this son of Abraham spread a paste of sulfur on the sides of the candles and cut through them below so that, as he explained to me, the flames would first flare up and then die, it is undeniable truth that God uses whom He may choose to do His will. Mayhap He chose one of the people of His first covenant to bring to account a sinner of His second."

With these words, Sir Henri was led away by the Reeve to await the Abbot's court on the morrow. Seward, feeling the shame of his master's fall from grace, left to return to the stable and work through his sorrow making Raven's coat gleam like silk.

Abbot Samson and Isaac of Cordoba walked slowly toward the west front of the Abbey church. It was a strange sight to see the two men, equally devout in their own ways but so different in experience and position, walking together in such accord.

Jude, placing his hand on his daughter's shoulder and telling her that he was proud to have such a steadfast and clever daughter, followed the two older men. The three of them had much to discuss in the matter of how to present the solution to the mystery to the people of the town in such a way that no further harm was done to any.

Prior Herbert came over to the four young people, who were hugging each other and congratulating themselves on reaching the end of a nightmare.

"When you came to me yesterday," he said to Aileen. "I did not wish to believe that your tale could be true. Yet you spoke with such authority that I could believe only that Our Lord was using you as His instrument of justice. You are truly blessed."

"Brother Prior," replied Aileen. "It was your heart that Our Father spoke to, for I think that few would have believed the word of a girl who works with the abbey linen. And if you had not decided that I should speak to the Abbot, perhaps the true thief would never have been known"

The monk laid his hand briefly on her shoulder and gave each of them a smile. "Now, the day is not yet done. Go, all of you. Go to work. I do not wish to hear the complaints of any that nothing can be done for lack of your assistance"

As the four friends walked out of the church door, a cloudless, bright blue sky greeted them.

"Look at the sky!" said Robert. "Yet at the moment when the candles flamed up in the shrine, all light was gone from the church. How could that be when all day it has been as clear and bright as it is now?"

None of the others could give any answer to that question.

CHAPTER TWENTY-EIGHT

It is essential to have an understanding
of evil in order to avoid it.

WORD OF THE CRUSADER KNIGHT'S confession seemed to spread like wildfire. Anger was accompanied by disbelief and embarrassment at having been so duped. The Abbot determined that there could be no delay in recovering the precious relic, though none could tell if that was due to his desire to ensure its safe condition or fear of someone else stealing it from its place of hiding.

Thus it was that, accompanied by the Abbot and a solemn procession of monks from the Abbey, the Reeve had gone out that very afternoon to retrieve the holy relic from the pond in the forest. Sir Henri had given Durand instructions as to where he could find the sunken trap, concealed under the twisted roots of the stump of a tree that had grown close by the edge of the pond, and, thus, there was no difficulty in locating it.

Having removed his boots, the Reeve slid into the water and cut the rope around the rock that held the trap in place. Then, carefully opening the trap, he grasped the casket with reverent hands, returned to the pond's edge and placed it into the anxious hands of Abbot Samson. Placing the box on the linen cloth the monks had brought with them, the Abbot unwound the folds of sodden fabric in which the casket was wrapped. As the box was revealed, the gold gleamed in the rays of the sun, drawing gasps of anticipation from those standing close by. Abbot Samson made the sign of the Cross over the box, uttering a prayer of thanksgiving. Then he dried the gold casket before slowly lifting the lid. The relic was safe and dry within!

With psalms of praise and thanksgiving, the procession began its slow journey back to St. Edmund's Bury. Word had spread to the manors and villages in the surrounding area, and, as the cart containing the golden box trundled past the increasing number of people lining the route, cheers went up and knees were bowed.

As soon as the monks of the Abbey received word that the procession had entered the gates of the City, they began to sound the bells both inside and outside the choir. A great throng of people, thus warned of the arrival of the precious treasure, began to gather. Although the whole town grieved the turn of events, and, this time there was no festive celebration or shining knights, there was a desire and a need for all proper ceremony in placing this great gift from God in its rightful place in the Abbey church.

Abbot Samson, as soon as he drew near the entrance to the Abbey grounds, was overcome with awe at the power of God and the piety of His people. He dismounted from his horse and removed his sandals. Barefoot, he walked through the gate to be greeted by the Prior and the monks of the Abbey. The company of monks entered the church, brothers of the house bearing a litter with the gold box in its place of honor following behind. Those guests of the Abbey who had remained in hopes of the relic being recovered filed into the church behind the monks. At the end of the procession came as many of the Liberty as could find a place within the great doors.

As the solemn procession made its way down the nave to the high altar, the monks chanted "Blessed be the Lord God of Israel" from the office for Trinity Sunday, and then the office for the Feast of St. Edmund.

Arriving at the foot of the high altar, the chanting and the bells were ceased, and the Abbot prostrated himself before the altar. Prior Herbert made the sign of the cross over him and then over the golden box, reciting "Almighty and eternal God, have mercy upon us now, and at the hour of our death."

The Abbot rose and led the way behind the high altar to the place chosen for the lodging of the holy relic, a small chapel beside the shrine of St. Edmund. As the monks sang the "Te Deum," the Abbot and the Prior reverently placed the relic inside the niche prepared by a master stonemason and closed upon it the door of golden bars fashioned by Robert's father, John Palgrave. A more permanent and intricate shrine would be fashioned in the years to come, but, for now, the relic of the cross of our Savior was accorded a place of safety and honor beside the saint who had been martyred in His name.

Turning to the congregation, Abbot Samson raised his arms and spoke a blessing upon all gathered there. The ceremony being complete, the townsfolk of St. Edmund's Bury were then free to return to their homes and fields, fervently hoping that all could now return to normal.

The day after the recovery of the relic Isaac of Cordoba and his companions returned to Fornham, free from the fear of immediate violence. They regarded the damage done to their homes with resignation and offered up prayers to Yahweh for their deliverance. Abbot Samson sent word that he would ensure that the undertaking given them before the shrine of St. Edmund would be fulfilled, and that there would be restitution for the losses sustained by the families.

Of the Crusader knight, little now was said. There was a rumor that his mother's family had sent a petition to the Abbot craving mercy for their kinsman, but the knight himself expressed his willingness to suffer

309

whatever punishment may be meted out to him in the Abbot's court. The word was that his very remorse might have more effect on the Abbot's decision than would the pleadings of his family. The Abbot was known to be harsh in his fury, but just in his judgments.

Now, after a busy day, Aileen and Robert were back in their favorite place, their worries of the past days behind them and the satisfaction of having completed a difficult task clear on their faces.

"I'm glad that Ruth and her father came to the Abbey yesterday." said Aileen. "Perhaps hearing the confession of the knight will be of some small recompense for all that they have suffered in the past days."

"It was fitting that they should be there," said Robert. "When Master Isaac said that he had a preparation that would force a man who believed in a righteous God to confess his sin, I did not know what he had in mind. But when he explained how the sulphur would make the candles flame up and spit out sparks, and how cutting through the wick would then extinguish the light altogether, I felt sure that it was God's will that he be present when the plan was carried out."

"That was truly something to behold," said Aileen. "I am so glad that you were able to smuggle our friends into the Abbey in your cart, for without Master Isaac's presence I really was not sure that the Abbot would be able to time everything correctly."

"I felt the same way," said Robert. "I know that Master Isaac said that the sputtering of the candles would be a warning that the Abbot had little time

310

before the church would be plunged into darkness. Even so, what Master Isaac proposed seemed so strange that I think my anxiety might have shown on my face had the physician not been there to make sure everything was placed as it should be."

Robert is right, thought Aileen. We are not well used to being other than we truly are. So many people depended on this plan being successful. The fact that Master Isaac was there to see that it went according to the plan eased our minds and helped us carry out our part without our faces showing concern. Mayhap Sir Henri would have sensed something was not as it seemed were we to appear otherwise.

"It is well that the Abbot accepted Master Isaac's help," Aileen said, returning to the subject at hand. "For there are not many in this town who would have trusted his word or permitted him to cross the threshold of the Abbey church."

"Sadly, that is true," Robert said. "But the Abbot told Isaac that he knew him to be a man of great skill and good will and that, even though Isaac and his family be not believers, he had faith that God's house was open to all who would seek out those who defiled that sacred place."

"What did Master Isaac say to that?" asked Aileen

"He replied in his gentle way that he was grateful to the Lord Abbot for his trust and shared his faith that Yahweh would use His servants to bring to light the evil than men do." Robert smiled at the memory of the two men's gracious greeting, though, even at the

311

time, he had sensed the words the two men spoke had currents that ran deeper than the surface meaning.

"I'm so glad Ruth thought of asking for her father's help," said Aileen. "I'm not sure we would have been able to surprise a confession out of Sir Henri otherwise."

"Speaking of being right," said Robert, suddenly remembering something he had been wanting to ask Aileen. "How did you come to know that it was Sir Henri himself who had stolen the relic? What was it that Ruth and I missed?"

"Oh, it wasn't anything that you missed," she responded. "Remember how I kept on saying that there was something tickling at the back of my mind, but it just kept slipping away? The first time was when we were talking by the River Lark, just before we had to run home."

"That was the night Sir Henri said he heard us," said Robert after a moment. "That twig you heard cracking was no badger, was it?"

"No," she said. "But I think what was troubling me that evening was the idea that the obvious motive for the theft of the holy relic was not necessarily the true one. I know I wasn't very clear when I talked to you about it, but my mind just wouldn't let go of that thought. I didn't have any suspicion of the Crusader at that time, though, or I would have mentioned it to you."

"What about later?" he asked.

"That night after we met with Ruth and Avraham, when we were walking home again, you said something about a spider's web ... "

"Did I? Oh yes, I think I said something about the spider catching the unwary who approach the web."

"Yes, you said that the riddle was like a web that traps the innocent," said Aileen. "It was those words that somehow started that train of thought again."

Robert, however hard he thought about it, couldn't see how Aileen could have come to the conclusion that Sir Henri was the thief based upon those words. His brown crinkled as he mulled it over, and Aileen smiled to herself at the way his nose always twitched when he was confused.

"It wasn't a solid idea," Aileen insisted. "Had it been so I would have told you, Robert. Really, I would. It was just the idea that not everything was as it seemed."

Robert said nothing, but merely nodded his head, encouraging her to go on.

"It was not until Will told me about the knight's horse being ridden the night of the theft that it all came together in my head. Suddenly, I realized that Sir Henri was playing a role."

"A role?" asked Robert.

"Yes, just like the performers who act a part on the stage at the fair," she said. "I realized that that was what I was thinking the night we walked home from the river on that first night. I was thinking how strangely some of the people we have grown up with are behaving these days, and how grateful I am that you're not like some of the boys that go around pretending to be something they're not!" Aileen let it all out in a rush

313

of words, and then blushed as Robert turned to look at her in astonishment.

"You see," she hurried on. "Sir Henri was like those boys in a way. He was pretending to be something he was not. Everyone I talked to told me about his ambition and his pride. So, that night in the stable it suddenly occurred to me that the humble knight we were all seeing was not the real knight. He wasn't humble, any more than the boys are grown up."

Robert's brow cleared, and he laughed. Aileen's lips quivered, and then she joined in. It did sound ridiculous, when put like that!

"Oh, Aileen," said Robert. "I've spent all this time going over and over all the clues we gathered, and the answer was in the silly games of children!" He could barely get the words out, he was laughing so hard, and it was some minutes before either of them could continue their conversation.

"Thank you for what you said just now," said Robert, after they had finally calmed down again. "I don't think of you as a silly girl, either."

I'm glad that Robert treats me as a real person, thought Aileen. Most men only think of women as someone to cook and clean. My father taught me that God gave women brains, just as He did men, and he has always expected me to use them. Robert is like that, and that pleases me.

Robert sought for a change of subject to fill the silence.

314

"Do you think that the people of the town will act differently toward the Jews of Fornham now?"

"I don't know," replied Aileen, equally glad to find something else to talk about. "The people I heard talking this afternoon seemed to want to forget about the whole ugly incident. I don't really think they are ready to admit they were wrong."

"Well, I'm just glad that Isaac and our friends were there to hear the words of the Abbot and the knight," said Robert.

"Yes," said Aileen. "It was important that they see that Christians follow a God of love, not hate. It has always seemed very strange to me that we are ordered to go out and bring people to Christ, but that many think we can do that by hating others. How do we show them Christ's love, when all we do is hate?"

"I don't know," said Robert. "But there's a lot of things I don't understand about the way people do things. Perhaps we'll understand better as we get older?"

"I'm not sure I want to understand things like hatred," said Aileen. "If I get comfortable with it, I might start feeling it."

"I don't believe that," said Robertstaunchly.

"At least for the moment we did something good," said Aileen. "And I learned a lot as well."

"In what way?" asked Robert.

"Ruth said something to me on the day that the knight arrived that really started me thinking. She asked why Christians need relics to believe that God works in our lives."

"But we don't!" said Robert.

"No, but in a way I could see why she would think that," said Aileen. "It's almost as though we have made of things we can see and touch the proof that God exists. But faith isn't really something that we can touch, is it?"

"No," said Robert, slowly. "Father always tells me that belief in God is something we can't prove to someone who won't believe, and don't need to prove to someone who does!"

"That's it exactly," said Aileen. "I talked to Prior Herbert today. He wanted me to know that he was grateful that I should have placed my trust in him and asked for his help."

"That was kind of him," said Robert, wondering how the Prior had come into the conversation.

"Yes, he is a kindly man," she said. "But I thought to ask him about true faith and how we prove the truth to ourselves and to unbelievers. He said that St. Paul told us we should fix our eyes on what is unseen, because that is what is eternal, and that if we do that we will not need physical proof. So, I keep on asking myself, if that is what faith is, aren't we doubting our faith when we look for something to see or touch?"

"Have you found an answer to your question?" Robert asked.

"I think so," she said. "At least I have an idea that seems to make things more clear to me." Aileen settled herself more comfortably on the grass, and smoothed her skirt, giving herself time to put her thoughts into words.

"God made us," she said finally. "And He knows all about us. I think He knows that we sometimes need something right in front of our noses that shows us clearly that we are going in the right direction. Sometimes it's a miracle of healing, sometimes it's a relic of His precious Son or a saint, sometimes it's a special gift that He gives someone.

"But that doesn't mean that we should make that relic or gift the center of our faith, or our worship. It seems to me that things like this are really just symbols, but they're nothing in themselves. Does this make sense?" she added.

"Yes," Robert said. "You mean that it's sort of like when a puppy leaves a bone by your foot. He might not be there when you see it, but he leaves it as a sign that he's thinking of you and loves you!"

Aileen laughed. Sometimes she felt as though her mind and her tongue were not connected in any way. It was so hard to explain what she was thinking in a way that others could understand. But Robert nearly always understood her tangled explanations. It seemed that he could always bring her back down to earth from her wildest wanderings.

"Well, I wasn't quite thinking of it like that, but you get the general idea!"

"I wish the priests could explain things as simply as that," said Robert. "Usually I can't understand anything they tell us!"

I'm glad he thinks it was simple, thought Aileen. He understands me better than I do myself, apparently.

Robert sat, lost in thought, for a moment. "If you take that thought a bit farther, you can see that what has happened is what so often happens when people get hold of something good. They want more and more of it, and then they make it into something that it isn't."

"That's right," said Aileen. "Relics have become so important in themselves, that people have forgotten what they represent."

"Oh well," Robert said, getting to his feet, and holding out his hand to help Aileen up. "I don't suppose people are going to change in a hurry, and it's just as well that God is so patient with us. And now that we've sorted that out, I think we had better go home."

"Yes, but can we stop by the Abbey school on the way home?" Aileen asked.

"Of course, but why do you want to go there? You know they won't admit girls to the school, however brilliant you are!"

"Very funny," Aileen laughed. "But it just so happens that I do know one of the scholars who attends the school. You do, as well."

Robert raised an eyebrow in inquiry.

"I'm talking about Hugh, the blacksmith's son," said Aileen.

"Oh, of course," said Robert. "I remember him. But it's a long time since I've seen him."

"Yes," said Aileen. "He sent a message to me this morning asking me to come and see him as soon as possible."

"Did he say why?"

"No, but it is passing strange that he should send such an urgent message. He was no close playmate of ours when we were young, and I have seen him only once since he began his studies. He hailed me in the courtyard a few days ago, as I was returning the mended cloak to the guest hall."

"Did he say anything then that might tell us what it is he wants to discuss now?"

"No," Aileen replied. "We didn't talk for very long, and then it was only about how it was that we should both have come to the Abbey at the same time. He did seem a little anxious about living up to his father's expectations, but he is doing well at his studies and I said there surely should be no need for him to worry. That was all."

"Well, then I suppose we had better go and see what it is that is so urgent he must send for the solver of all riddles!"

Robert ducked as Aileen playfully threw at him the core of the apple upon which she had been munching. They set off for the Abbey in the best of moods, looking forward to seeing Hugh again and thinking that the riddle of why the young scholar wanted to talk to Aileen was likely one that would cause them a lot less trouble than the one they had just solved.

COMING SOON

Penitent's Sword (Book Two of the St. Edmundsbury Mysteries) coming Spring 2022.

Anne-Marie Amiel joined the Royal Navy straight from high school, after which she attended law school. In addition to her career in England she has worked in France and as an attorney in several U.S. States.

In the course of her career Ms. Amiel has won short story competitions, been featured in several legal publications and has written for Cobblestone magazine and Devotions for the Public Servant. In her spare time, Ms. Amiel writes music and practices martial arts. Just like any self-respecting English woman, she also loves to drink hot tea and knit!